ABOUT THE AUTHOR

Iain Kelly lives in East Kilbride, Scotland. He works as a television editor and is married with two children. He has previously written a trilogy of novels set in the near future: *A Justified State* (2018), *State of Denial* (2019) and *State of War* (2020).

He has also written for screen.

For more information visit his website:
www.iainkellywriting.com

Follow on Social Media:

facebook.com/iainkellywriting
Instagram: @iain_kelly_writing
Twitter: @IainK_Writing
LinkedIn: iain-kelly-writing

By the Same Author

The State Trilogy
A Justified State
State of Denial
State of War

THE BARRA BOY

Iain Kelly

The Book Guild Ltd

First published in Great Britain in 2022 by
The Book Guild Ltd
Unit E2 Airfield Business Park,
Harrison Road, Market Harborough,
Leicestershire. LE16 7UL
Tel: 0116 2792299
www.bookguild.co.uk
Email: info@bookguild.co.uk
Twitter: @bookguild

Typeset in 11pt Minion Pro

Printed and bound in the UK by TJ Books LTD, Padstow, Cornwall

ISBN 9781914471933

British Library Cataloguing in Publication Data.

A catalogue record for this book is available from the British Library.

For
Chloe Dawn
and Caden Daniel

and Mum

PART ONE

EWAN FRASER

1

Lights flashed and flickered and sparked in the darkness. I stood frozen and motionless and gripped on to the pole and mumbled an apology to the lady I bumped into when the carriage swayed around a bend in the track. A cold sweat broke out across my forehead and drips of moisture ran down my back. A man standing opposite me stared. I tried to breathe inside the mask that covered my mouth and nose and looked at the blank white space above the window.

Had any of the regular commuters wedged together in the confined space noticed anything? The man standing opposite me turned away. No one seemed to be paying me any particular attention.

Screeching brakes announced our approach to the next station. It was my stop. I wiped my brow with my sleeve and my briefcase hit the shoulder of the unfortunate lady next to me. I murmured another apology and was met with a cool stare. She noticed the sweat on my skin and inched away from me. The train juddered to a halt and the doors opened. Politeness dictated a shuffling pace as I moved towards the exit. The human cargo disgorged itself onto the crowded platform and battled against travellers coming in the opposite direction, trying to board the carriage. I reached the door and stumbled over the gap onto the platform and stepped aside and steadied myself and found myself leaning against a white tiled wall. I dropped my briefcase and bent over with my hands on my knees and took deep breaths. There was a disapproving tut as someone navigated around me. 'Stay home,' they advised. I raised a hand in apology, but they walked on before I could explain it wasn't the virus.

Then quiet. Only a few people remained on the platform. A woman wearing a sari glanced at me. I tried to give her a reassuring look before she asked if I was okay. She moved away. I pulled my facemask down and sucked in the fetid air of the underground. I took a handkerchief from the chest pocket of my suit jacket and wiped my brow.

* * *

The morning had started like any other. I had woken up in the bedroom of my terraced townhouse. Autumn sunshine peeked in through a gap where the curtains met and highlighted dust particles dancing around the room. October had arrived but the final vestiges of summer were still clinging on. I looked out at clear blue skies and the treetops from the park beyond the row of houses were calm and still. I struggled through a twenty-minute run on the treadmill, before eating a slice of toast for breakfast and showering and changing for work. Outside the air was cool and crisp and the sun was warming away the morning frost as I walked along Mortimer Road and passed St Martin's Church. The leaves on the trees in Kensal Green had started to turn from green to orange and red. Traffic was building as cars filled with commuters embarked on their journeys. The chatter of children on their way to school imbued the day with a welcome lightness that had been missing when the pandemic had interrupted the life of the city.

Before reaching the gridlocked junction at the end of Mortimer Road, I slipped my facemask on and turned into the underground station.

During the lockdowns I had only travelled into the office once or twice a week. There had been fewer passengers during those months. Now the commute was as busy as it had been before the pandemic had reached London. The long summer holidays were over and children were back at school. Shops, banks, factories and museums were open again. Bars, cafés and restaurants were welcoming customers, and office workers were once again making their daily journey into the heart of the city. It felt like a normal Thursday morning. There were still reminders of the last awful year and a half, like the facemasks worn by those standing on the platform in Kensal Green Station. On the train I had to make do with a standing spot instead of a seat as we made our way along the Bakerloo line. By the time we left Paddington, the carriage was overcrowded and people crammed into tight corners and stray scarves and bags were caught in closing doors. There had been some advantages to lockdown. I missed the luxury of a seat and the chance to read a book or a paper on the way into work.

At each station everyone squeezed along to allow more people onto the train. I ended up in the central aisle between occupied seats on either side. Holding on to a strap that dangled from the ceiling, I stood facing the window as we pulled into Baker Street. There were apologies and polite nudges as those wishing to alight made their way to the doors. I was bumped on both sides and had to turn round to let someone pass. I found myself facing out onto the platform and that was when I saw his face at the window.

I held my breath. The bustling underground station faded into the background. Forty years drained away and I was looking at that same face on a windswept beach. A boy framed against a backdrop of turquoise sea and golden sand and waves rolling into rocks and beachgrass blowing on top of sand dunes. Now he stood on a train platform in rush-hour London. He had the same mop of dirty-blond hair with a fringe falling forward over blue eyes. Lightly freckled cheeks held on to the last fullness of youth, on the edge of hardening into teenage tautness. He looked straight at me. Neither of us turned away. It couldn't be the same boy. He would be in his early fifties now and those days of childhood were distant memories buried under the depths of time.

The carriage doors closed and a garbled announcement from the public address speaker broke the spell and the noise of the outside world returned. The underground train staggered forward with a jolt and the boy slipped away. I strained to look back but he was lost in the crowd. The darkness of the tunnel swept over me.

* * *

I was still on the platform when the next train pulled into the station. I waited until the crowd had passed and then followed them up the escalators and stairways and emerged into the daylight. I walked along Regent Street and turned up Little Argyll Street. Halfway along the narrow lane of terraced sandstone buildings was Argyll House. Holmes & Friend Solicitors occupied the fifth floor of the Georgian building. I took the stairs and was grateful that I met no colleagues on the way to my office. My assistant, Sharon, was not at her desk and I closed my office door behind me and stood leaning against the cold wood. I placed my briefcase on my chair and removed my facemask and coat and loosened my tie. The days of solicitors having a private bar in their office had passed, but a stiff shot of alcohol to steady my nerves was what I needed. Instead all I could do was look out the large window onto the street below and collect my thoughts.

The offices of the firm's solicitors, of which I was the longest-serving, were small but pleasant and ran along the side of the building that faced out onto Little Argyll Street. Looking down from the elevated position of the fifth floor, the commuters bustling past looked like a swarm of ants, an army of workers hurrying along. A row of bicycles in racks sat at the front of Argyll House. Occasionally a person would deposit one and someone else would pick one up. On the opposite side of the narrow lane was an identical Georgian townhouse with similar offices. Lisa appeared at her fifth-floor window and waved at me. This was our morning ritual. It had progressed from a shy wave between a solicitor and an accountant to a running joke and eventually a pleasant meeting one morning when we arrived at the same time to start work. One day I may tell her I had deliberately waited on her arrival in order to instigate the meeting. An invitation to morning coffee was accepted and we had now been seeing each other for almost a year. We were both in our early fifties, she widowed with two grown-up children and me a confirmed bachelor. It felt odd to describe Lisa as my girlfriend. We settled on introducing each other as our 'partner'.

I returned her wave and smiled. I noticed the flicker of concern. She could tell something was bothering me. Someone entered her office and she turned away. I sat at my desk and took out a sheaf of papers from my briefcase. A moment later my smartphone beeped. It was a text message from Lisa: *Everything okay?*

All fine, I typed in reply. *Coffee at eleven?*

See you then.

I put the phone down and began to read the top piece of paper on my desk. It related to the case of Mister Faruq Shah and the settling of his will and estate. Siblings from his first and second marriages were disputing the breakdown of his assets and it needed to be resolved before it got out of hand. I underlined a section in red pen and made a scribbled note or two in the margin. Sharon knocked on the door and entered.

'Good morning, Mr Fraser. Coffee or tea?'

Sharon had recently taken over as my personal assistant. She had been promoted from the team of clerical staff within the firm to replace Ms Whittaker, who had decided to take retirement after forty years with Holmes & Friend, the last decade of which she had spent as my personal assistant. The settled routine that Ms Whittaker and I had practised for so long was lost, and the youthful Sharon and I had still to establish a working relationship we were both comfortable with.

'Please, Sharon, call me Ewan,' I repeated, as I had done every morning for the last month. Ms Whittaker and I had always referred to each other by surnames. Ms Whittaker was ten years older than me and had been at the firm longer so the deference to each other seemed appropriate. Sharon was half my age. Every time she referred to me as 'Mr Fraser' I felt like a teacher being spoken to by a pupil.

'Of course.' She smiled. She wore a white blouse above a black pencil skirt and her dark hair was tied in a neat bun. She dressed the same each day, a monochrome professional hiding any clues that might reveal an individual personality. Ms Whittaker had always added a splash of colour to her outfit with a blue scarf or a green brooch or a red belt. I wondered if Sharon saved her personality for her gym wear. She arrived at work from the gym every morning and returned there for another fitness class every evening. The exhaustive effort showed in her figure and it had been that which had inspired me to try and halt my middle-aged spread with a regime of pre-breakfast jogs over the summer and autumn months.

'Tea or coffee this morning?' she repeated.

'No, thank you, Sharon.' I had always allowed Ms Whittaker to make my morning coffee. She knew exactly how strong my coffee needed to be first thing in the morning and how to gradually weaken the brew through the day. Sharon belonged to the generation who shunned coffee and caffeine for stimulation and instead relied on water and fruit drinks and exercise and healthy lifestyles. I found it easier to make my own coffee instead of trying to educate Sharon on the finer points.

'You have Sir Peter at ten,' she informed me. 'Nothing else for the morning.'

'Right. Thank you.'

Sharon backed out of the room and closed the door. One day I would be able to break the ice with her but so far I hadn't found a topic on which we shared any views. With Ms Whittaker it was easy because of our Scottish connection. Although she was from Edinburgh and I was from Glasgow, there was a bond of nationhood between us. Her soft Embra accent was a familiar comfort among the myriad dialects in the urban maelstrom of Central London. It manifested itself most often in our morning observations of the weather: a grey, wet day was 'dreich' and if the sun was shining it was 'braw'. Although I had lost the harsh sounds of the Glaswegian dialect of my youth, we could still slip into our native accents when chatting and return to formal elocution when clients and colleagues arrived. On Sharon's first day with me, I had arrived soaked from an unexpected downpour. I mentioned how 'drookit' I was.

'Pardon?' Sharon had looked up from her desk.

'Drenched. Soaked through.' I gestured at my sodden clothing. 'Drookit.'

She had turned back to her laptop monitor. 'We have the first mediation meeting for the Henderson divorce settlement at nine-thirty. I can get a change of clothes for you if you need them.' I hadn't tried to introduce her to any more of my native vocabulary since then.

I had an hour before I was due to meet Sir Peter Holmes and update him on the Shah case. I began to browse through the papers again and the unsettling emotions of the morning commute faded away. I had studied the documents the previous evening at home and knew all the information contained in them, but I liked to be well prepared and it helped to keep my mind off the face of the boy I had seen on the underground. Mr Shah had owned two residences, one a spacious apartment in Central London, the other a large family home in the Kent countryside. I had suggested the family home be left to the children from his second marriage who had largely grown up there. His London apartment could go to the older children from his first marriage. Neither party was happy with this solution and an impasse had been reached. The older siblings wanted to sell both properties and split the proceeds equally, the younger children wanted to remain in the family home and give nothing to their step-siblings. Mediation beckoned.

After half an hour I leaned back in my chair and pushed my glasses up and pinched the bridge of my nose to release the pressure in the corners of my eyes. I closed my eyes and the unsettling vision from the underground train flashed before them. I felt the stirring of panic and sweat broke out on the back of my neck again. How long had it been since I had last thought of him? How long since I had explored the memories of that summer? It was not the first time I had been reminded of him. It was not the first time I had thought about what had happened and what had become of him, but as the years had rolled by those questions and thoughts had faded. They belonged to a different time and a different life. They were a long-forgotten dream.

I opened the laptop on my desk. At some point I would have to transfer the notes I had made on the Shah papers into the document on the computer. I opened up the web browser and logged into my Facebook account. In the search bar along the top I typed in 'Laura Robertson'. A scroll of results appeared. In the social media world the easiest way to hide was to have a name so popular that the list of possible matches was endless. I had no idea if she had a social media presence on Facebook or Twitter or Instagram or any of the newer sites where we all exist now. We came from the generation before the social media boom. There was every chance she had never signed up to any of these platforms. I had no idea if she still had the same surname. I had no idea what she looked like now. I had no idea where she lived or what job she had. I had no information that I could use to narrow the search parameters. I only knew she had lived on the Isle of Barra until she was at least fourteen years old, and that we had spent one summer together there as friends. And that the boy I had seen standing on an underground train platform in London that morning had been there with us.

I scrolled down the list and looked at the thumbnail photographs of all the Laura Robertsons in the world. Old and young and middle-aged with black hair and blonde hair and brown hair and redheads. They lived in America and Canada and England and Scotland and Ireland and Australia and more. I closed the laptop and sat back in my chair.

There was a fine drizzle of rain outside the window, falling from light clouds that had covered the clear morning sky. Ms Whittaker would have described it as a 'smirr'. That was the rain I remembered falling when I had left Barra. I had been standing on the stern of the ferry and looking back at the village of Castlebay as it gradually slipped away. Before the jetty disappeared I saw Laura Robertson standing in a red jumper and jeans. She was soaked by the rain and stared at the ferry and at me. Her long dark hair was drenched and hanging limply over her shoulders and her pale face was unmoving. She did not wave a farewell. I was too naïve to think I would never see her again but looking back I think she knew differently. I had learned enough that summer to know the people on the remote island thought differently from those of us on the mainland.

Was she the reason I had remained a bachelor? She was my first love, though I only realised that in hindsight. I was the same age as her and just beginning to take an interest in girls. I never knew if she felt the same way about me. Did she remember me?

The awkward boy from the mainland who had arrived at the start of one summer and disappeared two months later? Did she search social media for 'Ewan Fraser'? I had been in plenty of relationships since then, of course. I had lived with women but never taken the final plunge of marital commitment. What had been stopping me? Had a small piece of me remained with her as she disappeared into the grey mist across the widening expanse of water?

Sharon's professional tone interrupted my daydreaming. 'Mr Fraser, it's time for your ten o'clock with Sir Peter.'

2

The café on the corner of Little Argyll Street and Regent Street was busy and this morning had the added noise of umbrellas being opened and closed and shaken at the door as people entered and exited. The drizzle had turned into heavy rain and the damp atmosphere hinted at the extended summer finally coming to an end. Despite the rain, there was a steady flow of pedestrians walking past the floor-to-ceiling windows, a reassuring return to normality after the eerie emptiness of lockdown when offices had been deserted and shops closed. We managed to get our favourite corner table that offered a modicum of privacy and comfy armchairs and provided the best view of the people passing by.

Lisa sat opposite me and we both removed our facemasks and took a sip of coffee and held the mugs cupped in our hands to absorb some of the warmth. Her shoulder-length, fair hair was streaked with encroaching strands of grey and was held back from her face by a pink clip. Her make-up was natural and professional. She was comfortable with her age and resisted the urge to disguise it. She wore a burgundy blouse that hung loosely over her slight frame and black suit trousers with heels. I continued to wonder why she chose to spend her time with a slightly pudgy solicitor with receding grey hair and no sign of committing to anything more than a casual relationship. She deserved better.

'Everything okay in work? You looked concerned this morning.'

'Yes, fine. Just another day at the office.'

'Really?'

I could no longer fool Lisa. After a year together, she was now able to read my inner thoughts and see through my innate West of Scotland stoicism. I had been trying hard to adopt the emotive conversation that went against the nature of my upbringing but was a recognised requirement of any long-term relationship.

'It was nothing. I saw someone this morning on the way to work that reminded me of something that happened a long time ago. That's all.' A long time ago was how I referred to my childhood in my homeland.

'From Scotland?' Lisa asked. I nodded. 'Did you talk to them?'

'No, just a face in the crowd on the train platform.'

'And why would that worry you?'

I had mentioned the formative summer of my youth to her before, but I had never told her what had happened there. 'It's hard to explain. You remember I once spent a summer living with my aunt and uncle on Barra?'

'Your summer on the island?'

'Yes. There was a boy who lived there. He was a little younger than me and we became sort-of friends.'

'And it was him that you saw?'

'Only he was still a boy. You see? He hadn't aged a bit, but I could have sworn it was him.'

'So it was just someone who looked like this boy.'

'I knew you would think it was silly.'

'Why would seeing someone who looked like this boy upset you?'

The barista fired up the coffee machine and made conversation impossible and all the other chatter from the café was drowned out.

The grinding noise grated and mixed with the swirl of memories that had been stirred up that morning. I gazed out the window and tried to hide my thoughts from Lisa behind repeated sips of coffee from my mug. It was too long a story to tell her over our morning break. Pedestrians eager to reach their destination and escape the autumnal showers hurried by. Many had been fooled by the early morning sunshine and were under-dressed without coats or jackets, unprepared for the vagaries of the London weather. Dark puddles were forming on the pavement. The coffee machine subsided and I made my excuses and put my still half-full mug back on the table.

'I really have to be getting back.'

'You said you had a quiet day.'

'Just remembered a meeting at half past. I better go.'

I fumbled some change from my pocket and placed it on the table and picked up my coat and left before she could stop me. I forgot to put my facemask back on as I hurried through the café. I was gasping for air. The panic that had affected me on the train that morning had returned. I squeezed between the tables and dragged my coat over a startled customer's head and bumped into a damp couple trying to enter through the glass doors as I hurried out. I didn't stop to apologise. Raindrops made wet blotches on my shirt and suit jacket before I put my coat on and turned and walked down Regent Street in the opposite direction from my office. The pavements were filled with people and the air was polluted. I could feel the city smog clawing at my throat. A car horn blared as I stepped onto the road to navigate around a woman waddling along with shopping bags. I spun round and saw the café door and Lisa staring after me with a look of concern on her face.

I had lied. I had no reason to get back to the office. I crossed Regent Street and carried on down Hanover Street, passing the art gallery and the bank and the department store. Finally the buildings opened out onto Hanover Square and the city felt less overbearing.

Another car horn blared as I stepped onto the pedestrian crossing and a red Audi hurtled past.

The middle of Hanover Square is a small space of greenery that has somehow escaped the developers as Marylebone, Fitzrovia and Soho have grown and expanded on all sides. It offers an oasis among the urban jungle, although it could hardly be described as a remote idyll. The city noise still surrounds it and cars encircle it and pedestrians rush through it, but it offered the space I needed at that moment. Tall trees and black railings created a boundary that tried to hold back the onslaught of central London. Green grass and bushes were neatly tended and small flowerbeds were filled with late-blooming colour. I found a vacant bench near the centre where the footpaths converged and the tall trees blocked out some of the surrounding grey stone and falling rain and I sat down. I leaned forward and put my head in my hands and slowly my breathing returned to normal. I tried to understand the panic that had come over me again. My thoughts and feelings had been buried for so long. Why were they now affecting me in such an acute way? One glimpse of a child's face and I had been reduced to an anxious wreck. Had I been fooling myself for all these years? Had my entire adult life been afflicted by what happened that summer? Had I been hiding that fact from myself? Perhaps I was never as well-balanced as I had thought. Or was I completely over-reacting? Nothing tangible had happened despite the thoughts and memories rushing through my mind. Lisa had asked the right question: *Why would seeing someone who looked like this boy upset you?* I knew part of the answer, of course: because I had never told the boy and Laura the truth after I had discovered it.

I sat for ten minutes and an idea came to me. A crazy idea. Lisa would not understand, but it felt like the right thing to do, and the more I thought about it the more I believed it was something I had to do. The only obstruction was work, but I had put in a lot of extra hours over the last few weeks and would not feel guilty about taking a couple of days off.

The rain stopped. I stood up and retraced my steps back to Little Argyll Street. I looked in the window as I passed the café. The corner table had been taken by tourists whose oversized rucksacks blocked the emergency exit door. There was no sign of Lisa and I would have to explain my sudden exit to her later.

Back at the office, Sharon noticed the damp patches on my coat and asked if I had enjoyed my coffee break.

'Do I have anything scheduled for this afternoon?'

'No, Mr Fraser.' Sharon caught herself. 'Ewan. You asked to keep this afternoon free to prepare for the Dawn Silo briefing tomorrow.'

Dawn Silo was a large agricultural firm which specialised in genetically modified crops that had recently been the subject of attention from Her Majesty's Revenue & Customs regarding discrepancies in historical tax accounting. As far as I could tell they had broken no laws despite utilising some questionable practices. Neither side was backing down and court proceedings loomed. One of the senior partners would soon be taking the files off my desk and I had been asked to prepare a briefing to bring them up to date.

'Could Harry take over the briefing? I need to take the rest of today off.'

A look of concern appeared on Sharon's face. 'Are you okay?'

'Just a little under the weather.'

'I'll check Harry's schedule.'

I left her tapping on her computer keyboard and raising the telephone to her ear to call Harry's assistant. Harry would not be amused to receive the extra work but I knew he wasn't rushed off his feet. It would be a small measure of revenge for the thrashings he meted out at our weekly tennis game.

I sat at my desk and considered the idea that had come to me on the park bench. Back in the austere surroundings of my office it seemed ridiculous. Could I just drop everything and rush off like this? I wondered why it had not occurred to me to do this in all the years that had passed since I had spent that summer in Barra. Was this a mid-life crisis? Was it a reaction to the pandemic and the enforced order to stay home over the past year? Whatever the reason, I needed to finally confront what had happened that summer. I wanted closure and I wanted to know what had happened to Laura Robertson and the boy whose face I had seen that morning. And I wanted to finally do the right thing, the thing I should have done all those years ago. I wanted to tell them the truth.

There were no restrictions on travel to the islands at the moment and when I looked online there was accommodation available and open to travellers from the mainland. The threat of the virus would be fresh in the minds of the isolated and elderly community, but Barra was open for visitors so long as they had taken the correct precautions. There was a flight leaving from Stansted Airport the following day that had seats available. It would get me into Glasgow in the afternoon. I clicked to confirm my booking and filled in the payment details before any doubts could change my mind. I was not used to being impulsive and it made me uneasy but now I was committed to my plan. There was only one flight to Barra each day from Glasgow and it would already have departed before I could make the connection tomorrow, but there was a seat available the following day. A night in Glasgow would give me a chance to revisit the places where I grew up and I now looked forward to spending time in the city of my birth. I found a hotel room in the centre of the city next to the River Clyde and booked it for one night. I found self-catering accommodation on Barra and booked it for the weekend. I had been back to Glasgow once in late spring when the lockdown restrictions had been lifted to visit Dad in the care home. He had looked frail and old, but all things considered he had been in fine spirits. I would visit him after my trip to Barra, on the return journey. I couldn't let anything distract me from the path I had chosen to follow. I picked up my coat and briefcase and left my office.

'Harry can do the Dawn Silo briefing for you,' Sharon said as I walked past her on the way out.

'Thank you, Sharon.'

'Are you sure you are okay? Can I get you a taxi?'

'No, I'll be fine,' I called over my shoulder and kept moving. 'Just need a good rest.'

I was being deliberately vague but I couldn't stop and explain to Sharon everything that was going through my mind. Ms Whittaker would never have let me leave without a full explanation followed by some words of wisdom. I missed her. She would have told me I was being a bloody fool and she would have been right. I had to keep going and rush headfirst into this course of action before my guilt told me to stop.

* * *

The underground train wound its way through the dark underbelly of London and as it passed through Baker Street Station I felt my chest constrict and my heart thump against my ribcage, but the platform was sparsely dotted with only a few Londoners and tourists and no young children. I still peered anxiously at the faces through the window and looked for those blue eyes. As it was the middle of the day I was able to sit in the carriage for the entire journey back to Kensal Green. I emerged into a chilly afternoon and trooped back to my townhouse. The brickwork that had shone in the golden sun that morning was now damp and dull. It was past lunchtime and I hadn't eaten anything since breakfast, but I could not bring myself to do something as mundane as eating while chaotic thoughts ran through my head.

I pulled the travel suitcase from the top shelf of the airing cupboard and filled it with winter clothing. Autumn in the west of Scotland could be unforgiving and on the exposed island even more so. Packing did not take long and by early evening I found myself with nothing to do but wait until I left for the airport in the morning. I contemplated just heading to Stansted, but the thought of pacing around a soulless airport terminal for the night was an unwelcome prospect.

My phone rang. I looked at the display and saw that it was the office. Sharon would be calling before leaving for her evening fitness class. I couldn't face her questions and dismissed the call. In the morning I would call and explain my absence. The ringtone sounded again and I was about to swipe the ignore button when I noticed it was not the office number. It was Lisa. I hesitated before deciding I had to answer.

'Hello.'

'Ewan, are you alright? Sharon told me you left at lunchtime today.'

'I'm fine.'

'What is going on?'

'It's nothing.'

'Is it still something to do with this boy you saw on the underground?'

'I've decided to go back there.'

'Go back where?'

'The island. Barra. I've booked a flight for tomorrow.'

She paused. 'What happened on the island? Was it something bad?'

'I don't know. Maybe. That's what I have to figure out.'

'I could come with you. I've always wanted to visit Scotland.'

'This is something I want to do on my own.'

'Are you going to tell me what this is about?'

'I will tell you when I have figured it out for myself. I promise.'

There was an exasperated sigh on the other end of the call and she made one last attempt. 'Can I come round tonight and you can tell me what this is all about?'

The thought of Lisa's company was tempting. I always felt better with her than when I was alone, which was hard to admit after years as a contented bachelor. A quiet evening with a bottle of wine and the comfort of each other's company was exactly what I needed, but something held me back.

'Ewan?'

'Sorry.'

'When will you be back?'

'In a few days. I'll tell you about it then.' I felt guilty. Over the last year we had slowly opened up to each other. We had been cautious at first. Lisa had lost her husband two years ago and hesitated about sharing her life with someone new. We guided each other and found a space we were both comfortable to inhabit.

'I'm worried about you.' Lisa's tone softened.

'Don't be.' I tried to reassure her even though I had no idea if she should be worried or not. I had no idea what might happen to me over the next few days. It would probably turn out to be nothing more than the forlorn wanderings of a middle-aged man around the ghosts of his past on a remote island.

'Well, you know where I am if you need me.' Lisa knew when to concede rather than fight a lost cause.

'Thank you.'

'Goodnight.'

'Goodnight.' She ended the call. This was how we always ended our conversations. We were both old enough to survive without telling each other we loved one another every time we parted. And yet tonight, standing in my living room with the patter of rain against the window and the sound of the cars rushing past and the dark sky holding no stars, I missed having her next to me.

3

I woke up in my bed. Through bleary eyes I looked around the room and saw the contents of the wardrobe strewn across the floor. Among piles of clothes were the boxes that stored the collected memories and mementos of my life, accumulated over time and left to gather dust on shelves. I looked over the various pieces that lay among my shirts, trousers and underwear. There were old postcards, an expired passport, cheap holiday souvenirs, childhood photographs, theatre ticket stubs and football programmes. Sitting up on the edge of the bed, my feet landed on the football programme from the 1982 cup final between Queens Park Rangers and Tottenham Hotspur. The clubs were near neighbours and their stadiums were equidistant from my townhouse in Kensal Green. As a thirteen-year-old I got the programme from a collector's catalogue and had no idea I would one day be living within walking distance of both these London teams. 1982 was the last time Queens Park Rangers had made it to the cup final. They had lost in a replay. The Tottenham team that year included the Argentinian Ricky Villa, who refused to play because of the Falklands War. While Tottenham and Queens Park Rangers had been kicking a football around Wembley Stadium in London and a war was being fought halfway around the world, I had been on Barra staying with my aunt and uncle. Since yesterday morning, everything seemed to link back to that summer.

After Lisa had hung up the previous evening, I had paced around my flat for half an hour. I kept picturing Laura Robertson standing on the pier in Castlebay and her sullen face and our unspoken farewell. Then I thought of the happier times we had shared running through the village and clambering over rocks and playing on the sandy beaches and swimming in the sea. It was our last summer of freedom before the weight of adolescent responsibility fell upon us. In my mind we had been alone, but there had been others, of course. There had been Uncle Tom and Aunt Cathy. There had been Laura's parents, Flora and Hamish. There had been the priest, Father Baird, ruling over his parish. Other names came back to me as I brooded over that summer. Robert MacNeil, who ran the post office and café with his wife, Marion. Alec MacLeod, the hard-of-hearing bank manager, and his wife, Mary Margaret, and their wheelchair-using son, Lachlan, who lived in the flat above the bank. And Alasdair Campbell, the harbour manager, with his hacking cough brought on by the tobacco pipe permanently lodged in his mouth.

And there was him. The face I had seen in the crowd on the underground platform in the centre of London. William Matheson. Billy. He lived with his mother on the east side of the island. I stayed along the road from them with my uncle and aunt. He was only a year younger than I was, but he was small, short and skinny. Over that summer Billy was left to his own devices by his mother, just as Laura and I were. I remembered first seeing him when I had discovered a small cave and he had emerged from inside it, startling me. I remembered the silent boy watching Laura and I as we flew a kite on the beach. I remembered him and his mother, Mhairi, and the four of us splashing each other in the cold Hebridean Sea.

That was when I remembered the photograph. It was in one of the boxes I kept stored away. Boxes filled with the collected souvenirs of life. Before the internet and digital cameras and smartphones and easy access to everything, photographs were valued possessions. They were treasured and kept as souvenirs of important moments and albums were filled with holiday snaps and family celebrations. And they were limited. A roll of film could take only a certain number of pictures. My old camera could only take twenty-four, before a new film roll was required. Once you had clicked the camera and wound the film to the end it could be weeks before you saw the results of your efforts. A film negative in the hands of an inexperienced shop assistant could be destroyed before you ever got to see the images you had taken. It seems ridiculous now, in the age of unlimited digital photography. One picture of Laura and Billy and me had survived from that summer and I had held on to it all this time. I could see it without looking at it. I was on the left, standing on top of a beach sand dune. In the middle was Laura. Both of us looked straight at the camera. I had an awkward smile and the wind had blown my dark fringe across my eyes. Laura's long black hair was damp and strands swirled around her face as she stared into the camera. She did not smile but looked determined and stared at the person holding the camera. And on the right sat Billy, perched on the edge of the sand cliff with his legs swinging over the void. He looked off camera to the right at something that had caught his eye and distracted him just as the button was pressed on the camera. Was the story of that summer written in those expressions? My naïve smile, Billy's inattentive innocence and Laura's direct stare at the woman taking the photograph, Mhairi Matheson, Billy's mother.

The photograph was sent to me after I had left the island. It arrived in the post at our house in Partick. The small island of Barra had no photograph-developing service. You had to leave your film at the main store and wait for it to be sent to Oban on the mainland, where they would produce your prints and send them back on the ferry. And then someone had sent this one photograph on to me. For years I kept it hidden behind the framed picture of my mother that sat by my bed. I had looked at it less and less as time passed. It became another one of those things that was carted about from childhood home to student accommodation to rented flat to first home, buried in a box and largely forgotten about. It was the only physical evidence I had of that summer on Barra, the only proof I had ever been there and that what had happened wasn't just part of my imagination.

I had to find that photograph and take it with me. A frantic hour of searching had ensued. A succession of cardboard filing boxes were taken from my wardrobe and emptied onto the floor of my bedroom. A grey layer of dust covered each lid. I found it tucked inside a plastic wallet along with a few other random items that I paused over and wondered why I had kept them: my first payslip from a summer job in a clothing store, an old toy compass, a pin badge from the Edinburgh Commonwealth Games in 1986 and two cinema ticket stubs from the ABC Cinema on Sauchiehall Street from 1987. The photograph was a little faded and curled around the edges, but it was still clear. It was creased where I had folded it to exclude Billy and leave just Laura and me on the sand dune. I remembered lying in bed in my room in Partick and using the picture to bring back memories of Laura running along the beach and swimming in the sea and smiling at me as we raced our bikes along the twisting road around the island. I flattened the crease as best as I could so that Billy re-joined us in the image. It was a cruel thing to have done. He was part of that story and those events and the summer that linked us together. I stared into the young brown eyes of the girl looking straight out at me and wondered if I would recognise that same face on a woman in her early fifties. I had fallen asleep with the photograph in my hand. Would those brown eyes remember me?

Now the photograph lay on the pillow of my bed. I picked it up and turned it over and looked at the writing on the back. The two words were still there, written by Laura: *Thank you.* I hadn't been sure what she had meant at the time. Was she thanking me for being her friend for those few weeks? For making that summer on the island bearable for her? Or was it something more, something left unsaid between us, about the truth of what I had learned that summer about her and her family? After she had sent the photograph to me, I wrote a letter in reply and posted it to her house on Barra. I never received a reply. Before emails and text messages and smartphones, the only other way I could contact her was by the house telephone. I never knew her number. I could have found it out, but I never had the courage to get that far. What would I have said to her? What if her parents had answered the call? As the weeks drifted into months and life in Glasgow settled into a new rhythm, she gradually slipped to the back of my mind, until too much time had passed.

I placed the photograph on top of the pile of clothes in my travel case and closed it. I got up and dressed in a casual shirt and denim jeans and ate toast for breakfast. I telephoned the office just before eight-thirty and left a message on Sharon's answering service to tell her I wouldn't be in the office today and that I was going away for the weekend. Then I locked my front door and made my way along Mortimer Road and wondered if anyone noticed that I wasn't dressed in my usual office clothing and I was carrying a travel case instead of a briefcase. It was another fine autumnal morning, although rain was expected later. I checked the weather forecast for Glasgow on my phone as I waited for the underground train to arrive at Kensal Green. A day of steady rain was forecast. That was how I remembered my childhood in the industrial city on the west coast of Scotland, blanketed under a curtain of perpetual rainfall.

When we reached Baker Street Station, I left the train and

crossed over to the Metropolitan line. Faces flashed by as I walked along and I looked again for the boy among the throng, but of course there was no sign of him. The hustle of Londoners and tourists swept me onto the train and in another quarter of an hour we arrived at Liverpool Street Station, where the Stansted Express would take me on to the airport. The crowd thinned on the express train and I took a comfortable seat next to a window. The train departed and was soon hurtling east before curving northwards through Bethnal Green and Cambridge Heath and Hackney. I looked out at the vast sprawl of London. I had lived here for almost thirty years and yet much of the city remained an unexplored mystery. Streets and buildings and alleys ran in all directions. So many lives unfolded in anonymity beneath towering blocks of flats and across vast housing estates. The elevated train track allowed me to look down on the cars and buses and pedestrians milling around the streets. The full variety of London was on display. I thought about the city I was heading towards and how it compared to the metropolitan capital. Glasgow was a city of only half a million people, not even a tenth the size of London, but Glasgow liked to be that way. It liked to be the underdog and the people liked to see themselves as the oppressed who punched above their weight and had no time for pretensions. Glasgow was at its best when it had a cause to fight for. I had lived there during the decline of the shipyards and the rise of Thatcher. I had seen the Poll Tax marches and the spread of the post-industrial wastelands. Glasgow was small and muscular. The streets were straight and true and at right angles to each other. Nothing sprawled or meandered until you came across one of the vast green parks dotted around the city that gave it its sentimental nickname, the 'Dear Green Place'. It was a different world from London, where I had made my home. It was because London was so different that I had made it my home. Neither of them compared to Barra. The small rural island where no street ran straight and everyone knew everyone else and their business. It was impossible to be anonymous on Barra. It was impossible to hide secrets for long.

London flattened out and the buildings turned into industrial estates. My phone pinged and I read the message from Lisa. *Safe journey*, was all it said. I couldn't think of anything to write in reply so I left it unanswered and promised myself I would send her a message when I had made it to my hotel room later that day. Throughout the night I had questioned my decision to make this trip. What was I really hoping to find? I was being irrational, all because of a face I had half-glimpsed through a train window, but now that I was on my way I felt I had made the right choice. Whatever lay ahead of me, I needed to do it and I should have done it years ago. There was only a slim chance that I would find the girl who had watched me leave all those years ago, but it was a chance worth taking. There was only a slim chance I would discover what became of Billy and his mother, but now that I was travelling back to that summer of 1982, I was determined to find out what happened to them after I had left the island.

We passed the reservoirs at Walthamstow and Enfield and green fields began to appear and we ran parallel to the M11 motorway for the final stretch before arriving at Stansted. The train journey had left London behind and the familiar hotels and hangars that surround all airports signalled the beginning of my flight north to Scotland.

4

Glasgow is a difficult city to love, even for someone born there. Grand Victorian and Georgian buildings stand next to modern glass and steel. Wastelands along the river that were formerly shipyards lie abandoned since the Industrial Revolution petered out, slowly being replaced with dazzling modern architecture. It is a city of cinemas and bars and cafés and nightlife and shops and people. There are leafy suburbs and the artisan West End with its parks and its baroque-style museum in the shadow of the gothic-revival university building. A thriving music scene grew out of the music-hall traditions in the first half of the twentieth century. The famous art school gave the world Charles Rennie Mackintosh and Alasdair Gray and Harry Benson, before it was destroyed by not one but two fires in the last ten years. Glaswegians are proud and tough and uncompromising and welcoming with a friendly smile that warns you not to get above your station. This is Glasgow now, confident and assured and renowned and outward-looking.

That was not the Glasgow I grew up in. Glasgow in the 1970s and early 1980s was a downtrodden, violent city. The grand buildings were covered in black soot and hidden by brutalist modern office blocks. Areas like Calton and the Gorbals in the East End were the most deprived places in Britain with widespread poverty and ill-health and vast swathes of demolished and crumbling buildings. High-rise flats interspersed with inner-city ghettos and unemployment and alcohol and drug abuse were rampant. Homelessness was rife. Gangs fought one another and stabbing and slashing victims filled the hospitals and morgues every weekend. The battle for control of the East End in the 1980s was given the prosaic name 'The Ice-Cream Wars' as ice-cream vans were used to peddle drugs and brought the sound of guns to the city streets. The 'Glasgow Kiss' and the 'Glasgow Smile' were the violent exports the city was renowned for. Glasgow was defined by a simmering violent rage that was always on the brink of exploding. The echoes of these times still resonate in Glasgow today despite the best efforts of the city leaders to move on. If you are a boy born in Calton today you will be lucky to reach sixty years old. Sectarianism still divides the city, lurking in the shadows and mingled amidst the rivalry of the football clubs and rearing its ugly head in public every year during the marching season when the Orange Order and the Irish Republicans parade along the streets of the city.

This city was the playground I grew up in. It offered plenty of opportunities for bravery and standing up and being a man. Only with age and distance did the hopelessness and false bravado reveal themselves to me. Glasgow was made by its people and like them it had a chip on its shoulder that distrusted authority. It was a city with a short fuse and a violent temper, a champion of the working class and a disrespecter of the powerful and the elite. It revelled in the reputation of the hard men that came from its mean streets. When I moved to London I would smile with misplaced pride at the sliver of uncertainty that would cross a Londoner's face when they recognised the harsh vowels and glottal stop of my Glaswegian accent. I had just enough height and bulk to make good on the reputation that preceded me. I didn't let on that I had not been in a serious fight since the early years of school. I shied away from confrontation and abhorred violence, but it suited me not to tell them that.

Looking out of the window of the taxi that took me from the airport into the west of the city, I saw little of the landscape that I grew up in. The forecast rain had passed, leaving the tarmac dark and damp. Passing through the streets of the old industrial heartlands in Govan and Finnieston I spotted remnants of the past, small ghosts of broken dockyards and rusted warehouses and tenement flats, but now there were new, modern flats and houses. The mighty Titan crane in Finnieston, once used to load cargo onto vast Clyde-built ships, now stood in the middle of a concert and tourist sector, a dark and silent silhouette among the bright lights of the modern metropolis. It was early evening and the sun was disappearing behind the buildings to the west. Crossing over the river the taxi pulled up at the front door of a non-descript hotel that was my accommodation for the night. The driver muttered something and hit a button on the meter and pointed at the price. He had offered none of the local 'Glasgow patter' on the drive through rush-hour traffic along the M8, the motorway that cut through the middle of the city. Perhaps it was the facemasks we both wore that discouraged conversation. I thanked him and deposited myself and my travel case onto the pavement and only just managed to close the door before he accelerated away.

Behind the reception desk a Polish woman wearing too much make-up and a facemask checked me in, gave me a key card and directed me to the lift. My room was on the fifth floor. It was a square box no bigger than the bedroom of my London townhouse with a small en-suite shower room. From the window I had a view of the side of the building opposite. The hotel offered no room service and a limited and expensive minibar in a small fridge that sat under a ledge, on which sat a kettle and a basket of various tea and coffee sachets. I turned on the television and flicked through the free channels, while glancing through leaflets for local tourist attractions, most of which were not in Glasgow. I decided to go out for a walk.

It took only fifteen minutes to walk into the centre of the city along a pathway that had been built since I had last been down by the river. It took me under the motorway that crossed the River Clyde on the Kingston Bridge. When I was born at the Rottenrow maternity hospital in the centre of the city, the Kingston Bridge was nearing the end of its controversial construction. It had split the city in two, running right through the heart of it and splitting up communities. It opened a year later and every day since had been gridlocked with rush-hour traffic until the months of lockdown brought respite for the commuters of Glasgow. Past the bridge, the Broomielaw, once the gateway to the shipyards of the city, had become the financial sector and was home to huge glass office blocks with corporate signage and revolving doors.

I turned up Oswald Street which ran into the junction with Hope Street and brought me to the main railway terminus, Central Station. The tall glass windows of the Hielanman's Umbrella, the bridge that carries trains over the main thoroughfare of Argyll Street, brought back memories of day trips with my father. He would announce he had a day off work as the yard was on reduced hours again and would let me stay off school so we could walk into the city and visit a playhouse to see a film or treat ourselves to an ice-cream at Tony's Café. I walked under the gloomy bridge and entered the train station. An escalator brought me up to the main concourse. The shops and bars had changed, but the famous clock still hung from the glass roof, a brown cube with white circles on four sides that had witnessed every reunion and departure on the platform below for over a century. I exited via the main entrance by the Grand Central Hotel that is attached to the station and headed north up Buchanan Street.

My childhood flooded through my mind despite the clean and modern facelift the city had gone through since then. I had returned to Glasgow a few times each year to visit my dad, first in our old family home and for the last few years at the care home where he now lived. Each time had been a fleeting visit, usually arriving on an early morning flight and returning to London that same evening. I had never felt the urge to revisit the heart of the city. However, in keeping with my journey back to Barra, I now had the inclination to see the place where that summer had begun and carried on walking up the slope and away from the river. At the top end of Buchanan Street, I crossed Nelson Mandela Place with the church in the middle of the road that encircles it. The name of the square changed from St George's Place in the mid-eighties in protest against South African Apartheid. The South African Consulate was based in the square. Its address had now included the most famous political prisoner of the regime. Glasgow likes to make a point without being subtle. I remembered the intersection for the pizza restaurant on one corner and the chip shop on the opposite one. It was another place my father brought me for a treat. The chip shop was still there, but now bedecked with a gaudy neon sign. The building where the pizza restaurant had been lay empty with a 'To Let' sign pasted across the window. I carried on into George Square with the impressive City Chambers building along one side and several statues and monuments on the red-paved public space. Queen Street Station, the second train station in Glasgow from which trains left to head to the north and east of the country, had undergone a recent renovation and its impressive new glass and steel frontage dominated the north-west corner of the square.

I entered the station and stood looking at the departure board. An evening train to Oban was due to depart in the next five minutes. The floors and roof looked new and fresh and clean, and nothing reminded me of the station I had known as a child, but it was here that my journey to Barra had started and, unknown to me, along with it, the end of my childhood innocence.

* * *

That day my dad had brought me into town and treated me to lunch from the chip shop. It was the start of summer, the first warm day of the year, and we sat on a bench in George Square to eat while he explained the reason I was being sent to stay with his brother on Barra. Mum had been in the Royal Infirmary for a month. I had already spent some time staying with my elderly grandparents while Dad was working in the shipyard. They were both in their eighties and no longer willing to take on the responsibility of caring for a young teenager.

'Ye see, son,' my dad said, while people passed through the square on their lunch breaks from the surrounding offices, 'wi' the schools finishin' fir the holidays soon ye need somewan tae look after ye aw day an' ma maw an' da are tae auld.'

'Will Ma no' be hame by then?'

He turned away. An old woman on the opposite side of the square threw bread to a flock of pigeons, who flapped and pecked around her. I knew Mum was ill. It only dawned on me in that moment that she may never come home from the hospital.

'Ah'm goin' tae be at the hospital wi' yer mum helpin' her git better an' when ah'm nae there ah'll be workin'. There's a new big order in wan a' the yards that'll keep me in work fir the summer.'

'Ah could help look after Ma. Ah could stay in the hospital wi' her.'

He managed a weak smile and squeezed my shoulder. 'Hospitals dinnae work like that. They're no' hotels ye can stay in, an' the nurses are tae busy wi' patients tae be lookin' after ye as well.'

'Ah wouldnae be any trouble.'

'Ah've arranged fir ye tae spend the summer wi' yer Uncle Tam an' Aunt Cathy in Barra.'

'The island?' I knew Dad's brother, Thomas Fraser, had moved to an island about two years ago and since then we hadn't seen them. I knew it was far away and took a long time to get there.

'That's right. It'll be great. Git out a' this city fir a few weeks an' breathe some fresh air an' make some new friends. It'll be an adventure. Ah've packed everythin' ye'll need.' He lifted the holdall that he had been carrying around with him.

'Ah'm goin' now?'

'The train tae Oban leaves in fifteen minutes. Here are yer tickets. Now dinnae lose them.' He handed me the slips of card. One was for the train and the other had a picture of a ship on it. 'That's yer ferry ticket. When ye git aff the train in Oban, Tam'll be waitin' fir ye an' he'll take ye oan the ferry over tae the island.'

'Kin ah no' say gudbye tae Ma?'

He must have seen the confusion in my face as I looked up at him. He stared straight ahead instead of meeting my gaze.

'It's better if ye go wi'out. She's very sick at the minute an' no' up tae havin' visitors. Ah'll call ye every week tae let ye know how she's doin'. Come oan, we dinnae want tae miss that train.'

I had looked back along the platform as I heaved the holdall into the open carriage door. Dad stood with his hands in his pockets and watched to make sure I got on safely. I was blocking the door as others tried to board. I managed a wave and Dad waved back and motioned me to get on the train. I boarded and stashed my holdall in the baggage area and found a seat next to a window. The train wasn't busy and I had a double seat to myself. The conductor's whistle sounded and the engine growled into life. The train began to move. I strained to look out the window to see if my dad was still there, but the platform was empty.

* * *

Standing on the platform where he had waved goodbye to me, I watched the evening train to Oban pull out of the station. It was just a regular service with the usual mix of commuters and tourists. It had been a regular service on the day it had carried one frightened thirteen-year-old boy away from his dad and the life he had known. I was being sent away to spare me the trauma of my mother's death. I was a naïve child in many ways, but I think I already knew I would never see her again.

I had never been alone on a train before. I remembered worrying if I would recognise my Uncle Tom when I arrived in Oban. I was travelling to a place where I knew no one else and had no idea what to expect. Was life on a remote island different from my life at home? If there were no shops or cinemas or other children to play with, how would I pass my summer? Forty years later, tomorrow would hold similar trepidation. I was older and wiser and knew what to expect from island life, but I was travelling without knowing what I would discover or who I might meet. I turned away from the platform and left the station. I wouldn't be taking the train to Oban this time and didn't have to face the five-hour ferry journey across the Sea of the Hebrides to Barra. Instead, I was flying direct from Glasgow Airport and would land on a strip of beach that served as a runway after only an hour in the air.

I hadn't eaten since having a prepacked sandwich for lunch at Stansted Airport that morning, so I stopped at the chip shop on Nelson Mandela Place and ordered a fish supper. The décor had changed, but the food still tasted and smelled the same.

'Dae ye wan' salt 'n' vinegar wi' them?' asked the middle-aged woman behind the counter.

'Please.'

The rapid volley of glottal stops, stressed vowels and dropped 't's and 'g's that she rattled at me across the piles of fried and battered food were like a different language. Being unable to see her mouth behind her face covering didn't help my understanding. I had lost the Glaswegian accent of my youth, replaced by the soft, articulate voice that suited the office of a London solicitor.

I ate from the carton as I walked back down the sloping street towards the river. Night fell as I reached my hotel. There was no one in Glasgow to reacquaint myself with, apart from Dad. I had called ahead and arranged to visit the care home on my return from Barra next week. There were no old school friends I'd kept in touch with and no other family. It had been a deliberate choice to leave the city and the people behind. I had wanted to better myself and leaving the streets of my childhood seemed the only way to do that. I thought of the boys I had hung around with. I remembered a few names and pictured some of their faces. Davie and Scott, Michael and Duncan and Gavin. We used to play by the river in the old shipyards and docks that had been left derelict, kicking a football around the patch of grass at the back of the flats I lived in. We walked the streets of Partick and picked fights with other groups of boys and annoyed the older girls. We didn't have a care in the world. We went to school together and grew up together and then grew apart as each of us moved on and found new interests. Some of those faces would still be around Partick. As the decades passed in London with only fleeting visits north to see my father, I gave little thought to the friends I left behind. Now I stood with only ghosts and whispers of my past life surrounding me and regretted not having kept in touch with some of the people that tied me to this city. The whole place felt alien to me. The country and city of my birth felt foreign and I was a lonely stranger passing through.

Back in my hotel room I undressed and climbed into the comfortable bed and removed eight of the ten pillows provided for me. I switched on the television and gazed at the news channel until I could feel my eyes closing. Tiredness brought calmness to my mind and I pictured a young boy scoring the winning goal on a piece of wasteland as the sun faded behind the tall block of flats in Partick before I was shouted in for supper and bed. I set the bedside alarm and slipped off to sleep. I dreamt of Glasgow and my father and cinema trips and chip shops and my mother lying in a hospital bed and of never getting the chance to say goodbye to her.

5

The small twin-prop aeroplane banked to the left and through the window I could see the island as we circled around. The pilot's voice announced the sea mist had cleared and we would be able to land before the tide came in. The news was met with muted cheers and some applause from the passengers. The small islet of Vatersay, at the southern tip of Barra, slipped into view. There was a causeway that linked the two islands, built a decade after I had stayed on Barra. I saw the pebbled coastline on either side of the narrow channel of water and pictured the small rowboat we had used to cross from one island to the other. I tried to pick out the old tree that was etched into my memory of that day, but there was no sign of it on the Vatersay side of the channel. It had been dead and decaying and it was not surprising that it should have gone by now. I wondered what other memories of my childhood visit had been washed away by the inevitable tide of time. The plane banked again and travelled up the east coast of the island.

A flight to Barra can leave Glasgow with sunny weather reported and, by the time the plane has made the hour-long journey, a sea mist could close in or wind speeds gust up to dangerous levels and the plane has to turn around and head back. This had happened to the flight yesterday. Some who had been on that aborted flight had been accommodated today, which meant the aeroplane was fuller than expected. Most of the passengers looked like tourists, a mix of students setting off on a tour up the Western Isles, or older adults on the way to visit friends or family. The airport is Barra's most famous landmark. The runway is a stretch of compact sand that is revealed at each low tide. The flight timetable is set by the rise and fall of the sea. We began our descent as we reached the north of the island and the beach appeared below, with the small terminal building and observation tower at the top of the bay. The plane landed on the sand with a soft bump and taxied to a standstill on the beach. Baggage claim was a small bus shelter on the side of the building and an SUV drove over the sand to collect the luggage and deposit it in the reclaim area. I followed the others disembarking from the plane and gratefully removed the mask from my face and felt the fresh air revive my skin. I walked across the sand and onto the tarmac and waited in line to pick up my travel case. A white and blue minibus was standing by to take passengers onwards. Most were heading to Castlebay, the main village at the southern end of the island. One or two were met by friends or relatives with cars and the only taxi was taken by a couple heading to the hotel in Northbay, a short drive from the airport. I replaced the mask over my mouth and nose and took a seat on the minibus. A man took the seat across the narrow aisle from me. He was portly and didn't wear a facemask. When I nodded a greeting to him his face broke into a keen smile.

'Been here before?' he asked.

'Once, a long time ago.'

'First time for me. I've always wanted to come. I'm travelling up through all the Western Isles. Then the whole family are coming up to spend the half-term holiday in Lewis.'

I couldn't place the accent, Midlands or Northern England, perhaps. I smiled politely, wondering how well the locals would accept tourists returning to the islands from further afield, even with the vaccine rollout.

'What brings you back?'

'Revisiting my childhood.' I turned to look out the window as the bus started to move. The man turned to watch the coast slip by from his own window.

The main road was a narrow single track. Vague memories stirred. Uncle Tom and Aunt Cathy had given me the use of a bicycle to get around the island that summer and I had cycled along this road. The geography of the island came back to me and I knew as we crested a hill and curved to the right that we were passing the turn off to Bruernish, where I had lived with Uncle Tom and Aunt Cathy. The windswept countryside had not changed from the memory that I had carried with me since boyhood. There were few trees. The flat, exposed land and harsh soil made it difficult for them to grow to any great height on much of the island.

The bus stopped by request only and no one alighted at Bruernish. The sandy beaches of the northern side were replaced by the rocky coastline of the east, filled with rockpools and coves. The road dipped down to sea level between sloping hills and was at risk of flooding during high tide. We passed through the houses that made up Brevig. I caught a glimpse of the Robertson house set back from the road as it had been in 1982. It must have changed since then, but I didn't have time to look closely before it disappeared behind us. Was it possible that Laura still lived there with her parents?

The in-plane magazine had told me that Barra is eleven miles long and six miles wide. I remembered it feeling much smaller. You could cycle from one end to the other in a couple of hours. A circular road loops round the central part of the island and connects the northern peninsula to the southern end where Castlebay and the ferry port lie. Most of the road and the land around the coast is flat and lies at sea level, which is where most people live. Inland, the island rises in a series of rolling hills with steep peaks, the tallest of which is Heaval, which towers over Castlebay. I had been forced to push my bicycle up the slopes of these hills many times as the steep road proved too much for my underdeveloped young muscles. The descents down the other sides made up for the struggles though, feeling the rush of adrenalin as I plummeted downwards, praying I wouldn't meet a car coming the other way.

The bus met a car now as it laboured up the side of Heaval. We pulled into a passing place and stopped. It seemed like the bus wouldn't be able to haul itself up the rest of the ascent when it tried to continue, but the complaining engine built up enough momentum to struggle onwards. At the peak of the road, cresting a shoulder of land halfway up the full height of Heaval, Castlebay emerged below and the road swept down towards it. The church still dominated the skyline above the main street and the castle sat surrounded by water in the middle of the bay, two hundred yards from the coastline. The large black and white ferry with two tall red funnels was departing as we descended, on its way to Oban on the mainland. It would be five hours before it reached its destination. The water in the bay looked calm and gentle waves lapped against the castle and rolled serenely into the harbour. Beyond the shelter of the bay larger waves rolled across the Sea of the Hebrides.

We passed the outlying houses and the church and reached sea level and then turned off the main road down the street that ended at the ferry terminal. On this road were the post office, bank and newsagent, each standing in the same buildings they had occupied forty years ago. There may have been extensions added and roofs replaced but to my eye the row of small, grey terraced houses appeared unchanged. The bus pulled in at the ferry terminal and all the passengers stood to disembark. I waited until the others had exited before following them. The bus pulled away and the new arrivals split up as each made their separate way towards the village. There was a cool breeze coming up off the sea and I pulled my coat collar up around my chin as I removed my facemask. I headed back along the street the bus had just brought us down and took a closer look at the row of old grey-brick buildings. As it was a Saturday the bank was closed. I looked up to the window at the top of the building. Above the bank was the flat where the MacLeods had lived. I expected to see Lachlan MacLeod staring down at me from his bedroom. He had watched that summer unfold from there. I had only been inside his room once and remembered how he moved around in his wheelchair. There was no face in the window today. The post office next door had been open that morning but had now closed until Monday. One doorway along, the newsagent was still open. The owner, Mr Anderson, had been in his eighties when I had last been here. There was no way he would still be leaning against his counter muttering over the newspapers. He was known as a grumpy old man with a short temper, but whenever I had gone into the shop with Aunt Cathy, he had slipped me a couple of sweets free of charge on the way out, accompanied by a conspiratorial wink and smile.

Dragging my case behind me, I turned right and began climbing back up the foot of Heaval, heading away from the bay. The road was steeper than I remembered and at the junction where the side road led to the church I paused for a rest on a boulder. It was mid-afternoon but already this far north daylight was beginning to fade over the bay below. I gathered myself and walked another fifty yards uphill to the next side road, along which stood three houses. They were all single-storey and made of wood, but each was individual in size and layout and separated by thirty yards between each one. Two of them had been there forty years ago, but the third looked newer. The middle house had a car parked outside it. A woman appeared in the doorway and gave an enthusiastic wave as I approached.

'Ye could've got the bus tae drap ye aff right here, save ye walking back up the hill.'

I smiled and tried to hide that I was out of breath. 'I wanted to see a little of Castlebay. Get a bit of fresh air after the flight.' After hearing her thick Scottish lilt I was conscious of my own diluted accent again.

She waited at the door until I stood next to her. 'Mary MacNeil.' She offered her hand and I shook it and felt the rough palm. She was old and portly and her skin was worn, but her eyes had the keenness of a younger soul. Her hair was white and cut short and she wore a woollen jumper under a bodywarmer with jeans and sturdy boots. A cloth mask hung around her neck, but she didn't pull it up to cover her face.

'Ewan Fraser.'

She turned and led me into the house, talking as she went. 'We wer surprised tae git yer bookin'. We wer jist about tae shut the hoose doon fir the winter.'

'Thank you for accommodating me.'

'No' at aw. After the last year wer grateful fir any payin' visitor we git. So long as they're healthy.' Barra had escaped the dreaded pandemic for a long time thanks to its remote location and stringent travel restrictions, but the lack of tourism had hit the small local economy. Just as the vaccines had arrived, so had the virus. Over fifty people had contracted it, and hundreds had been forced to isolate.

'Has it been bad?'

'It's no' bin gud, but what kin we dae? We want the tourists tae come back but no' bring the virus wi' them. Ah've given the place a quick clean an' hoover, an' ah've left ye wash towels in the bathroom. There's bread, milk an' eggs an' a few other bits an' pieces in the cupboard, but ye'll ha' tae stock up the rest yersel'.' She looked at her watch. 'The Co-Op will be open fir another two hours.'

'Whereabouts is the Co-Op?'

'Doon by the ferry port, o'er the hill tae the café an' school, doon tae the left, next tae the fitba pitch.'

I followed the direction Mary MacNeil pointed to through the window in the living room and could see the green rectangle that was the football pitch, and a square, modern brick building beside it.

'Yer first time oan Barra?'

'First for a long time,' I replied.

'Wit brings ye back?'

'A long story.'

'Sorry, ah'm pryin'. Ruairidh, ma husband, is always telling me aff fir gossiping wi' the guests. Well, anythin' ye need we live at the next hoose along.'

'Do you know if a Laura Robertson still lives here?' I asked before she could leave the room.

She thought about it for a moment. 'Dinnae know a Laura Robertson. Somewan ye used tae know?'

'Forty years ago, when I last came here.'

'A long-lost love story, is it? Well, there's Laura MacCormack who runs the tea shop, she'd be about ages wi' ye, ah reckon. An' Laura Sutherland who lives out at Brevig, though she might be a bit aulder. Laura Colquhoun stays o'er in Vatersay, but ah dinnae know a Laura Robertson. Ah could ask aroun', though, others will know better. Ah wis born here but moved away as soon as ah wis auld enough tae escape an' ah only moved back five year ago.'

'That's okay, thank you. You've been very helpful.' I regretted asking her. In this small community, my question about Laura would become the talk of Mary MacNeil's circle of friends before the evening was over, and would spread around the bay and beyond before too long.

'Ah'll leave ye tae git yersel' sorted then. Ruairidh an' ah would normally have ye o'er fir tea wan evenin', but, well, since the pandemic...' She trailed off with a shrug.

'I understand.'

It didn't take long to unpack my clothes and hang them in the bedroom. The house had a musty smell and a feeling of age. The décor was old and hadn't been refreshed in decades. The carpets were a dirty orange colour, the living-room suite was brown leather and frayed round the edges and the curtains a mustard yellow, but it was clean and cosy. There was no central heating but individual heaters to warm each room, the stove was gas and the water heater was a small tank that sat above the kitchen sink. I turned a kitchen tap to fill the tarnished-chrome kettle and pipes creaked and water gurgled before spurting out and then fading to a trickle. I checked my phone and found it had a weak signal. I hadn't called Lisa since leaving London. I wrote a text message to tell her I had arrived safely. There was no immediate reply.

The kettle clicked as the water reached boiling point. The milk in the fridge was fresh but when I opened the coffee jar the granules had congealed into a lump with a growth of white mould on the surface. I put my coat back on and locked the door behind me and set off for the Co-Op.

The cool breeze from the seafront had turned colder as I walked down the hill and through the village. I returned a nod of greeting from an old man and woman out for their evening stroll and remembered it was still the custom here to greet everyone with a polite acknowledgement. There was something charming and reassuring about this simple ritual that was lost in the sprawl of a big city. Other than the couple, the village was quiet. Everywhere was closed. A dog barked somewhere in the distance. I remembered one or two of the buildings as I passed by. On the other side of the street from the post office and bank was a small cabin that housed the local tourist information and shop. Across the main road was a town hall. Further on there was a small shed that seemed to be a craft shop and beyond that a factory and shop that sold 'Traditional Barra Tablet'. Further round the bay was a café and a children's centre and community hall, housed in a new building, and across the road a primary school that was a modern, squat cube. After passing them I turned off the main road and found the Co-Op supermarket and one or two other shops, with a small car park attached. The units and the shop were made of corrugated blue and grey panels. There were only two cars in the car park and both sat in spaces reserved for 'Shop Staff'. As the gloom descended further, I remembered how dark the nights were on Barra. Without the light pollution of a city the black expanse was endless. The welcoming lights of the shop were the brightest in the village.

I stepped inside and felt disorientated by the bright interior. It looked the same as any medium-sized supermarket on the mainland, with familiar signage and brands and goods filling the shelves and the same adverts decorating the walls. I picked up a basket and wandered down the aisle and found my preferred brand of coffee that I drank in London. In the small frozen section, I picked up a pizza that would be simple to cook in my basic kitchen. I gathered a few other pieces in my basket. No one else was in the shop until I reached the checkout and a bored girl of seventeen sat flicking through a celebrity gossip magazine behind a plexiglass screen. When she saw me approach she pulled a facemask up from her chin. I placed my basket on the counter and she began to pass the items through the till. There was no attempt at conversation.

'Fifteen-twenty. D'ye want a bag?' I told her I would need one. 'Ten pence extra.' Her accent was disappointingly neutral compared to the west-coast brogue of Mary McNeil.

I realised I had no cash with me and pulled out my debit card. 'It's contactless.'

I waved my card in front of the panel. I managed a cheery goodbye as I picked up my bag of goods, which was met with a circumspect nod, and I exited into the early evening, where the dark night had fully descended. A three-quarter moon shone and bright stars glinted in the clear sky.

I retraced my steps through the village and toiled up Heaval back to my guesthouse without meeting another soul. There were lights on in some of the houses that lined the main road and somewhere there was live music playing, which was the only hint that it was a Saturday evening, and a few of the locals had gathered in a pub. One car passed as I reached the road that turned towards my accommodation. The noise of its engine faded into the night and I noticed for the first time the quietness. Apart from the wild grass swaying in the night breeze there was no movement. The sound of the sea lapping down in the bay was all that broke the complete silence.

Back in the house, I heated the pizza in the microwave and sat eating from a plate balanced on my knees in the living room. The television was connected to a satellite dish and I had a similar selection of channels that I was used to in London. I recalled Uncle Tom battering the side of his old analogue television set as the picture distorted. There had only been three channels available then, and only the main one, from the BBC, had a reliable reception on Barra. I passed a couple of hours staring at the rolling news channel without concentrating. I decided to turn in for the night, but I forgot the trick of lighting the heater in the bedroom half an hour before going to bed to warm the room up. I pulled a second blanket from the airing cupboard and wrapped myself up under the duvet until enough heat was in the room so that I couldn't see my own breath anymore.

The absence of noise was unnerving. No cars streamed past the window, there were no voices in the street outside and there were no distant trains or sirens passing by. I could hear the ringing in my ears that was normally drowned out by the sounds of the city and seemed unbearably loud in the quiet night. When sleep failed to come, I switched on the bedside lamp and picked up the photograph that I had placed on the table when I had unpacked. I folded it down the crease that hid Billy and stared at Laura and those dark eyes stared straight back out at me. My eyes closed and I saw Laura cycling along in front of me, her long dark hair blowing behind her in the wind. I heard her laugh as she sped away from me. At some point I fell asleep. Billy joined us in the dream. We reached a sandy beach and ran up and down dunes, hiding from one another in the tall grass, splashing each other as we paddled in the sea, daring each other to venture out further.

6

The early light broke through the yellow curtains. The duvet pulled tight around me provided a cocoon of warmth against the cold morning air. I lay watching my breath condense into white puffs of cloud before shivering my way to the bathroom. Groaning pipes complained before the water dribbling from the shower turned hot enough to stand under. I washed and dried and pulled on layers of clothing. In the kitchen, hot coffee and toast warmed me up.

It was Sunday. Although not as strict as it had once been, much of the island would be closed for the day of worship and rest. I made a second mug of coffee and sipped it as I stood looking out of the living-room window. The sun shone over Vatersay across the narrow strait, while in the bay Kisimul Castle stood upright above the water and the black and white ferry was moored in the harbour. A handful of cars and passengers waited to embark. Mary MacNeil came out of her front door and walked along the road. It was too early for her to be going to the church. I gave her a wave as she glanced in my direction and went to catch her as she passed.

'Everythin' okay, Mr Fraser?'

'I was just wondering if anywhere was open today?'

'No' a church-goin' man? Dinnae worry, Ruairidh and I are no' wans fir the church anymare either.'

'I'm lapsed.' I hadn't been to church since my primary-school days, after which my mother had stopped making me go.

Mary MacNeil shared a conspiratorial smile and pointed towards the street leading to the ferry. 'The post office an' café are closed, an' the bank is shut, an' the castle is closed tae visitors fir the winter but the newsagent opens fir a half day. The Co-Op is open but the rest a' the shops an' the tourist information are closed until tomorrow.' She turned and pointed at the road disappearing over Heaval. 'The airport café'll be open if ye want tae see the plane landin' oan the beach an' the hotel at Northbay has a nice bar fir later.' I should have remembered about Sundays in the Western Isles before dashing up here for the weekend.

'The tea shop that Laura MacCormack works in, would that be open?'

Mary MacNeil glanced at her watch, 'Aye, at ten, an' Laura always works a Sunday tae.'

'The one opposite the school?'

'That's the wan. Ah'm heading that way tae pick up some fresh eggs. Ah kin stop by an' let her know tae expect ye if ye want.'

'No, thank you.' I answered hastily, knowing full well that Laura MacCormack would know someone was asking after her as soon as Mary MacNeil made it to the tearoom. Perhaps it was better for her to have some warning. Mary ambled off along the road.

* * *

The Barra Tea Room was busy for a Sunday morning. One table was occupied by three elderly ladies, and at another two young men in dirt-stained overalls were having hot-filled rolls before work. Religious customs were no barrier to the modern world and the seven-day working week. There were only five tables in the small room. I sat at one in a corner and slipped my facemask off and looked at the menu, which listed all the fillings you could have on a breakfast roll and a variety of hot drinks you could have to accompany it. Lattes and cappuccinos had made it to the Barra Tea Room. The delicious smell of cooked bacon and sausages filled the air. I glanced over to the serving counter. I had been here before. The décor had changed, but the layout of the counter and the kitchen were the same. Mrs Grant had run the tearoom back then. There was a young girl making up lunch rolls and placing them on trays for later that day. An older woman was bustling between the till, the coffee machine and a hatch that led through to the kitchen. Both of them wore facemasks which obscured their features. A couple of plates were placed at the hatch. The older woman picked them up and took them to the table of local ladies.

'Two full breakfasts,' she said, placing them on the table with a clunk. 'Yer no' treatin' yerself this week, Irene?'

Irene shook her head, 'Doctor says ah've tae watch ma cholesterol again.'

'Ach, doctors.' The woman waved her hand dismissively and left the ladies to resume their gossiping. She took a notepad and pen from her apron pocket and made her way towards me through the tables and chairs.

'Wit kin ah git fir ye?' She smiled.

'The full Scottish breakfast sounds nice.'

'Wi' toast?'

I nodded. 'Please.'

'Anythin' tae drink?'

'Just fresh orange.'

'Ah'll git that fir ye.' She walked away. I knew as soon as I had seen her, even with the mask obscuring the lower half of her face, that Laura MacCormack was not the Laura Robertson I had once known. She was short and squat, in her forties, with fading red hair and freckled skin.

She returned with a glass of orange juice after taking my order to the kitchen. 'You'd be stayin' up next tae Mary MacNeil?'

'I am. Ewan Fraser.'

'She came by this mornin' an' telt me ye wer looking fir Laura Robertson.'

'I thought she might mention it.'

She eyed me with suspicion, 'Well, it's no' me yer lookin' fir. Ah've always bin a MacCormack. Why would ye be lookin' fir Laura?'

'Do you know her?'

'That depends. Ah wouldnae want ye tae be causin' her any trouble.'

'I'm an old friend.'

'Ah've lived here ma whole life, ah've never seen ye or heard her mention any Ewan Fraser.'

'I haven't seen her in forty years, since we were kids. It was an impulse decision to come back and try and find her.'

My reasoning sounded weak, even to myself, but Laura MacCormack relented. 'Well, ah suppose Barra's small enough that ye'd find her easy enough if ye wanted tae, so there's nae point in no' telling ye. She's Laura Colquhoun now, lives o'er oan Vatersay, oan the southern side.'

'Thank you so much.'

There was a shout from the kitchen as a plate of food clattered onto the ledge. Laura walked back across the café and picked it up and brought it over to my table.

'Ye promise ye willnae bother her if she disnae want ye around?'

'Promise.'

She left me to eat my breakfast. I polished off a fried egg, a potato scone, a Lorne sausage and beans, leaving the fried mushrooms to one side. While I ate Laura kept guard at the till, eyeing me the entire time. Occasionally she muttered something to the young girl making the rolls behind the counter. My mind raced through a range of emotions. Could it be that easy? After forty years, could I have tracked down Laura with a simple enquiry at the local tearoom? But if Laura had never left Barra, why wouldn't it be that easy? Now the prospect of seeing her again was real. She was only a short walk away, over the narrow stretch of water on Vatersay.

The two workmen finished their coffees and paid their bill and left. A couple of hillwalkers entered. Laura served them and talked about the conditions for walking on the island today. The tourists had foreign accents, Scandinavian of some kind. I was grateful for the distraction and slipped up to the counter to pay my bill while Laura was talking to the new arrivals. The young girl came over and I paid and left. I politely nodded to Laura MacCormack on the way out.

The bells of Our Lady Star of the Sea, the church that sat at the foot of Heaval overlooking the bay, called the congregation to morning mass. I saw a few elderly folk shuffling up the road and cars pulling into the car park at the front of the old stone building. I wondered if Laura Robertson, or Colquhoun, as she was now, was among those gathering. Her family had been Catholic and when she was younger she had observed mass every Sunday with her mother. Her mother went to confession every day too, but her father had avoided the church. It was unusual back then that someone did not go to church at all, especially one half of a married couple.

While I watched the congregation gather, a feeling of elation rose within me. Laura was alive and the memories of that summer were within my grasp. Later that day I could be face to face with the girl who had been imprinted in my mind since I was a boy. The elation was followed by doubts. Would she want to see me again? Caught up in my impulse to confront my past, had I taken into account if anyone, including Laura, would want to be reminded of that summer? The community had dealt with the painful events of the past. The last thing they would want was a mainland fool blundering in and dredging up long-buried memories.

Rather than have my arrival announced by the island's network of gossip, I decided to waste no time in heading to Vatersay. If Laura was at the church service I could wait for her to return, but I was sure the headstrong girl I once knew would have given up on religion as soon as she was allowed to by her parents. I was Protestant and she was Catholic, but we had both agreed at that young age that neither variation of the religion was one we wanted to be part of. If I started walking now I could be there before midday. The weather was fair. The breeze from the previous evening had stiffened, but the sky was clear blue. Turning my back on the church and the bay, I set off along the road. I followed it for a mile before turning off at a junction onto the minor road that led to the causeway which joined Barra to Vatersay. I had forgotten how steep the hill down to the sea was and my feet sped away from me as I descended the slope. At the foot of the hill the causeway spanned the channel of water that separated the islands. The breeze tossed waves along the sides of the embankment and spray crested the road top, making it black and slick. It had been constructed at the end of the eighties and opened in the early nineties, long after I had last stood on this spot looking across the water. As I walked, I looked into the dark sea lapping against the sides and remembered the rowboat Laura and Billy had used to cross this same channel and our horror when we had started drifting away on the current. If only the causeway had been built two decades earlier. Had it been there, perhaps none of what happened would have taken place. I reached the other side and stepped onto Vatersay. I looked along the rocky, pebbled coastline to where they had found the body. Billy had shown us the exact spot. He'd lain down to show us where it had been washed up on the shore, caught between large rocks and the dead tree that was no longer there. I pictured Billy, his morbid reconstruction like a game to him as Laura and I watched on.

There was a modern, white two-storey house near to the stone beach. It had replaced an old derelict cottage that had once stood in the same spot. Laura, Billy and I had ventured into the cottage on the day we had been stranded on Vatersay. There was no sign of the old building now and the new house had a neat wall around a garden and a new Range Rover parked in the driveway.

Like Barra, the middle of Vatersay rose to a peak that was untrammelled, while the road curved round the lower ground along the coast and then looped back to head further south. The island was home to only a few people. There was no village, really, just isolated buildings dotted along the road. The vast expanse of scenery across the sea was breath-taking and the walk in the autumnal sun was enjoyable, helping me to stay calm as the moment of potential reunion drew nearer. The sound of the breeze and the waves against the shore, broken by the occasional call of a seabird, was tranquil and serene.

I met only one car and two sheep as I made my way round the central hill. Coming round a bend in the road, a small cluster of buildings gathered together on the lower land was revealed. Beyond them there was only the expanse of the blue sea on one side, and to the other, stretching south in a line, were the uninhabited islands of Sandray, Pabbay, Mingulay and Berneray. The next piece of inhabited land to the west was North America, four thousand miles away across the Atlantic Ocean. It felt like standing on the edge of the world. There was no sign of any people among the five or six low, wooden houses, but I could see some chickens pecking around in one of the gardens. The road ran up to these dwellings, then petered out into a dirt track and stopped.

Without knowing which house to approach, I walked up to the front door of the nearest one. I knocked and waited. There was no reply. I peered in a side window, but there was no sign of movement. I tried the next house. Only the chickens made any noise over the constant hum of the wind and sea. Again I knocked. This time I heard movement. The handle turned and the door opened.

I opened my mouth to speak and stopped. I felt the same surge of panic that I had felt on the underground train at Baker Street Station beneath the heart of London. There in front of me stood Laura Robertson, exactly as she looked in the photograph that was in my jacket pocket. Thirteen years old with long dark hair and penetrating brown eyes and pale cream skin.

She waited for me to say something. I stood with my mouth open.

'Hello?' she said.

PART TWO

THE BARRA BOY

7

I had never been on a ship this big before. The closest thing was the Renfrew Ferry that crossed only two hundred metres from one bank of the River Clyde to the other. Dad would take me on it, not to get anywhere in particular but as a treat in itself. The motion of this ferry made me queasy and Uncle Tom wasn't much help, telling me to man up and stop whining.

That morning I had expected to go to school, until Dad had announced my summer holidays were starting early. We set off for a trip to the city centre and I thought we would be going to the hospital and see Mum, who had been there for a week now. Instead Dad put some of my clothes into a bag and handed it to me at the station and packed me onto the train bound for Oban. Uncle Tom would be waiting for me at the other end of the line.

I felt like a grown-up, travelling on the train on my own and setting out into the big, wide world. I knew why I was being sent away really. Mum was dying. Tears escaped and ran down my face as I stared out of the window at the countryside rushing by. A woman sitting opposite asked if I was okay and offered a tissue. I took it from her and thanked her and made up an excuse about forgetting to bring my favourite book with me on holiday. Left alone for less than an hour and here I was greeting like a wean. Dad would have scolded me. Real men don't cry. But I had noticed the reddening round his eyes as we had sat in George Square that morning with the people of Glasgow bustling past. I had never before seen my father shed a single tear in the thirteen years I had known him. If it was okay for him to cry about this, then I could too.

I picked up the comic Dad had bought me from the shop in the train station and read while chewing on a sweet bar and drinking Irn-Bru from the glass bottle. It was after midday when the train pulled into Oban.

On the platform, Uncle Tom was waiting for me. It had been a couple of years since Tom and Aunt Cathy had sold their large house in Rutherglen and moved to the Isle of Barra. Cathy had been born on the island and had decided to move back. I spotted him straightaway because he looked like my dad. Uncle Tom was five years older, his hair was greyer and his skin a little rougher and wrinkled, but the family features were the same – the slightly oversized nose and ears and the lean stature, and they wore the same sort of clothes, casual jeans and long-sleeved shirts. I would have liked a reassuring hug from my uncle, but that was not his way. Uncle Tom had been a brooding presence whenever he had visited our home and rarely smiled or showed emotion. I had warmer memories of Aunt Cathy, who smiled permanently and had an infectious laugh and a sing-sing voice that chattered away even if no one was listening. I wondered how their marriage survived.

Instead of a hug I received a firm handshake and a pat on the head and a sympathetic, 'Hello, lad.' He smelled of tobacco and alcohol and I guessed he had passed some time in one of the pubs in the harbour while waiting for my train to arrive. The station was next to the ferry terminal. We went straight from one to the other and I only glimpsed the busy street that lined the bay. Fifteen minutes later the ferry set out across the sea. It was the first time I had ever left the mainland of Scotland.

Uncle Tom bought me a sandwich from the canteen and another bottle of juice. We sat at a table by a window and I ate my sandwich staring out at the coastline passing by. Leaving Oban behind, the ferry passed through the Sound of Mull with the island of Mull on one side and the mainland on the other. Tom nodded to a couple of people he knew from Barra who were returning with some shopping from the supermarket. He waited for me to finish eating my sandwich. The ferry left the Sound and headed into open water, between the small isles of Coll and Rum with the Cullins of Skye on the horizon to the north. Uncle Tom finally spoke.

'This isnae a holiday. Ye'll be expected tae earn yer keep aroun' the hoose an' dae yer chores tae help Cathy out. Ah won't have ye gettin' in her way, ye hear?'

I nodded.

'Speak up.'

'Yes.'

'It'll be "Uncle Tom" or "sir" when ye answer me. Did ma brother bring ye up wi' nae manners at aw?'

'Yes, Uncle Tom.'

'Runnin' aroun' that city filled wi' aw they young hoodlums. There's nane a' the likes a' that oan Barra.'

'Yes, Uncle Tom.'

We sat peering out of the window and, in a softer tone, he added, 'Ah'm sorry about yer mother. She's a fine woman who deserves better.'

I didn't answer. I looked across at him, but he carried on staring out of the window.

'Come oan, let's go up oan deck, the air is tae stuffy in here.'

The fresh air did little to help my churning stomach and even though it was a calm, mild day, my teeth began to chatter in the fresh air. It was a relief when land appeared ahead of us. Uncle Tom pointed out the islands that lay across the vast expanse of ocean. Vatersay to the south, Uist to the north and Barra in the middle.

We passed small rocky outcrops before entering Castlebay, the main harbour and village on Barra. A grey stone castle sat in the middle of the bay, built on top of rock that was barely above sea level with little land around the sides of the courtyard walls and a tower on one side. The loud noise of the ferry's horn took me by surprise as it announced our arrival. The pilot steered the ferry alongside the pier before the crew threw thick ropes from the front and back of the deck and men on the land tied them securely to huge metal cleats. The large stern door was lowered and became a ramp and the cars and vans drove off. The foot passengers left by a narrow side staircase and path along the pier.

Despite my sandwich on the ferry I felt hungry now my feet were on solid ground and my stomach had settled down. It was evening now and past the time Mum would have shouted me in for dinner. I followed behind Uncle Tom as he walked up the small street that led away from the harbour.

'Stop draggin' yer feet,' he called back as he unlocked the door of a rusty van. 'Git in the front.' He ducked in the driver's side and reached across and unlocked the passenger door. I got in and put my seatbelt on. Uncle Tom didn't bother with his. Riding in the front made me feel like a grown-up again, like taking the train on my own.

We rattled along a single-track road with a pot-holed surface and the suspension on the old van creaked and groaned. The climb up the steep hill leading away from the bay caused the van's engine to complain with a deep growl, but we made it to the top and freewheeled down the other side to let the engine cool off. Tom said nothing as I looked out of the window at the new landscape. There was not much to see. There was a rocky shoreline that might be fun to explore and a few small sandy coves. Dad had told me the beaches were extraordinary and a summer in Barra meant endless days playing on the sand and swimming in the sea. There wasn't much sign of that along this road and to my thirteen-year-old eyes the island looked bare and lifeless. There were hardly any buildings, only rough heather and moorland and the occasional grazing sheep or cow. What was there to do to pass the time stuck in this place for months?

'D'ye have a cinema?' I shouted above the clattering engine.

'A wit?'

'A cinema. Tae watch films in.'

'Ah know wit a cinema is. There's nae cinema oan the island. Or a swimmin' pool, or a games arcade. Ye kin forget about aw that sort a' nonsense until ye git back tae Glasgow.'

I sat back and let the events of the day hit me. The noise of the old van meant Tom couldn't hear my small sob. I had been torn away from my friends, my dad, my favourite places and my mum without warning. That morning I had woken in my own bed, in my own room and now it felt like a lifetime ago. I was alone and a sense of sadness that I had never felt before crept over me.

Uncle Tom turned off the main road onto a narrower track that took us through more rocky moorland, heading straight towards the sea. The van dipped up and down short, steep rises. At the bottom of one hill we rattled and juddered across a cattle grid. On either side of the cattle grid a wire fence ran off into the distance, its line marked by wooden posts. We drove out of this small dip and after another minute of jolting along the track, Uncle Tom parked the van outside a white house.

Aunt Cathy greeted me warmly and gave me the hug I had been looking for earlier in the day. Lennox, their Border Collie, jumped around in excitement at the new arrival. Dinner was ready so before unpacking we sat around the dining table and Aunt Cathy gossiped about the latest news from the island, while Uncle Tom ate in silence, offering only an occasional grunt or comment in response.

'That HMS *Ardent* they sunk wis built in Glasgow, ye know, only eight year ago. Pete Lorimer that works up at the fish factory, he worked oan it in the shipyard. Ah saw him today, distraught, he wis. An' Mary Morrison is still waitin' tae hear about her boy oan the *Sheffield*. Ah telt her today at the shop, nae news is gud news oan that front.' She leaned over towards me. 'He wis an able seaman oan it. They say some died when it wis sunk.'

I had watched the news about the war in the Falkland Islands, although I hadn't taken much of an interest in it. It had been on the front pages of the newspapers for the last few weeks and everyone was talking about it. I didn't understand the history or politics behind it, but I understood that Argentina had invaded the islands that we owned. Why we owned islands on the other side of the world I didn't know, but the Navy was sent to defend and reclaim them. Dad had dismissed the whole thing as senseless when it had started. The islands were right off Argentina's coastline, of course they should have sovereignty over them. What were we doing clinging on to some tiny scrap of land? 'Stuck oan the idea a' an Empire that's lang deid,' he said.

His brother Tom took a different view. 'We'll soon show them. Blast them back crawlin' under the rocks they came out a.' It was all he said on the matter and he returned to eating his shepherd's pie.

'So long as it's o'er quickly. The thought a' those young boys drownin' an' dyin' aw that distance away fae hame.' Cathy fell silent and then changed the subject. 'Everythin' okay wi' yer food, Ewan?'

'Aye, Aunt Cathy,' I lied. I was no fan of shepherd's pie. I picked at the lumpy potato and tried to separate it from the watery gravy and onions and raw carrot. I struggled to find any meat on the plate.

'Ye eat it aw up,' said Tom. 'Yer Aunt's bin slavin' in that kitchen aw day fir ye.'

'Yes, Uncle Tom.'

Under the table Lennox wagged his tail and his tongue hung from his mouth in anticipation of any scraps that might fall his way. I managed to scoop a couple of forkfuls to the grateful dog while Cathy chattered away.

Tom finished and left the table and went into the living room, where the sound of the evening news was soon heard coming from the television set. Cathy tidied away the plates, including mine, even though I had eaten only half of the shepherd's pie. She scraped the rest of it into Lennox's bowl in the corner of the room and soon he was lapping it up, although even he walked away without finishing it all.

I joined them in the living room to watch television. I sat on the brown sofa next to Cathy. Tom had his own armchair in the corner. The carpet was a garish orange-brown pattern of swirls and flowers. Cathy said they had still to decorate the living room since moving in two years ago. After the news there was a natural history programme, *Wildlife on One*. Aunt Cathy's gossip continued all through it and I was sure Tom only took an interest in the programme in order to deflect the constant chatter. Cathy insisted I have a bath before bed after my long day of travelling. While I waited for the bath to fill I unpacked my holdall in the guest room and placed my underwear in one drawer and my T-shirts and jumpers in another and my tracksuits and two pairs of jeans in another. Dad had forgotten to pack any pyjamas. I had no choice but to sleep in my T-shirt and pants. Apart from the clothes and a few comics, I had brought none of my belongings from home. I was about to put the holdall under the bed when I noticed a piece of paper at the bottom of the bag. I picked it up. It was a photograph. Dad must have put it in with my clothes. It was a picture of Mum. She was younger and she was smiling. She looked tired but happy as she stared up at the camera. It wasn't perfect; the shot was slightly blurry and too dark. In her arms she held a baby wrapped in a white knitted blanket, with a scrunched-up face and wide-open eyes looking at her. It was me on the day I was born. I remembered seeing the picture before in one of the photo albums that was kept in a box in my parents' bedroom at home. I turned it over expecting some message to be written on the back, but it was blank save for the date scrawled in the corner in Mum's handwriting – '14.02.69.' My birthday.

Cathy came into the room, knocking on the door first. 'Are ye decent?'

She saw the photograph I was holding.

'She wis a real looker back then, yer maw.' She took the photograph and set it on the bedside table, leaning it against the wall. 'How about tomorrow we find a frame tae put that in? Ah've a few aroun' here somewhere, or we could pick wan up at the store.' I nodded and Cathy put an arm around my shoulder. 'Come oan, the water'll be gettin' cold.'

I lay in the avocado-coloured bath until the water began to cool and the skin on my fingers wrinkled. There seemed to be little to do around the house. This part of Barra was called Bruernish. It was marked on the map of Barra that I had seen hanging on the wall in the dining room, but from what I had seen on the drive in, there was nothing here apart from Uncle Tom and Aunt Cathy's and a few of other houses. Tom and Cathy's house had been a Bed & Breakfast before they bought it. There were five bedrooms, three toilets, a large kitchen and a dining room and a living room. Their land was enclosed by a low, whitewashed wall that was high enough to keep out the sheep that ranged the grassland beyond and they had a small garden and an outhouse at the back. The nearest house was a hundred yards along the road. This was a guesthouse and over the summer would have different people coming to stay in it. Perhaps someone would stay there that I could make friends with. At the moment an 'obnoxious, loud American' was staying there, with his wife who was 'at least twenty years younger than him'. That was how Cathy described them. The American had got drunk the previous weekend at the hotel bar in Northbay and caused a bit of a stir with the locals. His wife seemed thoroughly miserable about her summer vacation in the Hebrides. The sooner they moved on, Cathy said, the better.

I got out of the bath and dried myself. From the bathroom window I saw a row of five or six houses sitting along the coast. I wondered if any children lived in those houses. When I had asked Cathy if there were other children on the island, Tom had cut her off before she could answer. I put my T-shirt and pants back on. I could hear muffled sounds from the living room downstairs. The voices floated up through the floor and I could pick out the odd word. They were talking about me. I heard the word 'mother'. I assumed it was my mum, but I couldn't hear anything more. Cathy moved into the kitchen and the cutlery clattered as she tidied away the clean dinner dishes. I pulled the plug out of the bath and the water gurgled away down the hole. I wasn't sure if I was expected to go down and say goodnight to them but decided to avoid them and walked across the landing and closed the guest room door behind me and sat on the bed. The room had a faded tartan carpet of dull green and blue. I guessed they hadn't got round to redecorating this room either. The bedsheets smelled fresh and clean.

I stared at the blackness outside the window. It was like nothing I had seen before. There had been one camping trip with the local Scout group when we had camped in a field in the middle of nowhere, but there had been a campfire that kept burning all night and torches and electric lanterns that hung in each tent and I had been with a group of eleven-year-old boys and surrounded by voices and laughter and in the distance we could see the streetlights of a small village. Here the darkness was uninterrupted. Only moonlight reflecting on the sea in the distance broke the void. I could no longer make out the houses further round the coast and none of them had any lights on. The only sound outside was the gusting wind that blew around the corner of the house. It was eerie and unsettling. I was used to the artificial orange glow of streetlights and voices from the street below and car engines and the constant hum of the motorway in the background. I was used to the sound of Mum listening to music from the radio in the kitchen. Here, there was nothing. At one point I was sure I heard hooves clicking along on the rough track outside the house. I heard a bird call, like the whistle of an owl, except I had only heard an owl's whistle on television before. This was the first time I had heard one for real.

In between those noises there was just blankness and my mind swirled. I lay down on the bed and as my head hit the pillow I felt the dampness of my short hair that I hadn't dried after the bath. A little moonlight entered the room and caught the photograph sitting on the bedside table. I looked into the tired eyes of my mother and thought of her going to sleep in a hospital ward two hundred miles away.

'Night, Ma,' I whispered, and then felt foolish for doing it. I had no idea how long it took my brain to stop churning and for sleep to come. Whatever happened over the summer ahead, I was sure my life would never be the same again.

8

Over the next fortnight I got used to the slow pace of life and settled into Uncle Tom and Aunt Cathy's daily routine. I was given a few chores to do around the house to earn my keep, helping Cathy wash the dishes or sweeping out the kitchen and keeping my room tidy and taking out the rubbish, but a lot of the time I was left to do as I pleased. Tom was set in his ways and Cathy continued to run the house in the same fashion as she had always done. Meals were served at regular times every day and every evening we would sit in front of the television for a couple of hours while Cathy updated Tom on the latest gossip.

Tom had been an electrician and plumber when he lived in Glasgow, with his own business that had employed three others, each with their own vans with Tom's name painted on the side. When they moved to Barra, he sold the business to one of his employees, who kept Tom's name on the vans. I still saw the vans driving around the streets of Partick. On Barra, Tom continued to work as an electrician and plumber but had also branched out into painting, decorating, roof-mending and other handyman jobs. Each morning he left the house as the sun was still breaking over the sea. I would hear the cough of the van engine and grinding wheels trundling off down the track as I lay in bed. Most days he didn't return until Cathy had the dinner ready, dumping his bag of tools in the hallway and quickly showering and changing out of his dirty overalls before joining us at the table. Twice he missed dinner altogether, arriving home late, muttering about a job that had needed finishing before he could leave.

While Tom was at work, Cathy kept busy with all manner of projects. She baked bread and cakes for the local cafés, she spent time in the garden with its small greenhouse and neat flowerbeds and took Lennox for his walks, she wrote endless letters and knitted and did puzzles and read and listened to the radio and did the housework.

As they had only Tom's van to get about the island, a trip into Castlebay for Cathy took up most of a day. On my first morning in Barra, after Tom had left for work, Cathy served me breakfast and announced we would be taking a trip to the village to get some essentials. I washed and dressed and we left the house and walked for twenty minutes along the track until we reached the junction where it joined the main road. We waited for fifteen minutes for the bus to appear, standing on the grass verge at the side of the road as light clouds drifted across blue skies. It was the only bus service on the island and it stopped when Cathy waved it down. The driver was an elderly man with the thickest spectacles I had ever seen.

'An' who's this ye have wi' ye?' he asked, peering at me with huge magnified eyes.

'This is Tom's nephew, Ewan. He's stayin' wi' us fir a few weeks.'

'Ah see now. Wid he be under sixteen years a' age?'

'He is that, only turned thirteen in February.'

'That'll be one adult an' one child then. Return?'

'Aye, return. Tom's workin' up near the airport the day.'

'Ah thought it wis his van ah saw parked up there.'

The driver punched some numbers on a little machine, peering down his nose to look at it, and two tickets scrolled out from the side of it, which he ripped off and gave to Cathy.

'Plenty a' spare seats the day.' Cathy and the driver laughed; there was no one else on the bus. He waited for us to sit down in the first double seat behind him before putting the bus into gear and starting to drive.

The bus took us back along the route Tom had followed the previous evening, but it took double the amount of time thanks to the crawling pace of the bus and the manoeuvring required when we met cars coming in the opposite direction along the narrow road. The scenery outside the window looked exactly the same as it had done the day before. The bus struggled up the final steep slope and then trundled down the other side into Castlebay. We got off near the ferry port. There were at least signs of life here. The small row of businesses that had been shut the night before were now open. There was a newsagent, a post office and a bank nestled together. The buildings were neat terraced houses, with signs above the doorways revealing the businesses inside. A handful of people came and went. In the harbour two fishing boats motored out of the bay, passing the castle sitting on its rocky perch. Over the noise of the sea lapping against the harbour, I heard laughter and followed the sound to see a low building on the other side of the bay with children playing outside. It was a school. It must have been morning break and the playground was filled with children.

Cathy had a letter to post. Rather than slotting it into the red pillar box outside the post office she took it inside the building. This was how things were done on Barra. The island moved at a different pace to the mainland and every errand was an excuse to meet and chat with other locals. I waited outside while Cathy went in for a blether. Later I appreciated how much these visits to the village meant to Cathy. She was lonely in the large house if she didn't get out to meet other people at least twice a week. She was outgoing and social by nature, and lack of human contact for two or three days at a time was hard for her. When she took a trip into Castlebay or to the airport café, they were vital moments of interaction that would see her through the following days.

I kicked stones off the kerb while waiting for Cathy to reappear. Next door was the bank, the only one on the island. An elderly man left the post office and smiled at me. No doubt he had learned who I was from Cathy. I wondered if he had had any need to go to the post office or if he was just visiting as part of a daily wander through the village. I looked up at the windows on the upper storey of the buildings. Above the bank I saw a boy's face staring out at me. He looked a little older than me, maybe fourteen or fifteen. Our eyes met for a moment and then his sad face disappeared.

He did not reappear at the window. I went back to kicking stones across the road. Cathy came out of the post office and we set off round the bay. We passed the school I had seen. The playground was empty now and through the windows I caught sight of the children in class. We carried on until we reached the local store. There were familiar food brands that I recognised on the shelves and some fresh fruit and vegetables delivered by the morning ferry. The store also sold things like clothes, toys, magazines, tools, light bulbs, gas canisters, bags of coal and wood and books. Cathy let me pick a couple of books and a football. They had no pyjamas in my size. As she counted out the notes and coins to pay for the shopping, Cathy spoke to the lady who ran the store, Mrs MacQueen. She said she was visiting the mainland the following day and she could pick up a pair of pyjamas for me from Oban. She asked what sort of pyjamas I would like. I told her I didn't mind, but green was my favourite colour.

It was lunchtime when we left the store and Cathy took me into a tearoom for something to eat. It was across the road from the school and the children were back outside again on their lunch break. There were about twenty children in the playground and they were a mix of different ages. This was all the pupils at the school. At my school there were more children in my class alone. The boys were kicking an old football around and chasing after it in an unruly pack. Others played a game of tig and some of the girls joined in this game. Another group of girls stood off to the side and were taking it in turns to do some sort of dance. One girl in particular caught my attention. She had long black hair and was as fast as the boys she was playing tig with. At one point the football landed near her and she shouldered a charging boy out of the way before kicking the ball back. The other boys cheered and laughed at the unfortunate one picking himself up from the ground. He gave the girl a petulant shove and ran back to the game. She turned away from them with a smile on her face and looked across the road towards where we sat in the window of the tearoom. I watched her point in my direction and say something to a freckled, red-headed boy next to her.

Cathy saw me looking at them. 'Dinnae worry, once school is finished fir the holidays ye'll git tae meet some a' them an' make new friends. A couple a' them live out near us at the hooses further roun' the road.'

I looked back and the girl had returned to playing the game of tig with the others.

After a sandwich and juice we left the tea room and walked the rest of the way back round the bay towards the ferry port. The ferry arrived while we stood waiting for the bus and the harbour became busy with cars, trucks and passengers disembarking and by those boarding to go in the opposite direction. The bus pulled up and it was the same driver with the thick glasses. Cathy showed him the return tickets he had given us that morning. Surely he remembered we had bought them? We were the only people on board again as the bus struggled up the hill and out of the bay and back along the coast to Bruernish. When we got back to the house Cathy let me to put on the television and watch the children's programmes that were just beginning and she set about making dinner with some of the food she had picked up from the store and a fresh piece of lamb that one of the local farmers had sold her.

In the hallway of the house on a table next to a notepad and a house plant was the telephone. It was red with a circular dial on its face. After a lamb dinner that second evening, which was much better than the shepherd's pie I had endured the night before, we sat down in front of the television when the telephone began ringing. Cathy rose to answer it. I learned it was always Cathy that answered the telephone, even though it was often someone looking for Tom to do some work for them. It was another routine of the house. Cathy would chat to whoever had called for five minutes before she called on Tom. Tom would mumble a couple of acknowledgements into the mouthpiece and hang up after twenty seconds.

'Are ye goin' tae dae it fir them?' Cathy would always ask.

'Aye, next week,' was the typical response.

On this occasion when Cathy called through to the living room it was not Tom she shouted on.

'Ewan, yer father is wantin' a word wi' ye. Jist tae make sure ye're settlin' in okay.'

I stumbled out of my chair to get to the telephone. Cathy closed the living-room door behind her and gave me privacy in the hallway. I wasn't used to talking on the telephone. We had one at home, of course, but I rarely made any calls or received any.

'Da?' I said, holding the handset to my mouth.

'Ye'll have tae speak up a little, son, it's a terrible line. How are ye? Did ye git there okay? Uncle Tom met ye aff the train?'

'Aye, Da. It wis fine.'

'Did ye enjoy the boat?'

'It made me feel sick.' I heard him laugh.

'Uncle Tom an' Aunt Cathy are lookin' after ye?'

The line crackled and broke up.

'Are ye still there, Da?' I was desperate not to lose the fragile connection.

'Ah'm still here.'

'Everythin' is fine, Da.'

'Ye'll behave now, won't ye? Ah dinnae want tae hear that ye've bin causin' trouble.'

'Ah promise, Da.'

'Cathy tells me ye went tae the shops wi' her today. Sorry ah forgot tae pack yer pyjamas.'

'That's okay, a woman's goin' tae bring some over oan the boat in a couple a' days.'

Another small laugh. 'It's a different world over there alright.'

'It really is, Da, really different.'

How could I tell my dad that I didn't like it so far and that I would be miserable spending my summer here? How could I tell him that I missed my friends and school and my own bed and most of all my mum? How could I tell him that I would rather be at home and visiting the hospital every day and that even if Dad thought what he was doing was for the best, he was wrong? I couldn't tell him any of that because I knew it would just add to his worries and make him feel bad.

'How's Ma?'

There was a crackling pause on the other end of the line.

'She's doin' fine. The doctors are doin' aw they can.'

Another silence. I couldn't think of anything else to say.

'Well, ah best be goin'. It's evenin' visitin' soon.'

'Wait, Da,' I called urgently before he could hang up. 'Tell Mum ah'm thinkin' about her an' ah wish ah could visit her.'

Dad sounded weary. 'Ah will do, Ewan. Ye take care an' behave yersel. Ah'll call again soon.'

'Bye, Da.' The line went dead and I stood for a moment with the handset to my ear before replacing it in the cradle. I didn't want to go back into the living room. Cathy came to the door after a minute.

'Everythin' okay?'

I could only manage a nod in reply. If I had tried to speak I knew I would have cried.

'Perhaps ye want an early night? Ah could fix ye a hot chocolate an' ye could take it up tae yer room wi' wan o' yer new books?'

9

Most days I went with Cathy when she took Lennox for a walk. We would follow the road that went towards the sea. After half a mile the road split. One fork led down to a small bay with a view of the fish factory on the other side. There was a red telephone box there, used by people who still didn't have a phone in their houses. On the water's edge there was a small slipway and a rundown boathouse that had two small fishing boats and an old rowing boat inside it. Cathy said they belonged to people who lived in Bruernish. The other fork in the road followed the shoreline and led to the row of houses that I had seen from the window of my room, but Cathy never went along that road. Lennox enjoyed having someone new to play with and we quickly became friends. I had little else to do and Lennox appreciated the undivided attention I gave him.

'Ye take him fir his walk oan yer own,' Cathy said at the end of my first week on the island. 'Ah can git oan wi' the hoosework.'

Lennox had to be kept on a lead because of the grazing sheep and cattle that roamed over the land. I felt sorry for him, seeing all that open space and not being allowed to run over it. He always strained at his leash, dragging me after him, and I was terrified that I wouldn't be able to hold on. The walks gave me something to do and got me out of the house, where I was constantly getting under Tom and Cathy's feet. I gave up kicking the football that Cathy had bought me around the garden after Tom came home and saw the round marks of dirt covering the whitewashed wall. Putting a fresh coat of whitewash on the garden wall was added to my list of chores.

I stuck to the left-hand turn that took me down to the old boatshed and tied Lennox to a signpost and sat and watched the occasional trawler going up the bay, depositing their catch at the factory or heading back out to sea. I threw stones in the water and tried in vain to hit an orange buoy that bobbed around just out of range. When I got bored doing that, I untied Lennox and walked him back to the house.

After a few days I decided to explore the other fork in the road. Lennox tried to pull me down the usual track, but after a battle of wills he gave in and I set off towards the row of houses.

As I got closer to the houses, they looked to be empty. It was the middle of the day and children would be at school and parents would be working. I passed the first two and peered in the windows and, not seeing anything interesting, was thinking about turning back when I saw a woman in the garden of the last house at the end of the row. She was hanging out washing on a drying line. Lennox tried to pull me across the road towards her as we passed by. I managed to haul him back, but not before the woman had looked up and noticed us. She smiled at me as I kept walking. She was in her late twenties, I guessed, younger than most of the adults I had seen so far on the island. I knew Aunt Cathy had grown up on the island, but when she had reached her early twenties she had moved to the mainland to finish her education and get a job. That was what most people did. The woman's face was fair and plain and she was slim and had shoulder-length hair swept back from her face by a blue headscarf. She wore a loose T-shirt with a wide neck that showed bony shoulders, and an ankle-length skirt.

I smiled back at her and waved without saying anything. I felt my face turning pink and allowed Lennox to drag me away. The track bent away from the house and went over a small rise of heather-covered land and hid me from the woman in her garden. A fence ran out to the coast and cut across the open land and the track came to an abrupt end. I followed the fence down towards the sea over some wild grass that had been flattened. When I reached the shore there was a small sandy cove hidden by rocks that surrounded it. I clambered over the boulders, managing to keep Lennox's lead wrapped around my hand as he jumped ahead of me. There were lots of rock pools to explore. The sea must have covered the sand and come right up to the rocks when the tide was in. Just as I reached the sand, I stumbled over a small rock and the leash slipped through my fingers. Lennox took off across the beach before I could grab the trailing lead. I picked myself up and brushed the sand from my trousers. Lennox bounded about and ignored my calls. I prayed he didn't go into the water. I would have to explain to Cathy why he was soaking wet when we got back to the house. He headed towards the rocks on the other side of the cove. There was a small opening, a cave that must have been eroded away by the sea, and Lennox bolted straight into it.

'Lennox, come back here!' He reappeared and I thought it was because he had heard the anger in my command, until I realised it was not my voice he was obeying at all. He was backing away from the opening and growling.

I stepped forward to retrieve him and picked up the end of the leash. 'Wit are ye growlin' at?'

It was the eyes I noticed first, a pair of clear blue eyes that appeared from the dark opening of the cave. Then the rest of the boy emerged. He had a mop of dirty-blond hair that grew wild over his ears. He was wearing a dirty T-shirt and shorts and was barefoot. We stared at each other. He was younger than me, perhaps eleven or twelve.

'Hi,' he said.

'Hi.'

With that he turned and jumped onto the rocks and scampered up them to the grassy top above the beach and ran away, disappearing from view. I looked after the departing boy. He should have been in school with the other children. He must have lived in one of the houses in the row above the cove. Did his parents know he was missing school? Why had he been hiding in the cave?

I made my way back up the rocks the same way I had come down and kept a tight hold of Lennox's lead and walked back along the trampled grass next to the fence. I had been away from the house for longer than usual and Cathy might start to worry about where we had got to. I reached the small rise where the track began and the row of houses came into view again. I was relieved that there was no sign of the woman who had been hanging out her washing. Bedsheets and clothes hung from the line being buffeted by the breeze. I saw movement behind one of the garden walls, but when I passed by and looked in the gardens there was no sign of anybody. Lennox pulled me back along the road and we hurried towards the house.

Aunt Cathy was in the garden, kneeling in front of a flowerbed and attacking the soil with a trowel. She looked up as I came through the gate.

'Gud walk?'

'Fine,' I replied, and Lennox pulled me away before she could ask anything else. I didn't mention the boy on the beach.

* * *

The following day was a Saturday. I took Lennox for his walk after lunch again. Tom had the day off and settled down to watch sport on the television. Cathy had taken the van and was meeting friends at the hotel in Northbay for lunch. This time I kept to the left-hand fork in the road that took me to the telephone box and the boatshed at the small bay. I would go back to the cove with the hidden cave another day to explore it and hope that the boy was not there. At the boatshed, I tied Lennox to the pole and left him enough slack so he could wander around. I collected some flat stones from the beach and skimmed them across the water, trying to get them to skip on the surface as many times as possible. My record was six, but the sea in the bay was too choppy and I only managed three with the last stone I had collected. A stiff breeze was blowing, stronger than it had been in the past week, and a cloud drifted in front of the sun and cast shade over the bay. I sat and rested my chin on my hands and huddled up against the chill. I didn't notice how long Lennox had been standing still, but I sensed that he had stopped sniffing around and when I looked over he had his head cocked to the side and was staring at the boatshed.

I stood up and walked towards the old wooden doors, wondering what had caught his attention. Green paint was flaking off the slats, revealing rotten wood underneath. Pieces had broken away and through the gaps I could see inside the shed. There was a solid metal padlock and chain on the door. Someone could only get in from the other side, which faced out to the sea and was filled with water as the tide was in. I placed my eye up close to one of the gaps. The wind whistled through the shed. All I could see was darkness and the water lapping around the edges of the shed, where a narrow walkway jutted out from the walls. My eyes grew accustomed to the dark and I could make out the two motorboats tied up, one along either side. The rowing boat was tied up at the far entrance. That might let someone get in from that end, if they could jump from the rocks to the rowboat and then clamber onto the walkway. A strong gust of wind blew in from the sea and the motorboats rocked from side to side, banging against the walkway and causing the whole structure to creak.

'It's jist the wind, ye daft dug,' I called back to Lennox, who was still static, head tilted, ears pricked. I was about to turn away when I saw a shadow pass along the far wall, interrupting the shafts of light that crept through the gaps. I pressed my eye up to the door again. Staring straight back at me was a clear blue eyeball. I sprang back and tripped and landed on my backside on the stony ground. Lennox started barking and strained forward on his leash. I picked myself up. The person inside was no longer trying to hide themselves. There was a clatter and a thud and the small boy from the beach landed on the rocks at the other end of the shed. He looked at me and ran off across the grass. After he had gone thirty yards, he stopped and turned back. He had a broad smile and his blond unruly hair blew around his face. He waved and laughed and then turned and ran again over the grass until it met the road and he carried on towards the row of houses.

'Cheeky wee…' I untied Lennox and calmed him down by patting him and rubbing him behind his ears. We walked back up the track and reached the fork in the road. There was no sign of the boy now. I walked Lennox back to the house and kept turning round, hoping to catch a glimpse of the boy behind us. I felt like I was being followed, but if he was there I couldn't see him.

* * *

Sunday was always a quiet day on the island. Aunt Cathy took herself to church in the van in the morning. The main Catholic church was the one that overlooked Castlebay, but other churches were dotted around the island. Cathy went to the small Church of Scotland building that was on the north-west side of the island. It stood on its own just off the main road. The minister lived in a manse joined on to the main church building, but there were few other dwellings nearby. I wondered why they decided to build it there, it made it a journey for everyone who wanted to attend. My mum and dad had stopped making me go to church back home and Tom had not been to a church since they had moved to Barra either, so I was not forced to go. Tom had some odd jobs to do in the outhouse, which sat just beyond the white wall at the side of the main house. I watched some television and read a magazine. Lennox lay at my feet. When he began to make a small whining noise, I took him out to the garden and threw a tennis ball for him to jump and catch. Ten minutes of that game was enough to tire the old collie and he slunk back inside for water and a nap. It was another fine day, although rain was now forecast for the week ahead. I threw the tennis ball against the wall for my own amusement. It was soggy with Lennox's drool. Sitting on the back step, I saw the football in the corner of the garden where it had sat untouched since the wall-staining incident. I felt an urge to kick it as hard as I could. I picked it up and kicked it out of my hands. It soared over the low garden wall and trundled over the wild grass at the back of the house before coming to a halt against the feet of the small boy.

He picked the football up and walked towards the garden with it. When he reached the wall he offered it to me and I walked forward and took it without saying anything. He smiled and opened his mouth and was about to speak when Tom came out of the side door of the outhouse.

'Ye git away fae here, Billy Matheson, ye hear. Git back hame wi' ye.'

The boy sped off across the grass and didn't stop to look back.

Tom turned to me. 'Yer tae stay away fae that boy, d'ye hear me?'

'Yes, Uncle Tom,' I answered, without understanding. I wanted to ask why I had to stay away from him, but Tom had already turned and gone back into the outhouse. The clattering noise of a hammer against a workbench rang out. I wondered what was so wrong with this boy called Billy. I went back inside as the first drops of rain started to fall.

* * *

Uncle Tom settled down in front of the television after we had eaten Cathy's Sunday dinner. I helped clean away the plates in the kitchen and told Aunt Cathy about the visit from Billy that morning.

'Uncle Tom came out an' yelled at him tae go away even though he wisnae doin' anythin'. Wit is wrong wi' him?'

Cathy said nothing as she scrubbed the dirty oven tray in the sink. 'Tom?'

'Naw, Billy, the boy. Why is Uncle Tom angry at him?'

She set down the tray on the drying rack. 'Ye have tae remember that this island is very small. There are lots a' rumours an' gossip an' things that upset people.' She saw the confused look on my face and tried to be more exact. 'Billy's ma did somethin' a long time ago that upset a lot a' people an' some people hold grudges fir a long time.'

She picked up the next dish and resumed scrubbing.

'Well, ah dinnae see why Billy should be in trouble because his maw did somethin' wrang.'

'It's best ye dinnae ask questions about it.'

That was the end of the matter as far as Cathy was concerned and we finished the dishes in silence before joining Tom and the television in the living room.

10

It was the middle of June and in Spain the football World Cup started. Tom and I sat together to watch the matches on television. It was good to have something we could do together, although I would much rather have been at home watching it with my dad. The first game was Argentina, who were the defending champions, against Belgium. It was played in the evening and I was allowed to stay up to watch it. Cathy had no interest in football and sat in the corner doing some sewing, only looking up when Tom shouted or made a comment. Belgium won by one goal to nil and even this wonderkid the commentators kept talking about called Maradona could do nothing to help Argentina. The Falklands War had been going on for two months and was still going on and the football commentators kept mentioning it as though the game was somehow related to the war. The studio pundits seemed happy that Argentina lost the game.

The day after the opening game the war ended. Argentina had surrendered. Pictures from London showed celebrations and Prime Minister Thatcher stood outside the black door in Downing Street and spoke of resolve and heroism and how wonderful the news was. News footage showed British troops running over fields and a white flag flying over Port Stanley. The ending of the war made little difference to life on Barra. There was no celebration in the village main street and no Union Jack flags being waved from windows. What happened in the rest of the world and the rest of the country didn't seem to have much effect on life on the small island. That summer the new American President Ronald Reagan visited London and spoke in Parliament and Princess Diana gave birth to a prince. Neither of these global events made more than a ripple to life on Barra. The one event that did make a difference was the visit of the Pope to Scotland. He had held mass at Bellahouston Park in Glasgow at the start of June, just before I had come to Barra, in front of three hundred thousand people. It was the first time a pope had visited Scotland. It was strange seeing the park on the news. Watching at home with my dad I recognised the park from riding my bike round it, and Dad and I had played football on the big grass fields before. Now it was filled with people as far as the camera could see. Father Baird, the parish priest from Our Lady Star of the Sea Church in Castlebay, and a small congregation, travelled over to be there. Laura told me later that all Father Baird spoke about in Sunday Mass now was seeing Pope John Paul II in Glasgow.

The good weather returned after a couple of days of rain, and with the end of the war and the start of the football World Cup, things brightened up a little. The football gave Tom and me something to talk about and Cathy became the quiet one at the dinner table as we discussed the day's games and looked ahead to the evening kick-off. Dad phoned a few times and we would spend half an hour talking about the football, especially when Scotland were playing. I think he liked the distraction of talking about the football. I would always ask how Mum was getting on and Dad would always say that she was doing fine in hospital and missing me and sent her love. I would send my love back.

The Scotland team beat New Zealand 5-2 in their first game and optimism grew that we finally had a chance of doing well in a tournament. Our next game was against Brazil. It was another evening game and after dinner I sat down with Tom to watch. Even Cathy paid attention and her sewing was left untouched by her armchair. Against all the odds, Scotland scored first. The ball fell at the feet of David Narey on the edge of the Brazilian box, a defender not known for being a skilful player. He smashed the ball and it flew like a rocket straight into the top corner of the goal. There was a moment of disbelief. Then Tom erupted out of his chair. His glass of beer went flying across the room. I jumped up too and we danced around the room, arms aloft and hugging each other. He lifted me up and kissed me on the cheek.

'Put the boy doon,' cried Cathy. She was on her knees picking up the empty glass.

After another lap around the room, we settled back down. The euphoria was short-lived. Brazil equalised soon after. In the second half Brazil scored three more goals to win 4-1.

Tom didn't seem to mind that we had lost. 'We wirnae expectin' tae win that anyway. That goal, though. Wit about that? Ah'll never forget that goal.'

* * *

Tom was due to start fitting a new kitchen in a house in Eoligarry, the village on the northern peninsula of the island, but the furniture had missed the ferry the day before and wouldn't arrive until the afternoon. When I came down for breakfast he had already eaten and disappeared into the outhouse. He spent the morning in there, emerging to eat lunch and then taking the van to Castlebay, where he had to get some spare parts from the hardware store. He got back and went straight into the outhouse again. I spent the day pottering around the house as usual and taking Lennox for his walks. It was late afternoon and I was helping Cathy set the table for dinner when Tom called for me.

'Oan ye go,' Cathy encouraged me.

Sure that I had done something wrong even though I couldn't think of what it might be, I opened the back door that led from the kitchen into the back garden. Tom stood on the path holding a bicycle in front of him.

'Here ye go.'

'It's fir me?' I stepped forward to get a closer look. It wasn't pretty. It was an old bicycle and the frame was covered in patches of rust that Tom had sanded down and repainted a slightly different shade of red from the rest of the bike. The wheel spokes and rims were dull silver and had blotches of brown rust on them, but the tyres looked new. One pedal was silver and the other black. There was a new shiny bell and rubber grips on the handlebars that looked fresh.

'It belonged tae the lad that lived here before us, when he wis a kid. He left it behind when he moved away. A bit worn an' tattered but ah've scrubbed it up as best as ah can.'

I beamed at him.

'Hop oan an' ah'll adjust the saddle.'

I threw my leg over the saddle and sat on it. It was the original saddle, old and without any padding.

'Right, needs tae come up a bit. Hold oan tae it a second.'

I stepped off and kept the bicycle upright while Tom turned the nut under the saddle and raised it an inch or two and then tightened it again.

'That should be ye. Ye kin ride wan a' these, ah take it?'

It had been a year since I had outgrown my bike at home. Mum being ill and Dad not working much had meant they hadn't been able to afford to get me a new one. I swung my leg over the saddle again and had a practice pulling the brakes and ringing the bell.

'Course ye kin,' Tom said, answering his own question. 'It's jist like ridin' a bike.' He laughed at his own joke and went back into the outhouse.

'Dinner in ten minutes,' Cathy called from the kitchen where she had been watching through the window.

'Jist need tae tidy up an' then ah'll be in,' Tom called back.

Cathy smiled at me. 'A quick shot now, then ye'll have aw day tomorrow.'

* * *

It rained for the next two days, a slanting deluge that didn't let up. The bicycle was stowed away in the outhouse. Tom went out in the van to start the kitchen in Eoligarry, leaving Cathy and me in the house. Even Lennox was reluctant to go out in the rain. Cathy let him into the garden and after relieving himself, he wandered straight back in and shook the water from his coat and settled into his warm basket in the corner of the kitchen.

Dad rang again and spoke to Tom before I was called to the telephone. There was no news. Mum was still fine and Dad was visiting her every day. I told him about the bike and how I was looking forward to going out on it as soon as the rain stopped.

It finally relented, leaving the ground soaked and large puddles in the uneven bumps and divots of the road. Cathy insisted I wait until the afternoon before taking the bicycle out, once the sun had had a chance to dry out the ground. I spent the morning staring out of my bedroom window. At the far end of the row of houses down by the shore I saw billowing sheets on the drying line and remembered the woman I had seen in the garden. She must have been waiting for the rain to stop to get her washing out to dry. I watched a small spider try to pull itself up a thread to reach its half-formed web in the corner of the window. After lunch and after helping Cathy clean away the dishes she finally relented and let me fetch the bike from the outhouse.

'Dinnae go tae far now. The main road an' nae further. An' dinnae be goin' tae fast either, ah dinnae want ye fallin' aff an' hurtin' yersel.'

With an initial wobble, I set off. My shoes and socks and the ankles of my tracksuit trousers were soon soaked from the spray the wheels kicked up from the uneven track. The hard saddle hurt my backside as I bumped over the potholes and loose stones. The old bike had no gears and at the tiniest uphill slope I had to stand up out of the saddle and push down hard on the pedals to keep going, but I managed to make it up each of the rises on the road without having to get off and push. On the downhill slopes I gained more confidence and began freewheeling without using the brakes. The wind in my face and the rush of excitement made me happy. At the end of one steep hill I careered round the bend and saw the cattle grid filling the road in front of me. There wasn't enough time to stop and on either side was a fence. The metal grid would throw me off the bike at this speed and if it didn't the thought of the hard saddle smacking my arse didn't bear thinking about. I took evasive action and threw the handlebars to the right and bumped into the rough grass and ferns that bordered the road. The uneven ground slowed me down, but not before my front wheel plunged into a dip and I went flying over the handlebars.

I landed on my back, looking up at the sky and feeling the wetness of the grass seeping through my clothes. Aside from my pride, I was unharmed, although there would be some bruises the next day. No one was around to witness my fall apart from a solitary cow, who stared at me and carried on chewing the grass.

'Dinnae tell anywan about this,' I warned him, and I burst out laughing lying there.

I picked up the bike and checked it over and was relieved to find it was undamaged. After that I took more care coming down the hills and used the brakes to keep my speed under control. When I returned to the house, Cathy spotted the dirt stains on my trousers and back and the graze on my right hand but said nothing.

* * *

I had seen no more of Billy Matheson since the day Tom had chased him away from the house. I kept taking Lennox for a walk down to the boathouse, but there was no sign of him or his mop of tangled hair.

Cathy was taking the bus into Castlebay one morning and I suggested I set off before her on my bike and cycle all the way there and meet her for lunch. It was about six miles from Bruernish to Castlebay and I reckoned I could make the journey in less than an hour, especially with the tarmacked surface of the main road being much smoother than the tracks around the house. Cathy agreed, with a warning to watch out for cars on the way.

I set off mid-morning. The ground had dried up by now, apart from the odd remaining puddle. I had forgotten how many steep climbs there were on the road heading to the south of the island. I didn't remember there being so many when the old bus had taken us into the village. I managed to get to the top of the first few uphill slopes and enjoyed going down the other side, but the next one forced me to get off the bicycle and push it to the top. I remounted and set off down the hill, but a car came in the opposite direction and forced me to swerve off the road to let them pass. The next hour turned into a struggle. By the time I reached Heaval, where the road crept up the foot of the steep side of the highest hill on Barra, I was ready to drop with exhaustion. I barely managed the first twenty metres before I dismounted and pushed the heavy old bike alongside me. The front wheel developed an irritating squeak. I finally made it to the crest of the road and looked down on Castlebay below. The view, followed by hurtling down the road into the village, was worth the climb.

We had agreed to meet at the tearoom across from the school building where we had had lunch before. The bus had not passed me along the road despite how long it had taken me to get there, so I knew Cathy had not arrived yet. I pottered around on my bike outside the tearoom, bumping up and down on the narrow pavement. The school bell rang and a moment later children spilled into the playground for their lunch break. I stopped cycling round and sat on my bike and watched them through the black railings. They played the same games I played at my school. The older boys tried to organise a game of British Bulldog and roped the smaller children into taking part. There was no sign of Billy Matheson and I wondered if he ever attended school. There was no other school on the island that I knew about. The last pupil to emerge from the building was the girl I had noticed before. She was slightly taller than most of the other children and her long dark hair was tied back in a ponytail. It seemed there was no uniform for the school and each child wore their own clothes. The girl wore blue jeans and a plain light-grey T-shirt.

She looked at the lines forming for the game of British Bulldog, with the two biggest boys in the middle who would be the bulldogs trying to catch the other children. She decided she did not want to take part and then she saw me by the fence and walked over.

'You the kid stayin' wi' the Frasers?' she asked without introduction.

'Aye.'

She stared straight at me and looked like she was deciding if I was worth talking to or not. 'Ma maw knows yer aunt. She says yer here because yer ma's goin' tae die.'

Everyone else had avoided saying those words out loud and it caught me off guard to hear it put so bluntly.

'Naw, she isnae. She's jist unwell in the hospital.'

She accepted this, or didn't care either way. 'I'm Laura.'

'Ewan.'

'That yer bike?'

'Ma uncle fixed it up fir me tae use. It's jist an auld wan.'

'Ah kin show ye roun' oan ma bike if ye want. School finishes this week so ah could meet ye here oan Monday.'

'Okay.'

'In the mornin'? Meet me here at the gates.'

'Okay.'

Just then the bus came along the road and stopped outside the tearoom. I wanted to talk more to her. Cathy hopped off and thanked the driver. She saw us standing on either side of the school fence and crossed the road to join us.

'*Feasgar math*, Laura.'

'*Halò*,' Laura replied. It sounded like hello, but in a slightly different accent.

'*Ciamar a tha thu an-diugh?*'

'*Tha mi gu math.*' Laura turned to me and switched back to words I could understand. 'See ye next week then?'

'Aye, okay.'

She ran across the playground and joined in the game of British Bulldog that was now in full flow with the older boys catching the younger children and wrestling them to the ground.

'Ready fir some lunch?' Cathy said, and we walked across the road to the café. I looked back over my shoulder to catch another glimpse of Laura. Once inside we sat down and ordered sandwiches and crisps and a cake each for dessert.

'Wit wis that ye said tae Laura?' I asked while we waited for our food to arrive.

'That wis Gaelic. Lots of people oan the islands speak it.'

'How d'ye know it?'

'Ah learnt it a bit fae ma parents when ah wis brought up here. Ah'm a bit rusty, but ah know enough tae get by.'

'Dae aw the children speak it?'

'Most a' them, though it's less common now an' ah'm nae sure if the schools still teach it. Laura's parents speak it. They speak in Gaelic rather than English in their hoose.'

'Laura wants tae meet up wi' me next week when the schools are aff an' go cycling roun' the island.'

'That'll be lovely. Although she's a handful, that Laura. No' in a bad way, she's kind-hearted but… spirited. Ye'll have a job keepin' up wi' her. Seems like ye've made a new friend.'

I suddenly felt shy, and I felt my cheeks blush.

11

The weekend dragged by. Rain returned in bursts of heavy showers. The forecast said it should clear by Monday. I thought about Dad, sitting on the bus, soaked after waiting at the bus stop, on his way home from another visit to the hospital. He hadn't called in three days. I had no idea if that was a bad sign or not, if it meant nothing had changed or things had got worse.

Monday morning arrived. Tom was still working on the kitchen in Eoligarry and had left early. The forecast had been right and bright sunshine streamed through the kitchen windows as Cathy watched me rush through my breakfast. 'She'll wait fir ye if yer five minutes late.'

I set off just after half past nine. As I struggled to the peak of a hill on the road, I stood up on the bike and pushed down hard on the pedals. They span round without resistance and I toppled forward. I ended up on the grass verge and the bike landed on top of me. Grazed palms and a scrape along my right knee were the only minor injuries. I kicked the bike off and picked myself up and looked at the damage. The cause of the crash was obvious. The metal chain hung free from the cog. Dad had always been on hand to fix this at home. I tried to remember how to get the chain back on. I looped it back onto the teeth of the cog and turned the pedals by hand until the chain wrapped itself round. It took several attempts. My hands became covered in thick black grease and dirt. Finally the teeth and chain slipped fully into place and I felt a sense of achievement as the back wheel started spinning again. I wiped my hands on the grass to remove as much grease as I could. The black stain smudged and refused to disappear. Without a cloth, I had no choice but to use my tracksuit top and rub my hands up and down the front of it until I managed to remove a thick layer, although my fingers and nails remained black. At least my top was dark navy, so the black stains did not stand out too much. I got back on the bicycle and felt the remaining grease on the new handlebar grips as I set off again.

It turned into a warm day and by mid-morning the sun was beating down from clear skies overhead. There was no shade on the road. I managed to get up more of the hills than I had done the first time I had cycled along the road, but with each effort sweat dripped down my forehead and I wiped my brow clear with my hands.

The climb up Heaval defeated me. I doubted I would ever be able to make it to the top of that slope. I was braver on the descent, though, and released the brakes and freewheeled to the bottom and along the road through the village. Laura was waiting for me at the school gate. Her bike was propped up against the playground wall and she sat on the pavement picking up small stones and throwing them across the road. When she saw me coming she stood up. I came to a stop in front of her and she burst out laughing. It wasn't the greeting I had hoped for, or had imagined.

Without explanation she grabbed my arm. 'Come wi' me.' I left my bike leaning against the gate next to hers. She dragged me across the road and into the tearoom, which was open as usual. I recognised the woman behind the counter who had served me when I had been in before with Cathy.

'Mrs Grant, kin Ewan use yer toilet?'

The woman looked up and her face broke out into a laugh. 'Goodness me. Aye, ah think he better. Oan ye go.'

Laura pulled me through the café to the small bathroom at the back. There was only a toilet and a small sink and barely room for one person to stand in the small room. She pulled the light cord.

'Ye better have a look fir yersel,' she said, and then stepped out, leaving me on my own. From the mirror my grease-smeared face stared back at me. Lines of sweat had made a pattern through the black smudges that had transferred from my hands onto my forehead when I had wiped sweat from my brow. Black patches had trickled down over my cheeks and nose. No wonder she had laughed at me. I turned the tap on and splashed water on my face and hands and scrubbed them with a well-used bar of soap. It took five minutes to clear the dirt away. There were still bits of grease on my fingers and under my nails and round the edges of my eyes, but it would have to do for now. I had to clean everywhere I had touched around the sink where dark smudges of dirty water had gathered.

When I returned to the tearoom, Laura was standing by the counter next to Mrs Grant, finishing off a roll and sausage.

'Aff ye go now,' said Mrs Grant. 'Dinnae be gettin' intae any trouble. You kids oan yer school holidays, ye run the place daft.' She disappeared through a door to the kitchen at the back of the counter.

Laura wiped her mouth with her sleeve and we headed back outside. 'Sorry fir laughin' at ye.'

'Ah dinnae blame ye. Ma chain came aff an' ah didnae realise ah had wiped so much grease ontae ma face. Ah looked like somethin' out a' *Mad Max*.'

'Ah havnae seen that. Ma parents wouldnae let me watch somethin' like that oan the television.'

'Ma da sneaked me intae the cinema tae see it.'

We picked up our bikes that were still leaning against the school railings. Laura's bike looked new; it was bright red and shiny. It put the old rusty one, which Tom had gone to so much effort to fix up for me, to shame.

'Where d'ye want tae go?' Laura asked.

'Ah dunno. Ah've only seen the village an' roun' ma aunt an' uncle's hoose.'

'Come oan then.'

Laura wheeled her bike round and set off along the road and I followed, leaving Castlebay behind us.

The main store was as far as I had been with Cathy. Past it, the road turned right and headed off across the bottom of the island. There was another track to the left. Laura stopped and I pulled up alongside her.

'Doon there is Vatersay.' She pointed at a hill in the distance. From where we were I couldn't see that it wasn't joined to Barra. 'It's a separate island. Wan day we could git a boat an' go o'er tae it if the water's calm enough, but there's no' much there. Hardly anywan lives there.'

With that she pushed down on her pedals and carried on along the main road and I followed behind her. She was wearing the same T-shirt she had worn for school, but now had on a pair of shorts and trainers, showing her long, pale legs. I couldn't help but notice the white strap on her shoulder that peeked out from her T-shirt collar. Either because of her longer legs or her better bike, I struggled to keep up with her as my old bike rattled over the mottled surface.

The road turned again and headed up the west side of the island and was flatter than the route between Bruernish and Castlebay. Once we had made it over a couple of steep slopes, it meandered up the coast. The shoreline changed and a series of small rocky bays gave way to the sandy beaches Dad had told me about. There were even less houses and no villages on this side of the island to interrupt the rolling grass and heather. Laura made light work of the uphill parts of the road that I struggled along. I was determined not to be shown up and was grateful every time she stopped and allowed me a rest as she pointed out a beach to play on, or a hill to climb, or a house that such-and-such owned. The deep blue Atlantic Ocean stretched off to the horizon while its waves rolled onto golden sands. My old bike didn't let me down and the chain stayed on and eventually I relaxed in Laura's company. We didn't say much to each other as we cycled along, sometimes side by side and sometimes in single file, but I didn't mind.

We passed the unimpressive Church of Scotland building where Cathy went each Sunday morning and the road turned again to cut back across the island. There was another junction and a road that turned north, which led to the peninsula at the top of the island and the airport and Eoligarry where Tom had been working.

'Hungry?' Laura called over her shoulder.

'Aye,' I shouted forward.

Laura swung off the main road and took the turning north. There were more rocky coves and twists and turns and then the coast opened out into a large bay. The tide was out and there was a large beach of flat sand and at the top of the bay was a building with a small tower and a satellite dish on top of it. We looped round the bay and I saw a sign for Barra Airport. Laura stopped outside the building and propped her bike against the wall.

'We kin get lunch here.'

I leaned my bike against hers. It was an unimpressive building compared to the airport back home where Dad took me to watch the aeroplanes. There was an orange windsock out in the bay to indicate wind speed and direction and a small shelter at the side with a sign above it that read 'Baggage Claim'. I had heard about the planes landing on the beach, but there were no markings for a runway on the sand. I followed Laura into the terminal building.

Inside there was a check-in desk on one side, and on the other, through a door was a café. Laura was already at the counter talking to a woman. There was an older couple at a table having scones and tea. I walked over to join Laura at the counter and she introduced me to the woman.

'This is ma mum. This is the boy ah wis tellin' ye about.'

'Pleased to meet you, Ewan. I'm Flora,' the woman said. She spoke with a refined accent, pronouncing each letter with a soft, lilting tone. She looked about the same age as Aunt Cathy, but she was thinner and healthier. She had the same long dark hair as Laura but flecked with a few strands of grey and tied back from her face in a bun, and she wore a red apron and blue plastic gloves for preparing food. She looked me up and down and I was conscious of the grease stains on my clothes.

'*Suidh sios is agus bheir mi dhut rudeigin ri ith*,' she said to Laura.

'*Tapadh leibh*.' Laura smiled at me and walked over to a table by the window. I sat down opposite her. The window looked out onto the bay and the wide sandy beach we had just cycled round.

'Wit wis that?'

'She'll bring us a sandwich over fir lunch, free a' charge.'

I looked at Laura across the table. Her hands played with the sauce bottles and salt and pepper shakers in front of her. Her pale skin was dotted with very faint freckles and on the side of her face, just above the cheekbone, there was a small birthmark that moved when she smiled. Strands of dark hair fell over her face and she tucked them back behind her ear. The sun shone through the window and her face and her pale skin seemed to glow.

At last I had a chance to talk to her. I wondered about her parents and the fact they chose to speak Gaelic. 'Wit dae yer parents think a' people who come fae the mainland?'

'Depends oan the person. They dinnae like the wans that buy hooses here an' then never live in them. A lot a' the hooses are empty most a' the year until the holidays. Dinnae worry. Yer Aunt Cathy is sort a' an islander, so yer sort a' wan tae.'

'Why dinnae they speak in English?'

'My da kin bore ye fir hours about how the mainlanders stole the land an' the culture an' tried tae make us aw speak their language.'

'Dis yer maw own this café?'

'The airport owns it. She works here three days a week.'

Flora arrived with two plates of sandwiches with crisps on the side and two cans of juice and put them on the table. 'Have you had a chance to see the plane coming in yet, Ewan?'

I shook my head. 'Ah hadnae seen much a' the island until Laura took me round this mornin.'

'It's due in now if you keep a lookout for it.'

Flora left us to eat our lunch and we stopped speaking while we ate. I kept looking out the window for any sign of the approaching plane.

'Are there many other children our age oan the island?'

'Some. The only other girl the same age as me is Fionn, but she disnae come out much. Ah suppose ye ha' lots a' friends at hame?'

I had never thought about what it would be like to not have friends my own age to play with. It was just normal living in a city.

'A few. Mostly we play fitba jist like the boys at yer school.'

'Ah like football, but the boys willnae let me join in.'

'There's a girl who plays fir our school team wi' the boys. We could play sometime.'

'Wouldnae be much a' a game, jist the two a' us.'

'Jist a kick about. If ye wanted.'

Laura took another bite from her sandwich and the conversation halted again. She pointed out the window. 'Here it's comin.'

A tiny spot in the sky grew larger. It wasn't a big jet aeroplane like the ones that took hundreds of people on holiday. It was small with two propellers on either side and short wings and wheels on fixed poles underneath. It swooped across the sky and disappeared behind the terminal building.

'Keep watchin' doon that way.' Laura pointed over her shoulder. 'He'll loop roun' an' come in tae land fae there.' She turned in her chair to watch too. It didn't take long for the aeroplane to come into view again, this time pointing towards us and getting lower and lower in the sky as it approached.

'Will it no' git stuck in the sand?'

'Dinnae be daft, they've bin landin' here fir years.'

The older couple in the café left their table and stood by the window to watch as well. Outside a small group had gathered at the edge of the car park with cameras and binoculars.

'It's the only airport in the world wi' a beach fir a runway,' Laura said. I watched the plane draw nearer, the sun glinting off its surface. It landed without fuss, just a couple of soft bumps on the sand, and taxied up to the terminal. The wheels left tracks in the sand. A tractor towing stairs pulled out to meet the plane as the door in the side opened and the passengers emerged. They walked down the stairs and across the sand and into the airport. A jeep collected a few bags on a trailer and took them to the baggage reclaim area at the side of the building. Another tractor appeared and drove across the sand, pulling a large brush behind it and smoothing away the wheel tracks.

'It'll take aff again in an hour,' Laura said, turning back to her lunch. A small petrol truck now approached the plane and started refuelling it for the return flight. I thought how easy it would be to sneak onto the plane. I would be back in Glasgow in an hour. I could get a bus from the airport into the city centre and then it was only a short walk to the hospital. I could be sitting chatting to Mum before dinner tonight. I imagined her surprise and the smile on her face as I walked in and hugged her.

There was a bustle in the café now that the plane had arrived. 'Are ye goin' tae eat that?' Laura pointed at the uneaten half of my sandwich.

'Ye kin have it.' Laura picked it up and ate it. I picked at the crisps on my plate.

'Wit are ye thinkin' about?'

'Ma maw.'

'Is she really ill?'

I nodded. 'Da willnae talk tae me about it, but ah think so.'

Flora came over and picked up the empty plates. 'Right, you two, we need the table now for paying customers. Out you go.'

We weaved through the tables and chairs to the door.

'I'll see you for dinner tonight,' Flora called after us. 'And you can bring your new friend too if you want.'

I felt a little beat of happiness at the invitation. Laura didn't say anything about it as we picked up our bikes that were still leaning against the wall outside.

'Where are we goin' now?'

'Have ye bin tae the beach here?'

'The runway?'

'Naw, come oan.' She took off and left me lagging behind again as I struggled to turn the heavy bike around and follow her. She headed past the airport and kept going along the road north where the land widened. We went over a hill and the road narrowed along the coast of the peninsula. There were a few cottages and bungalows along the road. I caught up with her as she slowed down at a small car park. Next to it was a wooden stile with a path beyond it that went along the top of sand dunes. Below the dunes was a large wide-open beach and the sea. Smaller islands were dotted off the coast, uninhabited rocky outcrops that interrupted the rolling waves.

We left our bikes against the stile and Laura led the way over the short grass path. Rather than leading us down to the beach, she veered off the path and through the long, rough dune grass. The dunes rose higher and the edges became like cliffs with steep walls of sand plunging down to the beach below. Laura stopped at the top of one of them.

'Are ye ready?' she asked. The wind swirled her long hair in several directions.

'Fir wit?'

She stepped over the edge of the dune and plummeted downwards. I watched her taking long, jumping strides down the sheer side of the dune, her feet digging into the wall of sand. Somehow she managed to stay upright until she reached the bottom, when she stumbled and fell and tumbled onto the soft sand of the beach with a cry. She ended up on her back and propped herself up on her elbows.

'Yer turn,' she shouted up.

I stared at the drop. It was about twelve feet. I took a step forward and peered down to the beach below.

'Wit are ye waitin' fir?' I could see her looking up at me. I knew I would have to do it. Laura had managed it; so could I. I took a deep breath and plunged forward. My foot landed in the soft sand on the side of the dune and sank in a few inches. I hadn't expected that. It threw me off balance. With my arms flailing, I tried to steady myself, but it was too late. My momentum threw my head and shoulders forward and I toppled over. I rolled over and over and over until I came to a stop at the foot of the dune with the taste of sand in my mouth.

Laura appeared standing over me. She was laughing and smiling. 'An interestin' technique ye have there. Kamikaze-style.'

She offered me her hand and pulled me up. I started laughing too. I spat sand out of my mouth and wiped it away from my eyes. I had made a mess of it, but at the same time I had won her respect. I was still wiping sand from my trousers when she took off again, running across the beach. I followed after her, heading towards the sea.

We spent the next hour on the beach, collecting shells and throwing stones into the water. Laura could throw them just as far as I could. I didn't mind; I was still thinking about the touch of her hand.

We returned to the dunes and as I got used to the soft sand under my feet I was able to match her clambering up the sides and managed to run down without falling over. Then it was time to start heading back. As we walked back along the path, she jumped up onto my back and I carried her with her arms around my neck and her legs wrapped around my waist. Some of her hair blew over my face. She was lighter than I expected and I managed to break into a staggering run with her on my back and she burst into laughter and shouted at me to stop as she almost lost her grip. She bet me that she could carry me. I put her down and we swapped positions. I jumped onto her back and she was able to walk while carrying me. I could feel her thin frame as I held on round her neck. She was satisfied that she had proved her point and put me down and made me carry her again, all the way back to the wooden stile. It was late afternoon when we got back to the bikes.

'D'ye want tae come back fir dinner?'

'Sure, okay.' I tried to hide my joy. 'We need tae stop in an' let ma aunt know oan the way.'

12

Over the next few days I became a regular at the Robertson house. Laura lived with her mum and dad in a little cluster of houses called Brevig along the road into Castlebay. That first evening Laura waited at the main road while I cycled back and got permission to go to her house for dinner. 'So long as it's okay wi' her parents,' Cathy said. She was pleased that I had made a friend. Lennox would have to do without my scraps thrown from the table.

The Robertson household was warm and cheerful. Flora enjoyed being the host and welcomed me like I had been Laura's friend for years. She suggested Cathy and Tom come along one evening for dinner too. They never did come, though. I was sure Cathy would have wanted to, but Tom would have taken a lot of persuading. Laura's dad, Hamish, was a builder, but he and Tom never worked on anything together. He was spending the summer working at the castle in the bay. It was being restored to become a tourist attraction. They were building new walkways and a visitor display and some of the old walls were being rebuilt after years of exposure to wind and sea had eroded them away. Each morning Hamish took a small boat trip across the bay to get to the castle on its small island. He told me some of the history of Kisimul Castle as we sat around the dinner table.

'A real shame it was abandoned. They took the original stones from the walls and used them for other things. Fishing boats took some for ballast and some ended up in Glasgow as paving stones.' He pointed his knife at me as he said this, as though blaming me as a mainlander for taking the old stones. 'It's still the seat of Clan MacNeil. Now the clan chief has decided he doesn't want it as a holiday home and he's opening it up to the public.'

They spoke their perfect English when I was there. Occasionally, Hamish and Flora would break into Gaelic when discussing some family or work matter, and whenever Laura and I left the living room I heard them switch from English to Gaelic without a pause in the conversation.

Most days from then on, if the weather was good, Laura and I would meet on our bikes. We became a familiar sight around the main village. Laura would have messages to pick up or errands to run at the shops while her mum and dad were working. Often it was a trip to the post office to pick up some package or post a letter destined for the mainland. Laura introduced me to Robert, who ran the post office. She didn't tell him why I was staying on Barra and I only told him I was on holiday with my aunt and uncle for the summer. The post office in Partick was a soulless place with cashiers sitting in dark cubicles behind glass panels. In Barra it was the heart of the community. It had a community noticeboard inside and it sold tourist souvenirs and cakes made by the locals and there was another café that Robert's wife, Marion, ran. Islanders sat around the tables drinking tea and chatting with each other and groups of tourists would come in and soon they would all be chatting together. When Robert wasn't serving behind the counter of the post office he would help out if the café was busy. They had an old stray cat that had wandered in one day and had been adopted. No one knew where it had come from, but it must have come across on the ferry. It didn't stay in their house but always appeared every day for some food and attention. Marion left out a saucer of milk for it each morning and afternoon and it soon became known as the post office cat and regular customers would stroke it on their way in and out. Cathy baked cakes to sell in the café and the cat benefited from any leftovers at the end of the week.

Next door to the post office was the bank. Alec MacLeod ran it and lived in the flat above it with his wife and son. He was a stern man. His hearing was bad and I wondered if this was what made him seem so unhappy. He passed us on the street one day as we went to the post office and scowled at Laura as she said hello to him.

'Wit's wrang wi' him?'

'It'll be because a' Lachlan,' she answered.

'Who's Lachlan?'

'His son.'

I remembered the face in the window above the bank I had seen on my very first visit to Castlebay with Cathy. 'Ah think ah've seen him, lookin' out the windae at me.'

'He stays up there aw the time. He's in a wheelchair.'

'He never leaves the hoose?'

'Of course he dis sometimes, but he cannae git out oan his own.'

'Wit happened tae him?'

'It wis a couple a' years ago. We were oan a church picnic. Father Baird had organised it. Mr MacLeod wis there tae an' about ten kids. Me, Billy Matheson, Lachlan, Rosie an' Arthur an' a couple a' younger wans. We were playin' oan some rocks an' lookin' in rock pools an' climbin' about. There wis this cry an' ah turnt roun' an' saw Lachlan hittin' the water. He'd fallen somehow an' his da had tae dive in tae save him. That wis how Mr MacLeod damaged his hearin' too, somethin' tae dae wi' the water pressure an' bein' underwater fir too long. He pulled Lachlan out, saved his life, but the way he'd hit the rocks when he fell had broken his spine. They had tae git a helicopter fae the mainland tae take him tae hospital. Ah remember Mr MacLeod pumpin' Lachlan's chest an' blowing intae his mooth tae keep him breathing before Father Baird telt us aw tae move away.'

'Ah guess ah kin understand why he's no' happy.'

'The odd thing wis Lachlan wis really gud oan the rocks. He wis gud at sports an' we used tae go explorin' together aw the time. That wis before he became best mates wi' Billy an' then ah didnae see so much a' him. Billy wis standin' right next tae Lachlan when he fell an' he jist stood there, frozen like a statue, while Mr MacLeod wis screamin' an' runnin' over the rocks tae jump in the water tae save him.'

'Ah've seen Billy Matheson hangin' aroun' our hoose. Ah'm sure he wis followin' me sometimes. Tom telt me tae stay away fae him.'

'He's a strange boy, always has been.'

'Why disnae he go tae school like the rest a' ye?'

'He used tae. Sometimes he still turns up. Mum says it's because there's nae discipline in his hame. His father died when he wis young an' he jist lives wi' his ma. My ma says she's too young tae know wit's best fir him.'

'He never says anythin' when ah see him.'

'He disnae speak much, he's like a mute, but he's harmless. Not many people talk tae him or his ma. She wis young when she had him an' she wisnae married. They dinnae come tae the church anymare. Mum says Father Baird wud welcome them if she wud jist admit her sin.'

'Mibbe she didnae dae anythin' wrang?'

'Havin' a child wi'out bein' married is a pretty big sin oan this island.'

I guessed Billy's mum must have been the woman I had seen hanging up washing in the garden in Bruernish. I knew a few young girls around Partick who had children and weren't married. Two of my classmates were already uncles. It didn't mean people stopped talking to them, or they couldn't go to church anymore, although it did mean they had a reputation.

Laura carried on with her story. 'We didnae see Lachlan fir a year or so after the accident. He had tae stay in the hospital in Glasgow. Dad helpt dae up their flat above the bank so that a wheelchair could get in an' out an' move around inside.'

'D'ye ever talk tae Lachlan?'

'No' much. He disnae come tae school now. He gets cared fir at home.'

I looked back at the window above the bank and tried to imagine a life stuck inside that small house with no chance of escape, staring out at the same view every day.

'Mibbe we could visit him wan day?'

'Sure, we could ask. Ah'm sure he wud like it, but ah'm no' sure his da wud let us.'

On the day Laura had told me about Lachlan MacLeod's accident I asked Cathy about what had happened while we were washing the dinner dishes.

'A terrible shame. Such a bright wee lad.' Tom was already in the living room and Cathy looked to the door to make sure he couldn't hear us. 'They were as thick as thieves, Lachlan an' Billy Matheson. Lachlan took Billy under his wing when nae wan else wud.' She paused again and decided not to tell me anymore. 'Never mind why. It wis a tragedy, but sometimes these things happen. Neither a' those boys has bin the same since it happened.'

I wondered why she said both of them had never been the same since the accident, but that was the end of the conversation as the last of the dishes were put away and we joined Tom in the living room.

* * *

No one seemed to mind a thirteen-year-old girl being left on her own during the day while her parents went out to work. When Flora was on shift at the airport café, Laura and I would stop in for lunch and other times we went to my house and Cathy would make us a sandwich. Lennox soon took to Laura, another new person to play with, and I was relegated to second best. He strained to walk next to her, so I gave up and let her take his lead when we took him for walks. He didn't try to pull away from her but walked calmly alongside her. At the end of each day we would make a plan for the next morning of where we would meet and what we would do. Most of the time we spent on our bikes visiting different parts of the island. We did play football together and I had to admit that Laura was better than me.

On the days when the wind dropped and the sun shone we would usually end up at a beach. We explored different coves and caves and rock pools and tried to catch small fish with nets we bought from the store, without much success. When we were in Castlebay we would see other children, but most of the time it was just the two of us and I was more than happy for it to stay like that. On the days when it rained or I couldn't meet Laura, which included every Sunday, I sulked around the house. When I was with Laura I didn't think about home so much, but when I was on my own with nothing to do I thought of Mum, and Dad's journey to the hospital for visiting hours every day and him living alone in our flat. The pain of what was to come was still there, but when I was with Laura I could push it to the back of my mind and ignore it for another few hours. The boredom of the early weeks spent hanging around the house with nothing to look forward to became a distant memory. Barra itself changed now that I had Laura to enjoy it with. It became an island of adventure and possibility instead of a lonely prison.

We were allowed to stay out late in the evenings and watch the sun set behind the ocean from the beaches on the west side of the island. It could be as late as eleven o'clock before we got home some nights. I was never allowed to stay out that late in Partick, even in the summer holidays. Traigh Eais was my favourite beach. It was on the other side of the narrow strip of land from the airport and it was reached by walking across the *machair*, a sandy, grassy plain of land that rose up into sand dunes. Once you reached the top of the dunes you looked down onto the clear blue water of the ocean. A house stood at the back of the beach.

'That wis built by Compton MacKenzie, who wrote a book called *Whisky Galore*.' Laura told me the first time I spotted it. 'They made a film a' it oan Barra tae.'

I had never heard of it.

'It's an auld wan,' Laura replied, 'black an' white.'

Laura's dad bought us a kite to fly on the beach. Neither of us had a clue how to fly a kite but we soon figured out how to get it up in the air on the strong sea breeze. It was when we were flying it one afternoon on Traigh Eais that we saw Billy watching us. We didn't know when he had started following us, but that was the first time we had spotted him.

It was a perfect afternoon for flying a kite with a stiff breeze coming in off the Atlantic, and not a cloud in the sky. We cycled round to the airport and, after Flora had given us lunch in the café, we had taken the kite onto the beach. It was easy to get the kite airborne. Laura took the spool and reeled out the line while I held the kite and walked away from her. I barely had to break into a run before the wind was pulling at the bridle and it soared up as soon as I let go. It danced on the air currents. We did not have the beach to ourselves that afternoon. Another couple were sunbathing in a spot sheltered from the wind by the sand dunes. A dog was running across the beach and splashing in and out of the water chasing a stick thrown by its owner. I watched Laura as she fed the line out. She increased the height a little at a time until she had reached the end of the line. The kite soared high above us. I stood next to her and waited for my turn to fly it. Laura offered me the spindle. I took it from her and felt the tug on the line as the wind tried to tear the kite from my hands. There was little skill needed in these conditions and I held the line and let the wind do all the work. Then there was a break in the wind and I felt the line go slack.

'Reel it in quickly.' Laura grabbed a length of the line and pulled it down, hoping to make it taut again. I started to do the same, but the kite continued to fall as the breeze slackened.

'Ah'll try runnin',' I said. I didn't see the loops of line that were now gathered around my feet. As I started sprinting, the line wrapped itself around my ankles. I twisted and stumbled and fell onto the soft sand, pulling the spindle and line down with me. The kite buoyed for a moment, then fluttered down into the dunes at the top of the beach. Laura was doubled over in a fit of laughter as I untangled the string from my feet. Rather than feeling embarrassed, I joined in the laughter. I was getting used to making a fool of myself in front of her. When I managed to get the line free she pulled me up and we set off to retrieve the kite from its resting place on top of the dune grass.

It was as we reached the kite that we spotted him. Billy was standing about forty yards away and was staring at us as we picked up the kite. He seemed to be waiting for something.

'Should we ask him tae play?' I asked Laura, despite what Uncle Tom had warned against.

She was wrapping the line back around the spindle. 'Ye can try if ye want.'

'Hey!' I shouted over the dune.

Billy didn't move. He just kept staring. I left Laura trying to untangle a knot in the line and started walking towards Billy. 'Hey!' As I closed the gap between us, Billy turned and ran down the other side of the dune. He came back into view when he got to the bottom and took off across the *machair*.

'D'ye want tae play wi' us?' I shouted. He stopped and turned and for a moment I thought he was going to come back, but then he took off across the grass again. I watched him until he reached the road and the airport. He picked up a bicycle and cycled off towards

Bruernish. His bike looked like a new BMX. The blond head cycled along the road around the bay before disappearing from view.

Laura came and stood next to me with the kite ready for its next flight. 'Telt ye. Strange kid.'

'Ye think he's followin' us?'

'Who knows?' She shrugged.

13

It was two days later when we met Billy again. The wind had changed direction and was blowing in from the Atlantic, gusting onto the west coast of Barra. We decided to go to the beach we had visited on our first cycle around the island, where the tall sand dunes provided some shelter from the elements. Despite the wind, the sun shone and it was a warm afternoon. We left our bikes leaning against the wooden stile and walked along the top of the dunes and ran down onto the beach. As far as we could see in both directions we had the beach to ourselves. We began exploring and soon lost track of time. Neither of us noticed Mhairi and Billy coming along the path on the dunes. We were busy inspecting a small cluster of broken shells when shadows moving across the sand caught my eye. I looked up and recognised the woman who had been hanging up sheets in her garden. Seeing her up close, I realised she was younger than I had first thought. She was holding Billy's hand, while her other hand held on to her white dress that blew in the breeze. It was a light cloth, a beach dress with straps over the shoulders and it stopped above her knees, revealing thin legs. Her dirty-blonde hair blew around her face and her blue eyes shone and she was barefoot in the sand. Next to her, Billy stood staring at us with the same blue eyes and blond hair. He wore an old pair of shorts and was bare-chested, his thin, pale body exposed to the sun.

'Hello,' she said.

Laura looked up at her and didn't answer.

'Hello,' I replied.

'Ah've seen ye passin' our hoose.' She waited for me to reply, but I couldn't think of anything to say. 'Ah'm Mhairi.'

'Ewan.'

'Hello, Laura. How are ye?'

'Gud, thanks.'

She smiled at Laura, then turned back to me. 'Billy tells me yer stayin' wi' Tom an' Cathy.'

'That's right.'

'Ye've had a good summer so far. Are ye here fir the holidays?'

'Aye,' I said, not wanting to go into the full explanation. I was sure Mhairi could sense I was hesitant. I heard Tom warning me not to get involved with the boy, and Laura had warned me Billy was strange. I wasn't sure I should be talking to him or his mum, but she seemed nice enough while she stood on the beach talking to us.

'It'll be nice fir Billy tae have someone tae play wi',' Mhairi said. How could I tell her that my uncle and aunt had made me swear to avoid him, and her? 'How are yer mum and dad, Laura?'

'Fine,' Laura said. I could tell Laura was reluctant to be drawn into a conversation too.

'Ye dinnae say much, do ye? Wit have ye found there?' She pointed at the shells we had been looking at and knelt down to inspect them, bunching her dress in her hand and revealing more of her legs as she crouched down. She let go of Billy's hand and started picking up the shells and inspecting them one at a time. She found a complete one, a white fan with a shade of sandy-brown across the rippled side. 'That's a pretty one.' She held it towards Laura.

Laura took it from her and knelt down beside her. 'Ah like this wan, even though it's cracked a bit.' Laura showed her a shell we had been looking at before they had arrived.

Mhairi held one up for Billy to see. 'They're beautiful, aren't they?' He didn't say anything. 'Billy said ye were flyin' a lovely kite at the beach the other day.'

'Ma da got it fir me,' said Laura.

'That wis nice a' him.' Mhairi paused. Was it just me or did her smile disappear for a fraction of a second? Then it was back and her face glowed again. 'A shame ye havnae got it wi' ye today, the breeze is perfect. We should ha' brought yer football, Billy, or a bucket and spade.'

'We could still build a sandcastle,' said the small boy. It was the first time I had heard him say more than one word.

'Come oan then, near the water so we kin build a moat round it,' his mum replied. 'D'ye want tae help us?'

Laura and I followed them across the soft sand. Nearer the water the sand became compact and darker. It seemed natural that we should join them. Something about her warmth and openness made me want to go along with them, despite what Tom and Cathy and Laura had said. I couldn't see any harm or danger in playing with them on the beach for an afternoon. There was no one else in sight anyway and Tom and Cathy wouldn't be out this way. There was no chance they would find out that I had been with Billy and Mhairi Matheson.

Billy didn't say much, but Mhairi laughed and chatted away as we helped to shovel the sand with our hands and dig out a circular ditch that would act as a moat. We piled up the sand in the middle of the circle and Mhairi took charge of shaping it into some sort of castle. Without thinking about it, we were having fun. Mhairi was like an older sister rather than an adult, organising our efforts and helping us. She and Laura joked with each other and I relaxed, helping Billy to shovel out more sand. In the space of an hour we became a gang of four, and Mhairi and Billy became our new friends. The sandcastle ended up lopsided and kept crumbling down. The repeated failure didn't spoil our fun.

'Come oan, we need tae get it finished before the tide comes in,' said Mhairi. The sea had been creeping back towards us while we had been building the sandcastle. I looked round and was surprised by the shallow ripples lapping against the entrance of our moat. 'Billy, run an' get ma camera, quick.'

Billy took off over the beach towards the sand dunes. There was a white beach bag lying on the ground. He reached inside and came running back to us. Laura and Mhairi put the finishing touches to the mound and I pushed a stick in the top. The water filled the moat. Billy handed the camera to his mum and she quickly wound the film round and snapped a picture. Just as she did, a wave of water broke the castle's defences and swamped half of it. I jumped back, trying to keep my trainers and socks dry. Billy and Mhairi stood with the water around their ankles.

'That's a shame. Ah wanted tae get a picture a' ye aw wi' it. Never mind, we'll have one photo tae remember it by.'

Billy jumped on top of the remains of the sandcastle and stomped the heap of sand down and the water washed over it and soon it was gone and the little stick I had placed in the top floated away. Mhairi walked away and put her camera back in her bag. The tide brought the water further up the beach. When Mhairi returned there was five feet of water between us and Billy, who stood where the castle remains had disappeared under the waves.

'D'ye think it's warm enough fir a paddle?' Mhairi said as she reached us and carried on walking into the water towards Billy.

I thought she was crazy. The water was freezing, despite it being a sunny and warm day, but Mhairi and Billy didn't seem to notice. I looked at Laura. 'D'ye want tae go in?'

Billy and Mhairi went out further. They tried to jump over the waves as the white crests rippled towards them. They were up to their knees. A larger wave took Billy by surprise and as he jumped it knocked him over and he disappeared under the water for a second before re-emerging. He spluttered and wiped water away from his face as Mhairi steadied him and checked he was okay. He was smiling and laughing. Mhairi's dress was wet around the hem where the edge of it dipped into the water. The white linen became see-through and I could see the line of her underwear and the flesh colour of her thighs.

'Come oan,' she called to Laura and me. 'It's so refreshin'.' She splashed Billy as he jumped around her. His pale, thin body was as white as her dress.

Laura started to take off her shoes and socks.

'Yer no' goin' in? It's freezing.'

'Come oan. Havnae ye bin in the sea before?'

'Naw,' I said, which was true, apart from a shallow paddle along the rocky beach in Largs with my mum once. I could manage a couple of lengths of the local swimming pool, but I was not a strong swimmer.

Laura unzipped her shorts and pulled them down. I tried not to look. I noticed her toenails were painted red. She stood up and pulled her T-shirt over her head. She had on a white bra with little red spots dotted across it and dark navy pants with a white lace waistband. She was thinner than I had thought she would be, and somehow looked fragile. I could see her ribs under her skin and she had sharp hip bones that stuck out. Her skin was smooth and pale and contrasted with the long, dark hair that fell across her back and shoulders.

'It's rude tae stare.'

'Sorry.' I looked up into her face and saw the glint in her eye as her mouth broke into a smile.

'Never seen a girl in her underwear before?'

'Well, ah...' I didn't know where to look or what to say. I had never seen a girl undress before. The pictures boys brought into school in magazines and newspapers that were passed around the playground accompanied by giggles were the only place I had seen a woman in her underwear before.

'Dinnae be so shy. Come oan.' She ran to the edge of the water and kept going, splashing through the shallow waves for a few paces until the water was around her knees. Then she waded in further and the dark navy pants disappeared under a wave, and when they emerged they were soaking and sticking to her and I could see the curve of her bottom. She turned and waved back at me, beckoning me to join her with a shout. Then she turned and dived into the water and did a couple of swimming strokes and then seemed to float with just her head and her wet, black hair above the surface. She reached Billy and Mhairi. Mhairi flicked water at her and I heard their laughter and shouting as Laura stood up and started splashing her back. Billy leapt to his mother's defence and Laura was outnumbered.

'Come oan,' she shouted at me. 'Ah need yer help.'

I pulled my trainers and socks off, and then my T-shirt, self-conscious when I looked down at my thin chest and skinny arms. I had pants under my shorts but decided to keep my shorts on. I walked to the edge of the water and let the incoming wave trickle around my bare feet. I hesitated and took a couple of small steps forward, letting my feet and ankles be covered by the cold water, then slowly I edged in further until the bottom of my shorts were wet. I sucked in my cheeks and kept going, and let out a sharp blow of air when the water lapped up to my waist. After that progress became easier. The three of them were still splashing each other. Mhairi's dress was soaked through and clung to her and showed the curve of her chest.

'Hurry up,' Laura shouted. She pushed her wet hair away from her face. I went to her aid and began throwing water at Billy while Mhairi and Laura splashed each other. Billy got me with a big spray of water and I felt the salt sting my eyes and tasted it in my mouth. He didn't stop to let me recover as I tried to wipe my face.

'Boys against girls,' shouted Mhairi, and she and Laura turned on Billy and me. Billy went after his mum, who grabbed him and managed to pick him up and tip him into the water headfirst. Laura charged towards me and slapped the surface of the water, sending a spray over me. I shielded myself and then retaliated and started splashing water back at her. I moved towards her and ended up right beside her, still splashing water into her as she held her arms out in front of her face. Then she lunged forward and her arms were around me, wrestling me. I grabbed her and we were locked together, our legs intertwining under the surface as we each tried to trip the other over into the water. I felt her smooth skin and the bones underneath and I was aware of her bra straps as I took hold of her shoulders and the wet material that covered her chest. Her hands were around my back and on my chest and her arms round my neck. She had the upper hand until I managed to twist her round and we both lost our balance and fell into the sea together, separating as we fell and slapping into the water before both coming up spluttering and smiling at each other. Before I could get back on my feet, she leapt on me again. I grabbed her and managed to lift her off the floor of the seabed. As I did so her arms went around my neck and my hand was on her bottom and the wet material of her pants.

'Dinnae ye dare,' she warned me.

I threw her and she let go of my neck and splashed into the water her arms and legs spread wide. The spray formed a rainbow for a split second as the sunlight hit it. She went under the waves before scrambling to her feet. I took off, trying to wade quickly through the water before she could catch me. I was too busy looking back at Laura to see Billy and Mhairi as they ambushed me and started splashing me and then all three of them were upon me and I had no choice but to stand and take it.

The battle continued for another ten minutes until Billy shouted and waved at the beach. The tide had come in further and reached where Laura and I had piled up our shoes and clothes. We raced back to the edge of the water to retrieve them and managed to salvage them before they floated away.

Soaking wet, we made our way back across the beach to where Mhairi had left her bag. Laura carried her shoes and socks and her clothes by her side. My eyes were drawn to her and I noticed again the small freckles gathered over her shoulders and the dark mole on her back that sat just above the strap of her bra. She walked beside Mhairi, whose dress still clung to her and showed the curve of her hips. I felt I was looking at something I shouldn't have been, that I was doing something wrong by staring at their exposed bodies. So this was what attraction felt like, or love. It was one of those things, I was sure of that. They happily chatted as they walked along side by side and thought nothing of it. Did they know the thoughts that were running through my mind? When we had been wrestling with each other in the water, had Laura felt the same feeling I had? Billy and I followed behind them in silence, content to listen to their easy conversation.

Mhairi pulled a towel from her bag and dried her hair before handing it to Laura so she could dry herself and put her clothes back on. Billy and I shivered as we waited for our turn. I let him take the towel before me and he wrapped himself in it and patted himself down before handing it to me. Laura pulled her shorts and T-shirt over her damp underwear. My shorts and pants were wet and sticking to me, but I wouldn't take them off in front of the others and had nothing else to wear in any case, so I dried the rest of myself and then pulled my T-shirt back on. I sat down next to Laura and we both wiped the sand off our feet and from between our toes before putting our socks and shoes back on. The sun and the breeze helped to dry us and although the clothes were damp, they stopped clinging to our bodies and the warmth in the air replaced the chill from the sea.

'Wit time is it?'

Mhairi pulled a watch from her bag and put it on her wrist. 'Jist after four. We better start walkin' back in time fir dinner.'

We climbed back to the top of the dunes. My short hair had almost dried in the sun, but Laura's was still damp and tousled and gathered together in a clump across one shoulder. My pants and shorts itched, and small droplets of water occasionally ran down my legs.

'Wait there,' said Mhairi suddenly, rummaging in her bag. She pulled out her camera. 'Ah need tae get a picture a' the three a' ye together tae remember this afternoon. Sit together oan the dune.'

We sat down, Laura and I together and Billy to the side, slightly apart from us.

'It's the last picture oan the film, so make it a good smile.' She put the viewfinder to her eye. I smiled as naturally as I could, although I had never found a comfortable expression that worked for photographs. The camera clicked.

'Billy, ye looked away,' said Mhairi.

The boy didn't answer. He had seen something at the car park that was still a distance away from us along the path across the top of the dunes. He pointed. Mhairi looked in that direction and saw the car pulling up. I didn't recognise it, but Mhairi and Billy did, and I suppose Laura must have as well.

'Thank ye fir a lovely afternoon, you two. We had great fun.' She smiled as she spoke to us and I could tell that the couple of hours we had spent on the beach had meant something to her, something more than Laura and I were able to understand. 'We'll walk along the path an' join the road at the other end a' the beach. You two kin go that way an' get yer bikes.'

With a final wave she turned and Billy wordlessly followed her, taking her hand again as they walked away. She hadn't said anything, or shown a change in her bright manner, but it was clear she wanted to avoid whoever had just arrived at the car park.

Laura started walking in the opposite direction towards the

stile and the car park. I looked after the departing woman and her son before jogging to catch up with Laura.

'Wit wis that about?' I asked.

'It's fine. This way Cathy an' Tom an' ma parents willnae find out that we spent the afternoon wi' them.'

'Who is she scared a'?' The car was still sitting in the car park, but no one had got out of it yet.

'She's no' scared. Definitely no' scared. She's doin' it fir our sakes an' fir Billy.'

As we got near to the stile, the car door opened. It was a dark blue Ford Escort. I remembered seeing one parked in Castlebay, and there couldn't be too many cars the same on Barra. From the driver's seat a small woman appeared. She was thinner and smaller than Mhairi Matheson, and despite the lingering warmth of the day she was wrapped in a long coat and wore jeans. I recognised her. It was Mary Margaret MacLeod, Lachlan's mother, who worked and lived in the bank with her husband. She waited for us to climb over the stile.

'Lovely afternoon tae be oan the beach. Have you two bin in the water?'

'Aye, it's very cold.' Laura answered.

'You be careful going in there oan yer own. Ye never know wit could happen.'

'Yes, Mrs MacLeod.'

I thought of her son, Lachlan, falling on the rocks and landing in the freezing-cold water. Mrs MacLeod climbed over the stile and walked along the path. We picked up our bikes and turned them round and set off along the road south towards Northbay, where we said goodbye and made plans to meet up the next day. The ride back was uncomfortable as my wet pants and shorts chafed against my skin on the seat of the bike. That evening my mind was distracted by memories of a clinging white dress and pale skin and small red dots on pure white cotton.

14

That was the last we saw of Billy for a few days. Maybe Mhairi decided to keep him away from us for a while, or maybe he decided to stop following us. Had it been a chance meeting on the beach, or had Billy told his mum about Laura and me and made her follow us and introduce him to us and spend the afternoon together? As much as Mhairi had said she enjoyed that afternoon, as much as she wanted Billy to have friends to play with, had she decided she didn't want Laura and me to get into trouble? Whatever the reason, we didn't see either of them again until a Sunday evening in the middle of July, the day of the football World Cup final.

The ongoing football tournament had not got in the way of my friendship with Laura. She liked to sit and watch the games as much as Tom and I did. Her parents were not as enthusiastic, so when there was a game on that we wanted to see, Laura would come round to Tom and Cathy's house and sit in the living room with us. Laura and I sat together on the sofa, and Tom had his usual armchair in the corner and we would join in with his enthusiastic shouting at the television. Tom even started to look a little disappointed anytime we decided to go out rather than watch a match with him. He never said it, but I think he enjoyed having someone to listen to his opinions.

After four weeks of games it came down to West Germany against Italy in the final. The Scotland team had already returned home after being knocked out in the group stage. The final was in the evening. The cafés, shops and pubs were closed on a Sunday, but for the occasion of the World Cup final the hotel at Northbay threw a party and got hold of a big screen projector to show the game on. A lot of the islanders were going along to watch it. Some people still had no television set and some struggled to get a good reception, but most were going to be part of the social occasion.

The hotel was an imposing building made with huge grey bricks. It had once been a small castle, built five hundred years ago. Almost all of it had been replaced and rebuilt since then, but some of the original features remained. On each corner at the front there was a turret with a pointed conical roof and along the top of the front wall there was a parapet with lookout gaps along it. The MacNeil Clan had used it as a home before it fell into disrepair. Eventually it had been bought by an American, who converted it into a hotel. Cathy had told me all this while we had walked along the road to get there.

Large concrete stairs led up to the front door and into the lobby and at the back a grand staircase led up to the guest rooms on the floors above. Off to one side of the lobby was the dining room where the big screen had been set up. The room had wide bay windows looking out over Northbay, a rocky part of the coast with only narrow sandy beaches. It had high ceilings and chandeliers hung from the roof. The carpet was a faded tartan pattern of green and blue and was marked with stains and cigarette burns. The dark wooden tables and chairs were scratched and chipped and cushions were patched up with tape. On the back wall was a bar, with rows of bottles along the back and beer taps at the front.

Tom and Cathy decided to walk the two miles from Bruernish to the hotel. When we arrived a few of the locals were already there. The Church of Scotland minister from Cathy's church was talking to Father Baird, who had come up from Castlebay and was wearing a replica Italian football shirt. Laura and her parents were there, and we pulled two small bar tables together and joined them. The room filled up as the start of the game approached and the sound of chatter and laughter and whisky glasses clinking together got louder. I recognised most of the people from around the village and the airport, and there were also a few tourists who were staying at the hotel. There was one couple from Rome, who were touring the Hebrides as part of their honeymoon. They became the centre of attention and, with there being no West Germans in the room, the Italian team gained the support of the Barra locals. On the big screen the coverage was building up to the game, but not many in the room were paying attention to it. Tom was watching it but couldn't make out what was being said and I saw him trying to hide his frustration. Cathy chatted to Flora and Hamish sat looking out of the window, uninterested in both the football and the conversation. Laura and I left our seats at the table and moved forward to sit on the floor in front of the screen where a few other children had gathered. Above our heads a thick cloud of smoke from countless cigarettes filled the room.

Alec MacLeod arrived as the two sides made their way onto the pitch in Madrid. He pushed Lachlan in his wheelchair. Mary Margaret followed behind them. We hadn't seen her since that day at the beach. We guessed she had never found out that Mhairi and Billy had also been there that day. At least, we never heard anything about it, so nothing had been said to Laura's parents or Tom and Cathy. The MacLeods took a table at the side of the screen near the front and positioned Lachlan's wheelchair so he could see the screen. I was sitting near to him and he looked down at me sitting cross-legged on the floor.

I smiled up at him. 'Ah'm Ewan. Ah saw ye in the window above the bank that day.'

'Lachlan.' His voice was weak and I had to strain to hear him over the noise of the room.

'D'ye like fitba?'

Lachlan shrugged his shoulders and rolled his eyes. Laura nudged me. I hadn't thought. It was an innocent question, but Laura had told me Lachlan had liked to play football before his accident. Could he really enjoy watching it now?

The sun was shining in Madrid and the heat on the pitch was sweltering, making the pictures look distorted as heatwaves came up from the ground. Cameras showed close-ups of the teams as they lined up to sing the national anthems and the players were sweating already. As the anthems finished the room behind me went quiet. The chatter faded away and only a couple of conversations carried on. I thought it was because the game was about to begin, but when I turned round I saw Billy being led across the room by his mum. The adults in the room had stopped talking and were watching them. Through the haze of smoke Mhairi looked even younger than she had on the beach and I wondered again how she could be old enough to have a twelve-year-old son. She wore a blue dress that was tight around her and I remembered what her body had looked like under the white linen dress that had stuck to her when she had come out of the sea. She strode across the room and sat Billy down on the floor, away from the other children. I saw her jaw clench and a look of defiance on her face as she noticed everyone staring at her. There was no sign of the relaxed smile that had seemed so natural that afternoon on the beach. She met the eyes looking at her with a stare of her own. When she spotted Laura and me I thought I caught a slight smile of recognition, but I could have just imagined it. She went to the bar and asked for a glass of wine and waited for it to arrive. People continued to stare at the back of her head as she stood there. I looked around and saw Father Baird and the minister staring at her. They were next to Cathy and Flora, who were looking as well. Tom continued to stare at the big screen, seemingly oblivious to what was happening around him. Hamish had gone back to looking out of the window. Noise returned to the room as people resumed their conversations. There were still looks towards Mhairi Matheson as she took her drink from the bar, walked back across the room and sat on a chair next to Billy, who was sitting on the floor. I was worried Billy might come over to join Laura and me, or worse, say something about our afternoon on the beach within earshot of Tom and Cathy, but he didn't leave her side and made no effort to acknowledge us.

Everyone focused on the football game when it started, but after the first five minutes the casual viewers in the room lost interest and general chat mixed with the voices of the commentators coming from the loudspeakers. Italy won a penalty and the Italian couple leapt to their feet in celebration. Then the Italian player missed the penalty and the couple sat down and joined in the laughter as the locals teased them. The first half ended without any goals.

'No' a classic,' was Tom's summation at half-time as he passed us on the way to the bar. Billy Matheson was still sitting on the floor beside Mhairi. I thought he had been sneaking looks at Laura and me during the game. Every time I glanced in his direction I caught him averting his eyes back towards the screen. I hoped the adults behind us had not spotted his glances. Then I realised it was not Laura or me he was looking at. It was Lachlan in his wheelchair behind us.

No one spoke to Mhairi. While there was the half-time break in the match, other tables mixed and mingled and conversations jumped from one group to another and there were shouts across the room between neighbours and friends, but no one said anything to Mhairi. She sat and sipped her glass of wine and didn't seem interested in what was going on around her.

'Come oan,' said Laura, standing up. 'We'll be back in time fir the second half.'

We picked our way past the other children sitting on the floor and squeezed between the groups of adults standing around the room.

'Where are we goin'?'

Outside the dining hall the air was cool and fresh and the dark cloud of smoke thinned out. Laura led me through a door into a reception room with a few low coffee tables and comfy armchairs arranged within more bay windows.

'Ah want tae show ye somethin'. Ma da showed me this when he wis doin' some work here.'

She walked across the room and stopped in front of the far wall. It was covered in large wooden panels that were freshly painted white and had decorative carvings around the sides. Laura pushed one of the panels.

Nothing happened.

'Wit are ye doin'?'

'It must be this wan.' She pushed the next panel along. This time there was a click as the panel popped open and swung outwards to reveal a dark space behind. 'A priest hole.'

'A wit?'

'Old buildings like this had them built behind false walls. Secret places fir priests tae hide in. The castle has wan too.'

'Why wud a priest need tae hide?'

'No' now, centuries ago. When the Catholics were bein' hunted by the Proddies.' My knowledge of religious history and persecution in Scotland wasn't great, but you couldn't grow up in Glasgow and not know that Catholics and Protestants didn't like each other. My mum was Catholic and Dad was Protestant and I had heard them talk about their marriage as a mixed marriage. I knew it was all to do with something that happened a long time ago, but beyond that I hadn't taken an interest. When the Pope had come to visit

Glasgow the Protestants protested in the city centre. It had always seemed daft to me.

'Wit's in there?' I peered through the entrance into the murky space behind the wall.

'Follow me. Yer no' afraid a' the dark, are ye?'

'Of course no.'

Laura led the way, stepping over the wooden siding board and into the small, dark space behind the door. She shuffled over and let me in. Then she pulled the door back into place with a small handle on the inside. The door clicked as it closed and we were plunged into complete darkness. The space was narrow, no wider than the width of my shoulders. I stood with my back against a cold brick wall. I felt Laura take my hand and could just make out her outline as my eyes adjusted to the darkness.

'This way,' she whispered, and started inching her way along the passage, moving sideways. The floor was uneven and every couple of paces there were raised bricks that my feet stumbled over. Laura let go of my hand as I struggled to keep up with her.

'Where dis it go?' I called into the pitch-black darkness.

'Right through tae the back a' the hotel. Come oan.'

I heard her stepping ahead and tried to keep up. I lost any sense of how far we had gone. Through the wall I could hear muffled talking and clanks and clangs and realised it must be the hotel kitchen preparing the dinner for the guests who had no interest in the cup final.

'Shouldnae we git back fir the second half?' I whispered. There was no answer. 'Laura?' I couldn't hear any movement and started to feel uneasy. Had she left me alone in the dark tunnel? Was this her idea of a joke? I kept shuffling along. The kitchen sounds faded. 'Laura,' I hissed into the blackness again, more impatient now. I must have been close to the other end of the passage by now. I could forgive Laura a lot, but this wasn't funny anymore.

Then I saw a sliver of grey, slightly lighter than the darkness of the tunnel, and saw Laura crouching down. She was waving at me to do the same and had her finger over her lips, telling me to be quiet. A breath of cool air came through the tunnel and I realised the sliver of light was coming from outside. Laura had reached the other end of the passage and was holding the door open by a tiny fraction.

'Wit is it?' I crouched down next to her and whispered in her ear.

Laura pointed out the gap in the door and again urged me to be quiet with her finger to her lips. Now I heard voices talking. The first was a male voice; it was deep and calm and had an Irish accent. The second was a female voice and she was trying to interrupt the man.

'It would be better if you just went home, Mhairi. Don't cause any trouble.'

'Wit trouble am ah causing? Ah came tae watch the game, jist like everyone else. Why shouldn't ah?'

'You know fine well what you are doing turning up here.'

'Ah'm tired a' havin' tae hide away fae the rest a' the island.'

'I know it's not easy for you, but you have to accept this is the way it is on the island.'

The woman let out an exasperated sigh.

The man continued, 'I've told you before, if you want I can arrange for you to move somewhere else, where you and Billy can leave all this acrimony behind. Wouldn't that be better for everyone? There are places for single mothers like you, homes run by the church.'

I adjusted my feet and strained over Laura, trying to peer out of the small gap to see who the male voice belonged to. I knew the woman was Mhairi, I could recognise her voice, but I wanted to see who the man was that was talking to her. I craned my neck and was able to see the side of her head and her blonde hair. She was standing close to the opening, leaning with her back against the wall with her arms crossed and blocking the view so I couldn't see past her to the man's face.

'It'd be convenient fir ye aw, wouldn't it?'

A hand appeared on Mhairi's shoulder. 'Mhairi.' She shrugged the hand away and stepped to the side. Now I could see the man's face and the blue Italian top he was wearing. It was the priest, Father Baird. His friendly smile slipped away as he struggled to grip Mhairi's shoulder. He had a look of menace. At that moment, whether it was my surprise at seeing Father Baird's face or because I was straining over Laura, I lost my balance. I bumped into Laura and she put her hand out to steady herself and in doing so nudged the door. It made a small creak that echoed through the still air and sounded as loud as a gunshot in the quiet night. Father Baird paused. Mhairi broke free and hurried away. Father Baird looked in our direction. Laura slammed the door closed and pushed me back along the tight corridor.

'Who's in there?' we heard the priest call from outside. As we scurried away we heard his hands on the door. He would be sure to know about the priest hole in the old building, but the door was designed as an escape door and could only be opened from the inside.

'Hurry,' Laura urged me on, 'we need tae git back inside before he sees us.'

I stumbled along the passage, scraping my knees and hands until I found the handle of the door panel we had entered through. I pushed it open and stepped back into the light of the lounge. Laura piled out after me and closed the door panel over. We turned to see Father Baird staring at us from the hotel lobby. Time froze for a moment.

Before he could say anything there was a loud cheer from the dining room behind him. The game had restarted and a goal had been scored. Laura and I took our chance and hurried past the priest. He followed us into the room. The look of fury on his face disappeared, replaced by his familiar serene smile as he re-joined the minister and others. The Italian couple were at the centre of a circle of locals. Italy had scored the first goal of the final.

Tom saw us and shouted over the noise, 'Wit a goal! Paulo Rossi again!'

No one had noticed our absence at the start of the second half. Behind us Father Baird joined in the celebrations. We took our place on the floor in front of the screen as the match continued. Father Baird took his place at the table next to Tom and Cathy and Laura's parents. I was convinced he would say something to them, but when I looked round they were paying us no attention and were engrossed in the game on the screen. Mhairi Matheson was back in her chair with a fresh glass of wine. Billy sat at her feet.

There were two more Italian goals, both met with enthusiastic celebrations in the hotel dining room. West Germany could only manage a late consolation goal. The full-time whistle sounded and the crowd broke into a confused version of the Italian national anthem, led by the delighted Italian couple. Mhairi stood up and took Billy's hand and walked out. As she left she passed Father Baird at the door into the lobby. She refused to make eye contact with him. I watched them leave and joined Laura and Tom in the celebrations.

After the Italian team had lifted the trophy, the hotel began to empty and people drifted away, heading home as the sun was setting. The Italian honeymooners were the last of the hotel guests to head up to their room. The Robertsons said goodbye and Laura arranged to meet me in the morning. We didn't get a chance to discuss what we had seen. Tom insisted on staying until the television coverage came to an end, so we were among the last to go, leaving Alasdair Campbell, the harbourmaster, at the bar, where he could usually be found until closing time, ordering another dram of whisky and puffing on his pipe.

15

I got up early the next day and cycled to Castlebay to meet Laura. Only the steep slope of Heaval still defeated me and forced me to push the bike uphill until I reached the top. Laura was waiting by the school gates as usual.

I stopped next to her. 'Ah thought we wer fir it.'

We started walking side by side, pushing our bikes. Laura was on the edge of the road and I walked along the pavement. We headed away from the village.

'He's a priest, he's no' goin' tae dae us any harm.'

'Ah wis sure he wis goin' tae shout at us, or tell our parents.'

A loud horn blared behind us. Laura pulled her bike onto the kerb as the bus rattled past. Mrs MacQueen was standing outside the store chatting to Pete Lorimer, the man Cathy had mentioned who worked at the fish factory. They looked up as the bus disappeared along the road and waved at us. I waved back. They went back to talking to each other and I wondered if they were talking about last night. Pete had been in the bar when Mhairi and Billy had shown up. Was he filling Mrs MacQueen in with the gossip?

'Wit dae ye think it wis aw about? Aw that stuff about her an' Billy leavin' the island tae stop causin' trouble?'

'Nae idea.' Laura shrugged and stepped back down onto the road. The pavement ended beyond the outskirts of the village. We walked in single file along the side of the road, Laura leading the way. 'Mibbe it has tae dae wi' Billy's da,' she called back over her shoulder.

'Wit about his dad?'

'His da died years ago, when Billy wis only a baby. Got drunk wan night an' drowned in the sea. Ah know Mhairi keeps stirrin' up trouble about it.'

'Wit sort a' trouble?'

'She says there wis mare tae it than jist drownin', or somethin'.'

'Wit dae ye mean?'

Laura shrugged. 'Ah dinnae really know. Ah wis only two or three at the time. Ah kin show ye where they found him if ye want. It wis oan the beach oan Vatersay.'

The image of Mhairi Matheson changed again. She was a young woman, a single mother with a son whom she raised on her own in a small community that shunned them for some reason, and now I added the fact that she had been a widow for ten years, since her early twenties, or even when she was still a teenager.

A car came towards us along the road and we had to pull our bikes up onto the grass verge to let it go past. When the road was clear we got on our bikes and started cycling. We reached the turning that Laura had shown me before, which led down the hill to Vatersay, and this time we turned off the main road towards the sea.

It was a steep gradient down the hillside before the road levelled off and followed the coast for a mile. Across the narrow stretch of water was the opposite shoreline of Vatersay. The islands were so close the sea was channelled into a river that separated the two banks. The River Clyde was wider than this when it got past Renfrew and Govan and started to open out at Dumbarton and Port Glasgow. Here, there was no more than about two hundred feet of water between the two shores. The road ran down to a concrete jetty that jutted out into the channel with two rowboats tied up to it. Both shorelines had narrow, pebbled beaches that sloped up to wild grass beyond.

Laura stopped at the end of the jetty and pointed across the water to the other side. 'He wis found lyin' oan the beach somewhere over there.'

It was an anti-climax. It looked like any other beach. I don't know what else I had been expecting to see.

'How did he end up over there?'

'Naebody knows. He'd bin drinkin' in Castlebay that evening. Nae wan saw him after he left the pub. Instead a' goin' hame he came doon tae the water an' tried tae swim across tae Vatersay.'

'Why wud he try tae swim tae Vatersay? Ah thought nae wan lived over there?' All I could see was an old cottage standing back from the shore and behind that the side of a hill with a track that went along the coast before curving inland.

'A few people live there, but that's aw.'

'Wis he tryin' tae visit somewan?'

Laura shrugged.

The voice came from behind us. 'He didnae know anywan oan Vatersay.' We both jumped and spun round and saw Billy perched on the saddle of his bike. He had come down the hill behind us and the noise of the sea and the ever-present wind had covered the sound of his wheels.

'Did ye follow us?' I asked. He didn't answer. 'If he didnae know anywan, why wis he tryin' tae git over there?'

'Ma maw says he wasnae tryin' tae swim tae Vatersay at aw.'

'How did he end up in the water then? Did he jist faw in?' asked Laura.

Billy shrugged. 'D'ye want tae go across an' see where they found him?'

'How wud we git across?'

Billy pointed at one of the rowboats tied to the jetty. 'That's wit they're fir.'

As always, I was wary of both Billy and the idea of us taking a small wooden boat out onto the water. I had never rowed a boat before. 'We shouldnae dae that ourselves. Wit if the wind blows us out tae sea?'

'Ah've done it hundreds a' times before.' Billy lay his bike on the ground and walked past us. Without his mum there to speak for him, he became more confident.

Laura gave me a shove. 'Come oan. There's three a' us. It's no' that far.'

I left my bike on the ground and followed after Laura. Billy untied a rope that was holding a rowboat to the jetty and stepped in. He pulled the rope so the boat stayed close to the side while the current tried to pull it away. Laura hopped in and the boat rocked as she shifted her weight and sat down at the front. I tried to step in just as the boat moved away from the jetty and a gap opened up. I saw the water between the boat and the side and stopped. Billy pulled on the rope and the gap closed again. I sat on the jetty and dangled my legs over the side of the boat and shuffled aboard. Billy dropped the rope into the back of the boat. 'Untie us,' he instructed Laura. She untied the rope at the front of the boat that was wrapped around a cleat. As soon as the boat was free it sprang away from land and began to drift out.

'Move over,' Billy said to me as he sat down on the plank in the middle of the boat. I shuffled to the back, not daring to stand as we rocked up and down on the waves. Billy picked up the oars that lay on the floor and put them through the metal rowlocks on the side. He was able to dip the ends of the oars into the water and, with his small arms extended fully, he began circling them round. I was no expert, but for all Billy's confidence I could tell it was a struggle for him to keep the oars in motion and working together. I doubted he had done this hundreds of times before and regretted our decision to follow him. We were drifting further out into the channel of water, but rather than heading straight across, we were being taken sideways by the current.

'D'ye want me tae take wan a' them?' Laura asked.

'Ah kin manage.'

'Gie it here.' Laura moved back and sat next to him. She took hold of an oar. With two hands on the top of the oar, they were both able to get their paddle deeper into the water and rotate the oar further on each stroke. Now we started to make progress forward rather than sideways. The boat started to veer right as Laura's strokes were longer and stronger than Billy's. She checked her stroke and allowed Billy to correct our course. We were halfway across. The current was stronger the further out we went and we drifted further away from the jetty on the opposite side. I had visions of drifting out into the ocean, lost at sea for days and washing up on a deserted island or disappearing forever.

It felt like an eternity but was probably no longer than ten minutes before we neared the other side and my anxiety subsided. We had been pushed so far along the coast that the jetty we had been aiming for was out of reach. Instead, the boat grounded itself on the beach of pebbles. I took the rope and jumped clumsily over the side and landed in shallow water. The cold gave me a shock as it seeped through my shoes and lapped around my ankles. I was just relieved to have made it to the other side. The boat pulled at the rope, straining to escape, but I held on and managed to take a couple of steps out of the water and onto dry land. Laura and Billy walked to the front of the boat and jumped over the side and the three of us hauled the boat further out of the water. When it was finally clear of the sea, Laura took the rope and looped it round a boulder that sat in the middle of the beach.

'It'll be fine there until we go back.'

Only when she said that did I realise we would have to do it all again in order to return to Barra.

'The current's a bit strong today, that's aw.' Billy defended himself even though neither of us had said anything. 'Follow me.'

He walked along the beach. We went after him and our feet slid over the mix of fine sand, seaweed and pebbles.

Billy stopped and pointed at a large tree. 'It wis jist here they found him.'

The tree was dead and lay on the ground, the wood frayed and brittle and pale grey, nestled between a group of large rocks.

'How d'ye know this wis the place?' Laura asked.

'Mum brought me an' showed me. We put flowers doon. He wis lyin' here, like this.' Billy lay down on his back and wedged himself into a small gap between the dead tree and a boulder with his head up and his arms out and knees folded up in front of him. He closed his eyes and opened his mouth and let his tongue loll out.

I felt a chill run up my spine. 'That's enough.'

'Blind drunk, they said.' Billy opened his eyes. 'He wis tangled up in some auld fishin' nets. Mum said he had a big cut oan his head. They said he must've bashed it against the rocks when he wis washed up.'

'Don't ye miss him?' I asked.

'Ah dinnae remember him much. Ah wis four or five before Mum telt me about him. Ah think ah wis only wan or two when he died. Ah know he worked oan the fishin' boats so he wisnae about that much. That's probably why ah dinnae remember him.'

'Ma maw telt me he used tae go tae church wi' yer mum. Angus wis his name, wasnie it? Angus Anderson.'

'Ah thought yer name wis Matheson?' I asked Billy.

'It is, that's ma maw's name.' Billy got up from the rocks. 'Anyway, this is where they found him.'

'We saw yer ma arguin' wi' Father Baird last night.'

'He disnie let her go tae the church anymare. Mum says she disnae want tae go anyway.'

'Why disnie he let her go tae church?'

'Ah think it's somethin' tae dae wi' me, because ma mum and da werenae married. People dinnae like her very much.'

'She seems nice tae me,' Laura said.

'She wis only sixteen when ah wis born. She says ah wis the best mistake she ever made.' Calling someone a mistake wasn't very nice. The picture of Mhairi Matheson shifted again. Sixteen was only three years older than me and Laura. I couldn't picture Laura with a swollen stomach with a baby inside. I couldn't imagine being a parent when I was still that young. And if she was a mum at sixteen she must have had sex before that. Thinking about sex was a relatively new thing for me, but I knew a little and I heard what other boys in my class said, and their older brothers and sisters. I had heard what some of the older brothers and sisters had done. I looked at Laura and wondered how much she had thought about it, or had she tried anything like kissing another boy? Then I remembered how I had felt on the beach when I had seen her in her underwear and how it had felt when we had been wrestling in the water. Was that how it started? Did it start with having fun and playing and cycling around and then grow into love and then when two people loved each other they had sex? But I also knew sex didn't have to involve love. I had a good idea what was involved in sex, enough to know it involved being naked with the other person and kissing and touching and where you were supposed to touch them. Would I enjoy that? I thought about that day on the beach again and what it would be like to have kissed Laura when we had been playing in the sea.

I forced myself to stop thinking about it, realising where we were and why we had come there. I felt sorry for Billy, standing next to where his dad's body had been found. I thought about my own mother in the hospital. 'Ah'm sorry about wit happened tae yer da. Ye kin play wi' us anytime if ye want tae, ye dinnae have tae follow us aroun'. But ma uncle said ah wis tae stay away fae ye, so dinnae come near the hoose.'

'Mum says ah should ignore wit anywan says about me or her.'

'We could meet oan our bikes,' Laura offered.

'Ah'll dae witever ah want.' He walked down the beach towards the water.

Laura shrugged at me and followed after him. I looked once more at the dead tree and rocks and the space where Billy's dad had been found. What a place to end up. Had he been found straightaway, or had he lain there for a few days before anyone saw him?

I caught up with the other two. Having seen the spot where Angus Anderson had been found, there wasn't anything else to do on Vatersay. We picked up stones and threw them as far as we could out into the water. Laura threw hers the furthest. After a while doing that I noticed the water had moved up the beach. The tide was coming in. How long had we spent looking at the dead tree and throwing stones? I had a sinking feeling of panic in my stomach and looked back along to where we had left the rowboat. It was still there, but it was afloat on the incoming tide. I yelled and pointed. 'The boat!'

Laura and Billy saw what I was shouting about and the three of us ran as fast as we could, scrambling over the loose shale. The top of the small boulder that Laura had looped the rope over was about to disappear under the water. If the rope floated off the rock then there would be nothing to stop the boat drifting away. As we got nearer the boulder disappeared under a wave. Laura got to the boat first and waded out after it, but the current took it out of her grasp. She put her hands in the water, feeling for the end of the rope. I joined her and did the same. We couldn't find the rope anywhere. Laura looked at the water around her and saw the end of it floating away on the top of the waves. She dived after it, into the freezing-cold water. I saw her head disappear under the waves. She stood up, gasping for air. Her hands were empty. The boat continued to drift away out to sea. Billy caught up with us.

'Wit dae we dae now?' I couldn't hide the panic in my voice. 'Kin ye swim out tae get it?'

Laura shook her head. 'The current's too strong.'

'Come oan,' said Billy, 'it might come in near tae the shore further along.'

We trudged back along the shoreline, keeping pace with the boat. It drifted further out into the middle of the water rather than coming close to the shore again. When it reached about halfway across the channel the current got hold of it and it shot ahead of us.

'It's nae use, it's gone.' Laura was shivering and her hair and clothes were soaking from her dive into the sea. I couldn't help but notice how her T-shirt and shorts clung to her and pictured the thin, pale body underneath again.

'Wit are we goin' tae dae now?' I repeated. We were stuck on the island. What if no one realised we were gone? We hadn't told anyone where we were going. How long before anyone started looking for us? Would we have to spend the night on the island? What would Tom and Cathy say when they found out what had happened?

'There might be another boat at the jetty,' Billy suggested.

My spirits rose. Of course there would be another boat. So long as we got back to Barra, then we could make up a story about what had happened to the missing rowboat if anyone asked us about it. Even if Tom and Cathy and Laura's parents did find out what had happened, I would just be happy to get back to Barra and then worry about my punishment. We started walking back the way we had come, glancing back at the disappearing rowboat, just in case it changed course. It was soon just a dot in the vast blue sea. It cleared the end of the channel and there the waves became bigger and it bobbed up and down and dipped out of view. We reached the jetty and there was no sign of a boat. Laura stepped up onto the concrete when we got there and looked over the other side.

'Nothin'.' My heart sank. We were stranded. On the opposite

shore we could see the other rowboat still moored to that jetty and our bikes lying on the path next to it.

'We cannae stay oan this island. Nae wan knows we're here.'

'Ah could try swimmin' it,' said Laura.

'Ah cannae swim that far,' I answered. There was no way I would make it over the choppy sea to the other side of the channel.

'We could try the hoose.' Billy pointed to the old cottage, the only building that was visible. It was about half a mile along the road. 'Nae wan lives there, but it might ha' a telephone.'

'It willnae ha' a telephone if nae wan lives there,' Laura said.

'Ah guess we'll jist wait here until somewan else rows over then.'

Laura was rubbing her arms, trying to warm herself up. The sun was high in the sky and providing some warmth, but the water had been freezing cold. At least the cottage would give us some shelter from the eternal breeze. 'Let's go an' see,' I suggested. 'We'll keep a lookout in case anywan comes across the water.'

Billy ran ahead. He still thought of it as an adventure. How could he not be worried about what might happen to us? I wished I could feel the same way. I wished we had never agreed to row across the water.

The house was a squat building which might once have been a pretty cottage but was now rundown. The plaster on the walls was cracked and falling off and the roof had gaping holes in it. Gusts of wind blowing through the gaps made a howling noise that got louder as we got closer to it. There were wires running down the side of the hill on wooden telegraph poles and one wire ran into the side of the house. Perhaps there was a telephone after all.

The front door was shut, but when Laura turned the handle and pushed against it, it opened with a creak. Everything was covered in a layer of dust and dirt and there were cobwebs around the door frame. We stepped inside. Laura led the way, followed by Billy and me. I took one last look back at the jetty, but there was no sign of anyone coming to our rescue. The hallway was dark and smelled of damp, and it was obvious no one had lived in the house for a long time. There was no furniture and the floor was bare wooden boards. A lightbulb hung from the ceiling. I pressed a light switch on the wall. It clicked, but nothing happened. The floorboards creaked with each step we took. Shafts of sunlight crept in through small gaps in the roof and cast shadows into the corners of the hallway.

'Hello?' called out Laura. Unsurprisingly, there was no response. A stairway was at the end of the hall. The roof space must have been converted into an upstairs room. Some of the stairs were missing and broken. On either side of the narrow hall, doors led to other rooms. Billy opened one and peered round the door and then stepped into the room.

'Kitchen,' he said. I looked over his shoulder and saw a sink covered in brown muck. The window was broken and glass covered the worktop. The cupboard doors were falling off or missing.

Laura went through another door which led to a living room. I followed her. There was a tattered sofa and armchair and a broken side table and a fireplace. The remains of a carpet were still on the floor, worn away in places and soaking wet so that our feet squelched as we stepped on it. A corner of the roof had fallen in and across the walls was a black stain of damp.

'There's a telephone.' It was sitting on the floor in the dry corner of the room and a white cable snaked from the wall into the back of it. Laura knelt down and picked up the handset and held it to her ear and frowned. She tried turning the dial on the front of it a few times. 'Nothin.'

'Ah telt ye it would be useless,' I said. 'Wit dae we dae now?'

Laura left the room to go and check out the rest of the house. Billy stood at the living-room window, which was still in place but was cracked and covered in brown smears and had green moss growing around the edges. It was the first time I had been alone with him. I took in the small frame and dirty-blond hair. I thought back to the previous evening and the looks I had seen him giving to Lachlan throughout the football game, and the story Laura had told me about Lachlan's accident.

'Wit happened between ye an' Lachlan?'

He knew what I was talking about. I guessed he had been asked the same question before. 'It wis an accident. He slippt an' fell.'

'But why don't ye talk tae him anymare? My aunt says ye were best friends before the accident. Ah saw ye lookin' at him last night.'

'Ah cannae talk tae him. His dad doesnae let me visit him an' he hardly ever leaves his room.'

Why would Lachlan's dad stop his best friend from visiting him? I was about to ask Billy that question when he ducked down below the windowsill.

'Sssh! Somewan's comin'.' He crouched along into the corner of the room. Laura came back from the hallway and quickly knelt down beside me.

'Wit if they could help us?' I hissed.

'Sssh!'

The front door creaked as it opened and we heard the visitor's footsteps in the hallway.

'*Seadh. Tha fios'm gu bheil thu seo. Thig a-mach.*' It was a man. He didn't sound angry, but he spoke with authority. I started to stand up but Laura stopped me. '*Trobhad.* Come on. This is private property, you shouldn't be in here.'

'This is ridiculous.' I pulled away from Laura's hand and stood up. 'Sorry, mister, wer comin' out.'

I walked into the hallway and the man was standing near the front door. He was tall and broad and blocked the doorway. He had a red moustache and beard that covered most of his face and reached down to the top of his chest and wore a heavy mackintosh jacket and matching cap, despite the warm sunny weather. He carried a shotgun, which was slung over his shoulder.

'Where are your friends? I saw the three of you walking up to the house.'

'They're in here tae.'

'Out you come, all of you.' The man stepped back outside to wait for us to follow him. Laura and Billy came out of the living room. Laura glowered at me. I followed them out the front door.

'Right then, what are you three up to?'

'Nothin', sir, honest. We wer jist lookin' fir a telephone tae use.' I answered.

'You'll not get a working telephone in there, no one's lived there for ten years or more.'

'We know that now,' said Laura. 'We needed tae call somewan tae come an' get us.' She told him about the rowboat and pointed out our bikes, which were still sitting on the jetty in the distance, with the sunlight glinting off the metal frames. 'We jist need tae git back across.'

'That'll be one of old Cameron's boats that you've lost then. He won't be happy about that. We'll need to tell him and your parents. What are your names?'

'Ah'm Laura Robertson, an' that's Billy Matheson, an' he's Ewan Fraser who's over visitin' fae the mainland.'

'You're the Matheson boy?' He looked at Billy who stood behind Laura and me. 'Mhairi Matheson's son?'

'So wit if ah am?'

The man raised an eyebrow. 'Do any of your parents know that you are out here?'

'We didnae plan tae take a boat across,' I pleaded, 'an' we didnae mean fir it tae float away.'

'D'ye live here?' Laura asked him.

'Aye, I do. Moved over from Barra a few years ago. How's your mum doing, Billy? A shame what happened to your father and her. Not right, the way they were treated.'

'Ye knew ma da?' Billy stepped forward now, more interested in the stranger.

'Aye, best friends growing up, we were. I'm George Stewart.'

'Never heard a' ye,' Billy said.

'I don't expect you would have, you were only three or so the last time I saw you. Come on. I've a boat moored a small way away. I can get you back over to your bikes.'

We followed George Stewart along the track, heading further away from the jetty. There would still be the wrath of Tom to deal with if he found out about the missing boat and the time spent with Billy, but at least we had a way to get back to Barra now. George Stewart seemed like a nice man and kept talking to Billy as we walked after him.

'Do you remember Angus, your father?'

'No' much.'

'He was a kind man. He stuck with your mother through everything, all the gossip and rumour. That's why I moved away from Castlebay. I couldn't stand to hear her spoken about in that way.'

'In wit way?' Laura asked.

'Ach, you kids don't need to worry about things like that yet. It's all in the past now and can't be fixed. Sometimes it's no good having everyone know everyone else's business. I'm not surprised your mother is still there, though, she always was a stubborn one.'

'Ye dinnae see ma mum anymare?'

'Once in a while I might bump into her in the store, but I don't go over to Barra much. I prefer keeping away from other people.'

Coming over the crest of a hill we saw a small dinghy with an outboard motor tied to a wooden pole alongside a small pier.

'There she is.' George pointed at the boat with the end of his shotgun.

We reached the bottom of the slope and clambered from the pier into the boat. After a couple of attempts the engine sputtered into life. I sat at the front of the boat and Laura sat next to me. Billy sat in the middle. The noise of the engine made it difficult for any more conversation. Compared to our struggle earlier in the day, it took no time at all for the return crossing. In five minutes, George was steering his boat alongside the jetty on the Barra side of the channel and tying it up and helping us get up onto the walkway.

'You best tell your parents what happened before they hear it from old Cameron. He'll be sure to get in touch with them about his lost boat. You hear?'

'Thanks fir the ride.'

'Don't be trying anything like that again, you of all people should know how dangerous this water can be, Billy.' His stern look softened. 'Say hi to your mum for me.'

'Ah will.'

We watched him untie his boat, put the engine in gear and turn round to head back over to Vatersay. White spray kicked up from the front of the dinghy as he skipped over the waves. When he reached the point where the island curved away, he looked back and waved. We waved back until he disappeared from view.

'Wit wis aw that about yer maw an' gossip an' rumour?' Laura asked Billy.

'How should ah know? Ye've seen how people talk about her behind her back. Ye said ye saw the priest arguin' wi' her last night. Probably he meant the fact her an' Da' werenae married.'

'That cannae be the only reason people dinnae like her, especially after wit happened tae yer da in the end.'

'Why dinnae ye ask her?' Billy challenged Laura.

'Mibbe ah will.'

We collected our bikes and mounted them, ready to cycle up the hill.

I pointed at Billy's shining BMX. 'Is that new?'

'Got it fir ma birthday last month. Mum went tae Glasgow an' bought it an' got it delivered.'

'Aren't they expensive?'

'Nae idea. Ye jealous?' He looked at my rusted old bike.

'Ah've ma own bike back home,' I lied. 'This is jist fir while ah'm stayin' oan Barra.'

'We better get goin' an' face the music before this old Cameron guy finds out his boat's missin' an' calls our parents.' Laura led the way up the track. Billy was able to keep up with her, while I fell behind as usual. At the top of the hill, where the track re-joined the main road, Laura waited on me to catch up. By the time I reached her, Billy had gone ahead on his own.

16

It was late afternoon by the time we got back to Laura's house. On the way we decided not to tell Flora and Hamish what had happened. Maybe the old man who lost his boat would just think it had slipped away on its own and the current had taken it out to sea. Hamish was working at the castle and Flora was at the airport café, so we had the house to ourselves. We made sandwiches and took them up to Laura's room. Laura had her own turntable in her room and put on a new record by Duran Duran that Hamish had brought back from Oban for her. Laura sat on her bed and looked at the record sleeve and hummed along to the music. Her room had yellow walls that were covered with posters of Duran Duran, Blondie, Bowie and The Human League and movie posters of *Jaws* and *ET*. I wandered round looking at her shelves and her desk. She had a lot of cool stuff. I picked up a Rubik's cube and idly turned the sides. I'd never been able to figure out the trick to completing the puzzle. She even had some *Star Wars* figures. Her room was a mess. There was a pile of laundry heaped in the corner. I was surprised Flora let her keep it like this.

I couldn't stop thinking about Billy's dad and the way he was found on the beach. 'D'ye remember anythin' mare about Billy's dad dyin'?' I asked her.

'Ah vaguely remember goin' tae the funeral, but ah dinnae really remember him. Whenever anywan dies oan the island almost everywan goes along tae the funeral because everywan knows each other.'

'D'ye think he wis tryin' tae swim over tae Vatersay?'

'Mibbe he wis jist drunk. Mibbe he made a bet wi' somewan that he could make it across the channel.'

'Ah still dinnae understand why everywan is so mean tae Mhairi an' Billy, especially after wit happened tae Angus.'

Laura slid another record from its sleeve and carefully placed it on the turntable. This one was Blondie. My mum had liked Blondie but she said their new album wasn't so good. Laura read the album sleeve while I thought about Mhairi Matheson. Apart from having Billy when she was young and before she was married, she hadn't done anything wrong. The people of Barra would get a shock if they ever decided to go and live in Glasgow. It had all happened over ten years ago; surely that was enough time for people to get over it? And then she had lost her husband and Billy had lost his father and shouldn't people feel sorry for them and help them out? There had to be something more to it, but no one would talk about it. Cathy, Tom, George Stewart, they had all shaken their heads and said it was nothing for children to worry about. I remembered the look on Father Baird's face when we walked past him into the hotel dining room. Was he angry that we had seen him acting that way with Mhairi?

'Wit will ye dae when ye see Father Baird at church oan Sunday?'

'Perhaps he'll have forgotten about it by then.' It was only Monday, so it was almost a full week before Laura would have to see him again.

'He didnae look like he wis goin' tae forget about it.'

'If nothin' else happens mibbe he'll think we didnae really see anythin', or he'll know we havenae said anythin' tae anywan. He probably wants tae forget about it as much as we dae.'

I couldn't forget the way the priest had been speaking to Mhairi and how he had held her forcefully by the shoulder. There was something more to it and it was linked to how everyone dealt with Mhairi and Billy, but I had no idea what it was about.

Laura got up and started moving round the room as the next song came on. We didn't hear the front door opening and closing over the loud music, but there was no missing the shout that followed.

'*Laura, a bheil thu shuas an sin?* Turn that music off and get down here right now. You too, Ewan Fraser.' My bike was parked outside the front door, so she knew I was here. We knew from the tone of her voice that the story of our morning adventure must have already made it round the island and reached Flora in the airport café.

Laura stopped dancing and took the stylus off the record and turned the turntable off. I followed her down the stairs. Flora stood waiting for us at the bottom. The look on her face confirmed our fears. Her hands were on her hips.

'I've just had a conversation with Father Baird.' Laura stood with her arms folded. I looked at the floor. 'Do you want to tell me anything?'

I felt a small wave of relief. It wasn't about this morning after all, it was only about last night and we hadn't really done anything wrong last night; we'd only overheard a conversation.

Laura answered her mum. 'It's no' our fault. They wer jist there at the same time as we wer.'

'Sneaking about in secret passages and eavesdropping on private conversations. I thought I had brought you up better than that, Laura Robertson. Perhaps this boy is having a bad influence on you.' She turned to me. 'Is this what you were brought up to do?'

'We didnae mean tae listen in.' I was surprised at the anger with which Flora was talking to us. All we had done was overhear a conversation we shouldn't have. We didn't even know what it was about. And it was true, we had only listened in by accident. I wondered how angry Flora would be when she found out what had happened this morning.

'We wer only playin' an' then we saw them standin' there arguin',' Laura pleaded.

'Luckily for you Father Baird is a reasonable man. He wants to make sure you haven't misunderstood what you think you heard and saw. I am furious with you.'

Laura stood up to her mum. 'We know wit we saw. We saw him shoutin' at poor Mhairi Matheson an' grabbin' her an' tellin' her tae leave Barra.'

I stepped to the side to avoid the hand that flashed past and slapped Laura across her face. Mother and daughter stood staring at each other. Laura stuck her chin out in defiance as the skin on her cheek turned red. Her eyes began to water but she did not back down. I held my breath, shocked at the unexpected and sudden temper that Flora had shown.

'You will never talk about Father Baird in that way, young lady, and you will certainly not feel sorry for Mhairi Matheson. Don't you ever think she is an innocent victim in all this.' Flora trembled as she spoke and her voice wavered. She pointed her finger in her daughter's face. 'Get up to your room this instant.'

Laura did as she was told and stormed up the stairs.

'Ewan, I think you best get back to your house and stay away from Laura for the rest of your time here.'

Laura stopped at that and turned. 'Wit?'

'Don't you "wit" me. Get upstairs.' Flora left Laura in no doubt that it was best to do as she was told. I hadn't moved. I couldn't think of anything to say. As much as I wanted to plead with Flora to change her mind, I could tell there was no point in arguing with her. I slipped past her and out the front door. I turned back as I exited and over Flora's shoulder saw Laura. Our eyes met before

Flora closed the door on me. I waited on the doorstep and heard footsteps going up the stairs and a door slamming.

* * *

On the cycle back to Bruernish, I tried to gather my thoughts. There was something about Mhairi Matheson and Billy and his dead father, and perhaps Father Baird too, that I didn't understand. It had to be more serious than Mhairi having Billy out of wedlock. As much as The Church frowned upon such things, it didn't make sense that Mhairi and Billy were still being punished for it. Was it to do with Angus Anderson and his mysterious death? What could have happened that meant a woman and her son were not welcome in the church? George Stewart had said Mhairi was being wronged somehow. Cathy had stopped herself from telling me too much and Tom had told me not to go anywhere near Billy. Everyone in the hall last night had shunned them. There had to be some secret behind it all. Maybe there was an innocent explanation for all of it, but it was something they didn't think children would understand. A couple of days ago my summer holidays had been turning out better than I could have hoped for in the circumstances. Now the rest of the summer looked bleak. Without Laura to spend time with I would be stuck in the house with Cathy with nothing to do except wait for Dad to call and tell me Mum had died. The beaches and rocks and sea that had seemed like a big adventure now looked grey and barren and empty. The wind picked up on the exposed ground before the dip that led to Bruernish and the bus trundled past, heading towards the airport. The driver gave me a wave. On the surface everything seemed friendly and quaint on this island. Everyone knew each other and got along and was part of the community and looked out for each other. Except for those that were cast out for some reason.

I got back to the house and left the bike lying in the garden and entered the kitchen. Cathy was up to her elbows in flour with her baking apron on and various bowls and ingredients spread over the worktop.

'Ah wasnae expectin' ye hame fir dinner. Ah thought ye were at Laura's?' At least Father Baird and Flora had not yet been in touch with my aunt. 'Ah'm jist bakin' fir the post office tearoom. The last lot selt oot already. That's wit happens when it's the summer an' the tourists keep comin'.' She sprinkled some water on a slab of doughy mixture and rolled it flat with a wooden rolling pin.

I watched her and decided to ask her straight out. 'Wit happened wi' Mhairi Matheson?'

The rolling pin stopped momentarily and then slowly carried on. 'Wit d'ye mean?' She didn't look up.

'Last night everywan ignored them an' Laura an' I overheard Father Baird arguin' wi' her about somethin'.'

'Wit d'ye mean, arguin'? Wit wer they arguin' about?' The rolling pin had stopped, but her hands gripped each side and she kept looking down at the worktop.

'He wis tellin' her she should leave Barra an' take Billy wi' her. That she had caused enough trouble. He grabbed her. Billy said they're no' welcome at the church.'

'Ye've bin talkin' tae Billy?'

It was too late to go back now. 'Laura an' ah went doon tae Vatersay oan our bikes an' he followed us. He showed us where they found his dad.'

The rolling pin spun across the worktop and clattered off the edge. She took two steps towards me and grabbed my arm and pulled me into the living room.

'Now listen tae me fir yer own gud, Ewan. Ye stop listenin' tae Billy Matheson an' ye forget any silly rumours an' gossip ye might hear. These things dinnae concern ye. Things happened a long time ago, before Tom an' I even moved here, an' people wud like tae try an' forget these things an' move oan. D'ye hear?'

I wrenched my arm free. 'No wan is lettin' Mhairi an' Billy forget. Why dinnae ye talk tae her? Yer nice tae everywan else, ye talk tae everywan else aw the time. She seems like a nice woman tae me.'

'How wud ye know anythin' about it? Yer jist a child. Father Baird is right. It wud be best if they left an' let everywan move oan.'

'Why will nae wan tell us wit happened?'

'Things happened that ye wouldnae understand. In a few years ye might.'

'Ah'm old enough tae understand now.'

Cathy forced herself to calm down and I was sure she was about to tell me something when the front door opened and Tom came into the house. He found us standing in the middle of the living room.

'Have ye heard?' he asked Cathy.

'Heard wit?'

'Wit this wan's bin up tae this mornin'.' Tom pointed at me.

'He's only jist owned up tae trouble he wis gettin' intae last night, eavesdropping oan Father Baird.'

Tom looked at me. 'Seems like ye cannae help but git intae trouble. Ah got a call fae Cameron lookin' fir me while ah wis at the airport. Seems wan a' his boats doon at the Vatersay jetty has disappeared.'

I prayed for the carpet to open up and swallow me. 'We thought it wud be okay. Billy said he'd rowed across before.'

'Ah telt ye no' tae go near Billy Matheson.' Tom didn't raise his voice; the low, simmering anger made him more menacing.

'Ye went out oan a rowing boat intae the sea wi' jist Billy?' Cathy exclaimed.

'Laura wis there tae. Billy wanted tae show us where they found his da.' Tom stepped forward. He towered over me and for a moment I thought he might strike me the way Flora had slapped Laura. Instead he knelt down and his face was level with mine.

'Listen tae me, Ewan, this is fir yer own gid. Yer tae stay away fae Billy Matheson an' ah will hear nae mare about his da or anythin' else tae dae wi' him. Is that clear?'

He looked me straight in the eye and I nodded.

'Dis Laura's mum know about this?' Cathy seemed concerned rather than angry now.

'She sent me hame because Father Baird had telt her about last night. Ah dinnae know if she knows about wit happened this mornin'.'

'I'd better call her.' Cathy went into the hallway and closed the door behind her. The telephone dial spun back and forth as she dialled the number and then she spoke in a whisper that I couldn't make out.

Tom put a hand on my shoulder. He talked in a soft voice. 'Ah spoke tae yer father this mornin'. Ye'll likely only be here fir a couple mare weeks. Promise me ye'll stay out of trouble until then?' He had a look of sympathy in his eyes as he spoke and I knew it had something to do with my mum.

'Ah havnae done anythin' wrang,' I protested one more time.

Tom sighed. 'Ah know ye havnae done anythin' that bad. It's jist this place. Dinnae get involved in things that dinnae concern ye, okay?'

'Ah'm no' a child, ah'll be fourteen in a few months.'

That brought a half-smile to Tom's face. 'Oh, yer a man now, are ye?'

'Near enough.'

'In that case how about ye come tae work wi' me fir the next couple of days? Ah've got some jobs that ye kin help me wi'. Ye can think of it as yer punishment if ye want an' it'll keep ye out a' trouble. Plus ye kin earn some a' the money ye'll need tae pay Cameron fir his rowboat.'

I had no choice but to agree. Without the chance to see Laura, I had nothing else to do anyway. I pictured her after Flora had hit her. I hoped she wasn't in too much trouble. The reaction from her mum was so different from the easy-going fun person she was normally. There was no way to contact Laura or arrange to meet her. Would I even see her again before I went home?

Tom left the room and spoke to Cathy in the hallway. The front door opened and from the window I saw Cathy get into the van and drive off. Tom appeared on the pathway that ran along the side of the house. He wheeled my bike into the outhouse and locked the door when he came back out. It was clear that I wasn't going to be allowed to cycle anywhere anymore. The final chance to see Laura again evaporated and I slumped onto the sofa.

Tom came back in. 'Cathy is getting us takeaway fae the chip shop fir dinner. She disnae want ye cyclin' aff an' getting' intae any mare trouble.' He walked over to the television and turned it on and flicked through the three channels and found a gameshow and settled into his chair.

'Ah'm goin' up tae ma room.'

I climbed the stairs and sat on my bed. The photograph of my mum holding me when I was a newborn baby still sat on the bedside table. We had never got round to putting it in a frame. Tom thought I would be going home in a couple of weeks. I knew it wasn't because my mum was getting better. It could only be that she was getting worse and it would soon all be over. Tears started to trickle down my face. I wiped them away and put the photograph down and lay on the bed, waiting to hear the van return with dinner and wondering if this summer could get any worse.

17

The following morning Tom woke me at half-past six. I washed and dressed and Tom gave me an old jumper that was suitable for painting and decorating work and was too big for me. The van windows fogged up in the crisp morning air and the sun was only just beginning to appear as we left the house and Tom drove us out to the airport. He was fitting new electrical wiring to the airport terminal and new digital screens for the arrival and departure boards. Did they really need them when there was only the one flight in and out each day from Glasgow? To lay the wiring for the signs and some new lights, Tom had removed plasterboard from the walls and ceiling and replaced it after the wires were laid. Now the walls needed a fresh coat of paint. It was Tuesday and I knew Flora didn't work in the café on Tuesdays. She wouldn't be back in until Friday and I hoped we would be finished by then so I wouldn't have to face her.

On the way, we stopped at the fish factory. One of their ships had brought paint supplies over from the mainland for Tom. I helped him load the industrial-sized tubs, three of white undercoat and three of mint-green topcoat, into the back of the van, before we carried on through Northbay to the airport.

The plane from Glasgow was not due to arrive until early afternoon when the beach was able to be used as the runway. The café was open and the smell of crisp bacon and sausages filled the room, but the airport was quiet. Tom left me to carry the paint tubs from the van into the room we were painting and then I joined him in the café and we ate breakfast. The radio was on, playing a mix of music, and in between songs the DJ chatted. The news came on and talked about Iran and Iraq. They had been fighting for the last two years and now the Iranians were launching an offensive into Iraq. Britain had agreed to return Argentinian prisoners after the Falklands War.

Before we could start painting, the fresh plaster had to be smoothed down. Tom worked up a ladder with a power sander, while I crawled on the floor on my knees and sanded along the skirting boards. I used sanding paper and after ten minutes my arms ached and my fingers were scratched and grazed by the rough paper. I wasn't used to manual labour. By lunchtime I could see the blisters on my hands. Apart from telling me what I had to do, Tom didn't say much. We could hear the radio coming from the café. At lunchtime we got a sandwich and took a half-hour break. I wandered outside to get some fresh air and crossed the road and the *machair*, and walked to the top of the sand dunes. The ocean rolled into Traigh Eais beach, waves breaking over the white sand. A surfer was paddling out into the water, dipping down and bobbing up as the waves swept underneath them. I walked along the beach for a few minutes and found a spot out of the wind and sat down and listened to the constant sound of the breaking waves and watched a seagull glide on the breeze. If only I could sit here forever, away from the rest of the world. If no one ever found me then I could carry on believing that Mum was alive and well. No one would ever be able to tell me otherwise. And Laura could come and visit me and we could fly her kite or build a sandcastle for the ocean to wash away as the tide rolled over it.

I returned to the airport and we carried on working until evening. We began to paint the walls and ceiling of the entrance hallway and the terminal side of the building. Tom worked up the ladders again and used a large roller to cover the ceiling in white undercoat, while I painted the skirting boards and around the corners of the walls. Then we each took a roller and covered the mustard-beige walls in bright clean white. It was satisfying to cover the dirty walls with a fresh coat, rolling over a section at a time and seeing the pure white cover up the blemishes. When the plane from Glasgow arrived we took a break to watch it land. An hour later it took off on the return journey and we watched it run along the sand, picking up speed and lifting into the air.

'Mibbe ah could fly back tae Glasgow?'

'It isnae cheap,' was all Tom said.

It was after six before we got home. I took a bath and scrubbed the paint from my arms and face and hair. The water in the bath turned a cloudy white as I washed myself clean. We ate at the table and afterwards Tom settled in front of the television. I took Lennox for his evening walk after I had made a promise not to take the road that led to the Matheson house.

Wednesday was much the same as Tuesday. We added a second layer of white undercoat to the walls. My arms felt stiff from the previous day. The plane landed and took off again. The same DJ played music that sounded the same and the news talked about Iran and Iraq. We got home, I had a bath and dinner and walked Lennox.

On Thursday we applied the pale mint-green topcoat to the walls. It took us until mid-afternoon and then we were finished and just had to clean away all our stuff. The smell of the turpentine made me feel sick as I cleaned the rollers and brushes. Tom removed all the sheets and ladders and his tools. At the end of the day we stood back and admired our work. Tom put an arm round my shoulder. 'No' bad at aw. An' ye get Friday aff tae.' Alongside my satisfaction, I was relieved I wouldn't have to see Flora the next day.

Tom returned to the airport on his own on Friday morning to oversee the furniture and signage being added to the freshly decorated room. I wondered if Flora would talk to him about Laura and me. I spent an aimless morning in the house with nothing to take my mind off my mum or distract me from wondering what Laura was doing. I walked Lennox down to the old boatshed and wished Billy would appear just for a moment, but there was no sign of him. Cathy went into Castlebay after lunch and I was left on my own.

Lennox started whining and padding between the front door and the back door. I got his lead and took him out for another walk. This time, when I reached the fork in the road I headed towards the row of houses, ignoring the consequences if Tom or Cathy caught me along here. The house at the end of the row stood still and silent. No washing hung in the garden. I walked up to the fence at the end of the track and followed it along the worn grass to the shore and the small cove and climbed down the rocks onto the sand. I let Lennox off his lead and he ran around the rocks, sniffing and exploring. The tide was in and cut off the cave entrance where I had first seen Billy. I threw some stones into the water and hung around in the hope that Billy might wander down from his house, but there was no sign of him. Knowing Cathy would return soon to start cooking dinner, I called Lennox over and re-attached his lead and retraced my steps back to the road. I took my time passing the house at the end of the row, peering into the windows. Was there someone moving inside? Was that a flash of blonde hair in the downstairs room? Perhaps it was a trick of the light or my imagination. I headed back to the house and another evening with my aunt and uncle.

By the weekend my punishment seemed to be over. The bike remained locked in the outhouse, but Cathy and Tom decided we would all go to Castlebay together for the day. We took the van and I sat perched in the back among Tom's work tools. There were no windows in the back so when we passed the Robertson house on the way, I only caught a brief glimpse of it through the front windscreen. I saw their driveway, but nothing else.

We parked in Castlebay. Tom had decided I should make the climb to the top of Heaval, the highest point on the island, at least once while I was on Barra. We left the road and carried on walking up the path that wound its way up the hillside and got steeper the higher we went. Cathy had prepared a picnic for us to eat and we stopped for lunch perched on rocks that sat among the wild grass and heather. When we finished Cathy insisted she had come far enough and would sit and wait while Tom and I continued to the top. We passed a statue that sat alone on the hillside, overlooking the bay and the village below. It was a strange place to have a statue, all on its own. It was white but covered in dirty patches. It showed the Madonna holding her child. It was called Our Lady of the Sea, Tom told me. It made me think of Mhairi, outcast from the community below, supporting her child. It took another half hour of climbing to reach the peak. My legs ached. The grass and wildflowers became sparse. Sometimes the slope was so steep that I used my hands to help clamber over the rocks, but I made it to the summit. It was cold even in the warm sunshine and we were exposed to the wind from all directions. Tom put his hands on his waist and took in an exaggerated breath. 'Wid ye look at that.' He spread his arm wide at the horizon all around.

It was impressive. To the west was the vast Atlantic Ocean and to the north the rest of Barra stretched out and in the distance the outline of Uist and the other Western Isles. Then to the east there were small rocky outcrops, and I could just make out Rum and Coll, the islands which the ferry passed between on its way to Oban and the mainland. There was a dark line on the horizon which I guessed was the rest of Scotland, although I wasn't sure if you could see it from this far away. Down below, Cathy was standing where we had stopped for lunch and was waving at us. I waved down to her. We stood for another five minutes taking in the view in silence. Something about the peace and the vast landscape drew me closer to my uncle and I summoned up the courage to ask if I would be allowed to get the bicycle back.

'Mibbe tomorrow,' Tom answered. I thought about asking him about my mum, but I didn't want to ruin the nice moment between us.

We descended the steep slope and joined Cathy again and the three of us walked back down to Castlebay. We stopped in at the café at the post office and Tom and Cathy had tea and a cake and I was treated to an ice-cream. Cathy chatted to Marion MacNeil. On the way out I looked up at the window above the bank. Lachlan was there in his usual position, looking out at the unchanging view, stuck inside those same four walls. In comparison my few days of punishment were not so bad. Tom and Cathy had walked ahead. I waved at Lachlan. He didn't return the wave but I saw a slight nod of recognition as he stared back at me. After a walk round the bay, we stopped in at the chip shop and bought fish suppers for dinner again. It had been a good day and the best time I had spent with Cathy and Tom since I had arrived on the island. We drove back in the van and I held the hot parcel of food in my lap, feeling the heat on my legs.

We passed Laura going round a cove, where the road dipped and rose up again. I saw her out the window as she pulled her bike into the verge to let the van pass. Tom and Cathy didn't say anything, but they must have seen her too. She looked straight at the van, but there was no way she could have seen me perched in the back. Tom turned his head to look in his side view mirror but didn't make any other sign that he had recognised her. I kept quiet. She was okay and was allowed out on her bike again. Had she been to the house in Bruernish to see me?

We ate our fish suppers in front of the television and I helped tidy away the dirty dishes. It was a mild evening and I spent an hour at the front of the house playing with Lennox and kicking a football around without much purpose. I glanced at the track that led to the main road, hoping Laura might appear freewheeling down the slope. There was no sign of her. At eight o'clock I went inside and up to my room. I flicked through a football magazine. I looked at the picture of Mum. I read a couple of pages of the book I had bought with Cathy on my first day in Barra and had hardly started. It had been over a week since Dad had called, although Tom had said he had spoken to him. The sun began to dip behind the island at the back of nine. I looked out the bedroom window. In the still-blue sky the white moon was clearly visible.

I turned away and the windowpane rattled. Then it did it again as a shower of tiny stones hit it. I went back to it and looked down. Outside the garden wall, Laura stood with her arm raised, about to throw another shower of stones. She saw me and dropped the stones and beckoned me to come outside. I nodded, then worried about how I would get past Tom and Cathy.

The sound of the television came from the living room and floated up to the top of the stairs. They were watching a comedy show with a loud laughter track. I crept down the stairs and paused halfway when one stair let out a groan as I put my foot on it. There was no sign of any movement and I carried on and reached the hallway. My trainers were lying on the mat at the front door. I tiptoed past the living-room door and I dared to peek through the gap as I passed. The top of Cathy's head stuck out above the back of the sofa. Tom's usual chair was out of sight and I prayed he was still sitting in it. In the kitchen, Lennox was in his basket, head lying on his front paws. His wide eyes watched me cross the room. I put my finger to my lips and pleaded with him to stay where he was and not make a sound. He let out a whine when I reached the door but didn't get up. The rubber seal around the door made a sucking noise as it opened and I slipped out onto the step and closed it behind me. Laura watched from the gate as I slipped my trainers on and hurried across the garden path to the wall, looking back at the house to make sure no one had heard me. It was colder now and my breath turned to vapour when I spoke.

'Ah thought ye might've bin comin' tae see me.'

'Why are ye whisperin'?' she asked.

'Ah shouldnae be talkin' tae ye.'

'Are ye grounded? Ah saw the van go past.'

'Ah'm no' grounded, it's jist that they dinnae want me gettin' intae any mare trouble. Ma bike's locked up in the shed. Tom made me go tae work wi' him at the airport. D'ye no' git intae trouble?'

'Mum wis furious but she calmed doon the next day. Dad found out about the missing boat but he didnae say much. He never gits angry wi' me.'

'Why wis yer maw so angry? I couldnae believe she slapped ye.'

'She gits like that sometimes. Probably because she wis embarrassed wi' Father Baird comin' tae speak tae her. She disnae like people gossipin' about her.'

'It's no' that big a deal, is it? Did she tell ye why Father Baird wis talkin' tae Mhairi that way?'

Laura shook her head and wiped stray strands of her long hair away from her face. 'Naw, but she says Father Baird wants tae talk tae me after church tomorrow.'

'Ah know wit we saw.'

'It's probably nothin'. They stopped ma pocket money fir the next few weeks tae help pay Cameron fir a new boat.'

'That's why ah had tae help Tom at his work.'

'When d'ye think ye'll be allowed out again?'

'Mibbe tomorrow, but they willnae want me cyclin' aff an' spendin' the day wi' ye again. Tom says ah could be goin' back hame in the next couple a' weeks.'

'Ye need tae make up an excuse so ye kin come out.'

'Like wit?'

'Ah dinnae know. Think a' somethin.'

'Ah'll try,' I promised, although I had no idea what I could tell Tom and Cathy. 'Ah hope the priest doesnae gie ye intae trouble. Wit if he threatens ye like he did Mhairi?'

'Dinnae be daft, ah haven't done anythin' bad.'

'Neither has Mhairi as far as anywan is telling us.'

'Look out.' A light clicked on in the kitchen window. Laura ducked down behind the wall. I had no choice but to leap over the wall and crouch down next to her. I caught my foot on the top of the wall and landed in a heap next to her. Laura put her hand over her mouth to stifle a laugh. After a minute the light in the kitchen went out. Laura raised her head to peer over the wall. 'Aw clear.'

'Ah better git back inside before they notice ah'm gone.'

'Mibbe ah'll see ye Monday then.'

'Mibbe.'

Laura picked up her bike and pulled it around before getting on the saddle. She waved as she pedalled off down the track. I watched until she disappeared over the rise then crept back inside. Tom and Cathy were still in the living room and the television was still on. Lennox raised his head and I gave him a pat of thanks. I slipped my trainers off at the door and made it back to my room and into bed without being caught. At least I knew Laura was okay, although I worried about what Father Baird might say to her the next day. If I could get the bike back I could cycle and wait outside the church until the service finished and see Laura coming out. That way I would know everything was okay with Father Baird. Cathy would be away at her service on the other side of the island with the van, but Tom would be in the house. It would be impossible to sneak away.

18

In the winter months the westerly winds that blow in from the Atlantic Ocean bring with them the tail end of tropical storms that batter the British Isles. In the summer months the storms are quieter, but they still bring to the Western Isles unseasonal rain and a constant stiff breeze, and stop the temperature climbing much above twenty degrees Celsius. It's thanks to this, combined with the northerly latitude, that the islands remain free of sun-worshippers and families on package holidays. The locals learn to live with the unsettled weather, and enjoy the peace and quiet.

On that Saturday night I lay in bed and listened as the wind began to howl round the corners of the house, increasing in volume and power as the latest weather front rolled over Barra. I heard the garden gate blow free from its latch and begin clanging open and shut until Tom went out and closed it. Ten minutes later it had blown free again. I drifted off to sleep. I dreamt of Father Baird and Mhairi Matheson arguing and Mhairi would change into Laura. The priest was holding her roughly and shouting at her and telling her she was causing trouble and demanding she leave the island. I saw myself in the dream, watching the priest and Laura, but I did nothing; I just watched as he slapped her across the face the way her mother had hit her. The storm gathered force outside and woke me in the early morning. It took me another hour to fall back to sleep.

When daylight broke the storm had subsided, the weather front already making its way over the Hebridean Sea towards the mainland. As I made my way downstairs for breakfast, I heard the van engine start and from the living-room window I watched it bump along the road with Tom behind the steering wheel. Cathy was in the kitchen preparing breakfast, already dressed for church.

'Where's Uncle Tom aff tae?'

She buttered a slice of warm toast. 'That wind last night blew an auld chimney doon at the Morrison's place. Came right through their roof.'

'Wis anywan hurt?'

'Mercifully, no, but Tom'll likely be out most a' the day makin' it safe an' patchin' the roof up until he kin git the right materials tae fix it properly.'

She carried on talking about poor Mary Morrison and all that she had to worry about without having this on top of everything else. I kept listening but my mind was thinking about the opportunity this presented. Tom would be away for the day. If Cathy was still going to church then I would be alone for the morning at least and free to do what I wanted. Perhaps I could get to Castlebay after all.

'How will ye git tae church?' I asked as casually as I could.

'Dinnae worry about that, Dot MacNeil is goin' tae pick me up oan her way round. She'll be pickin' me up early, though, as it's her turn tae help set up.' Cathy didn't see the smile that passed over my face. Dot MacNeil was an elderly woman who lived in the row of houses at Bruernish.

'That's good, ah'll stay an' look after Lennox.' I patted the old dog as he padded into the kitchen to join us.

'Ah may be a little later back than usual tae. Dot likes tae stay an' have a tea wi' the minister an' some a' the others. Ah've made up a sandwich fir ye fir lunch jist in case ye git hungry.'

Even better. 'Nae rush, ye take yer time. We'll be fine, won't we, boy?' I kneeled down and ruffled Lennox around his collar and ears.

Half an hour later Dot MacNeil's small blue Vauxhall crawled away with Cathy in the passenger seat. I waved them off at the door with Lennox on his lead. I even took a few paces along the road before the car disappeared over the rise just for good measure. Lennox looked at me in confusion when I yanked on his lead and took him back inside the house. He lay down in his basket with his head on the floor. I threw some dog food and water into his bowls to try and make it up to him. 'Later, boy. Ah've got somethin' important tae dae first. Ah've got tae make sure Laura's okay.'

The main obstacle now was getting the bike out of the outhouse, where it was still locked away. It was nine o'clock. I had plenty of time to get to Castlebay, if I could just get into the outhouse. The service started at ten. If I started walking now I could still get there just in time to see everyone leaving at the end of the Mass, but I would have no chance of getting back home before Cathy returned from her church. I went outside and tried the door of the outhouse just in case, but as expected it was locked. Tom kept one key to the door on his keyring along with the key to the van. There was a spare in the house, though; Cathy used it to get into the outhouse when Tom was out, and she kept it in a drawer in the kitchen.

Lennox watched me open the drawer. It was filled with odds and ends. In amongst the sewing pins, threads, needles, scissors, tape, string and buttons, I found a small metal tin that was filled with various keys for different doors and drawers and padlocks around the house. I took the full tin to the outhouse door. The breeze gusted around as I knelt down and tried one key at a time, trying to judge which one might match the lock. On the fourth attempt, a key slid smoothly into the slot and the notches clicked into place. The key turned and the metal bolt slid across and the heavy wooden door opened. The wind tried to blow it closed before I could wedge the doorstop into place. I ran back into the house and put the tin back in the drawer.

'Ye understand, boy, don't ye?' Lennox didn't stir as I hurried back outside. The outhouse was dark and only a small amount of light came through the door and a small window at the far end. A light cord hung just inside the door. When I pulled it a bare lightbulb in the middle of the room flickered into life. There was clutter all around: shelves stacked with paint cans, tools, plastic and metal pipes and building materials. The bike sat against the far wall. I clambered over old sheets, boxes and planks of wood to reach it and struggled to lift it back over the obstacle course. I made it back to the door and kicked the doorstop out. I didn't lock the door. I planned to be back before Cathy and Tom and I would put the bike back and lock the door and replace the key, before they discovered the bike had ever been used. A car coming from Bruernish passed by. I hid behind the low garden wall until the noise of the engine faded away. There was a fair chance that someone on the island would see me cycling along the road and word would get back to Cathy, but there was nothing I could do about that other than hope it didn't happen. I swung my leg over the saddle and pushed off down the driveway and onto the single-track road.

* * *

The steep incline of Heaval defeated me once again, but I completed the journey to Castlebay in record time. Halfway down the hill, I braked and swung into the road that led along a gentle slope to Our Lady Star of the Sea Church. Cars were parked along the side of the road and in the car park at the front of the building. The church sat on a rocky crag that jutted out from the hillside, with steep drops on three sides. The sound of an organ playing and muffled voices raised in song came from inside the thick grey walls. I reckoned it was about half-past ten and they would be halfway through the service. I was sure from previous conversations with Laura that the service lasted an hour and would finish at eleven. I got off my bike and pushed it along the final yards towards the church and the car park. I had no plan of what to do next. I just wanted to see Laura and make sure she was okay after Father Baird had spoken to her. The church was made up of a tower and a nave. The tall tower dominated the skyline of Castlebay. It was taller than any other building in the village. I had seen it when I approached Castlebay on the ferry, but this was the first time I had come close to it, and the grey walls were solid and foreboding.

The road ended at the side of the church. To the right was the manse where Father Baird lived. It joined onto the side of the nave, where the congregation was. The singing and organ had stopped and I couldn't hear anything from inside now. Father Baird would be delivering his sermon, or perhaps they were taking communion. I didn't know much about a Catholic service, but I knew at some point they all queued up and got a wafer and a drink. The tower was at the end of the nave, overlooking the small car park and facing out onto the bay. A black clock face with gold markings was halfway up it and the long golden hand pointed just past the half-hour mark. Above the clock was a long, thin window that was repeated on all sides of the tower. The nave and the manse had black pointed roofs of slate. I walked round the sides of the building, pushing my bike over the gravel. I had spent little time in church at home recently, beyond forced school visits at Easter and Christmas, but I was no stranger to the buildings. Every other street in Glasgow had a church. Not far from our house in Partick there was the squat, rectangular St Paul's Whiteinch Church and facing it right across the road was the Church of Scotland Gordon Park, which had closed the year before and was now disused. Both of those churches were bigger than the one I circled now, but this one stood out more in its isolated surroundings. None of those other churches dominated the community in the way Our Lady Star of the Sea seemed to.

I was unsure what to do. Why was I even here? If Father Baird insisted on talking to Laura and giving her into trouble, what could I do about it? The singing started up again inside and the organ played along. I returned to the front of the tower and looked up at the clock. Ten forty-five. Fifteen minutes until the congregation would be leaving. Next to the road that led up to the church was a field separated from the manse by a grey stone wall. I lifted my bike over and left it leaning against the wall inside the field, hidden from view of those leaving church. Two sheep stopped chewing the grass to look over at the new arrival in their field.

I looked for a spot where I would be hidden from those leaving the church. I didn't want Flora or Father Baird to see me. The main door was on the side of the tower at the front of the building. On the opposite side was a smaller door. This seemed like as good a place as any. If the door was open I could slip into the church unseen while the worshippers left along the road. There was a ramp that led up to the small door, with a small wall alongside it. I reached the door and crouched behind the wall and waited. If anyone decided to exit through this side door there was no way for me to escape them. I started to think of a plausible explanation. I couldn't think of one, so decided if that should happen I would have to run away as fast as I could. The wall provided a corner of shelter from the breeze that swirled around the outcrop of rock.

The organ reached a crescendo and died away. There was a final murmur and then shuffling footsteps from behind the door. The service had finished. I heard the main doors open on the opposite side of the building and voices became louder and clearer as parishioners spilled out into the courtyard and car park. I caught the odd, 'God bless you, Father,' and, 'Lovely sermon, Father.' How long to leave it before I tried opening the side door? The chatter from the car park died away. It was now or never. I reached up and turned the handle. When I pulled it the door opened without a whisper or a creak. I opened it just wide enough to allow my head in the gap and peered inside. There was a small square space and another door. I stepped inside and closed the outer door behind me. The door in front of me had a small glass rectangle through which I could see wooden pews, and turning my head I could make out a viewing platform at the back of the nave and a staircase that led up to it. I put my hand on the door and pulled it open and stepped into the main body of the church. Then I immediately drew back and ducked behind a pew as an elderly lady appeared on the opposite side of the nave. If she had looked she would have seen me staring right at her, but she was intent on tidying and replacing hymn books and brushing seats, getting the church ready for the afternoon mass. I didn't move for fear of being discovered. She made her way up the aisle, sorting each pew in turn on the right-hand side. When she got to the front, she turned and came back down, doing the same to the pews on the left side. Satisfied with her work, she picked up her coat from the back pew and carried it to the main door. As she opened it Father Baird appeared, having waved off the last of his congregation.

'Thank you, Mary Therese, what would I do without you?' He smiled at the old lady.

'All set for the afternoon, Father. I'll see you later. Will you be going out for your lunch today?'

'Not today, no. A rest and some contemplation. It's a rare thing that none of my flock have requested my presence for Sunday tea. I hope the Lord will forgive me for being thankful for a quiet Sabbath for once.'

'I'm sure He sees how hard you work, Father, He wouldn't begrudge you that. Bye for now.'

'Goodbye, Mary Therese.'

Father Baird watched her go and then sat on the front pew with his head leaning against the wooden back and his eyes staring up at the ceiling. I held my breath. We were alone in the church, just the two of us, and the silence was deafening. I couldn't move for fear of making the slightest sound that would echo around the white walls. All I could do was wait. There was no sign of Laura. Had I already missed her? If Father Baird was to sit there all afternoon I was stuck there too. If I was caught snooping around by Father Baird for the second time within a week, and inside the church this time, I would be in serious trouble. My legs began to cramp up and when I shifted them I felt pins and needles creeping up my lower limbs. I imagined Laura laughing at the ridiculous situation I had put myself in, if I ever got to tell her about it.

Then the door behind me, the side door I had sneaked through, began to open. I had no time to think; I had to move. I darted up the small staircase that led to the viewing platform and kept going until I reached the top. At the top was another door, exactly the same as the one on the floor below. I opened it and stepped out onto the platform that ran across the width of the rear church wall. On the opposite side was another door which must have been an entrance into the tower. The platform was empty save for a small table in each corner. The edge of it was lined by a bannister, with gaps between wooden pillars holding it in place. I guessed it was used for a choir to stand and sing from, or perhaps extra space if the pews below became full. From here I could see the whole of the nave laid out below me. There was the modest altar at the far end and two large crosses on the wall in between large stained-glass windows. Next to the table was a font and a small pulpit, and there were two large candlesticks on either side of the table. Down either side of the central pews ran arches made of white pillars with more pews beyond them in the wings of the church. Along the side walls were clear arched windows and shafts of sunlight spilled through them. It was light and airy rather than oppressive. The light bounced off the white walls and varnished wood panels. At the front of the seats on the right-hand side of the church was what looked like a large wardrobe with two curtains at either side instead of doors. I recognised this as the confessional box. Laura had told me about the embarrassment of sitting inside it with Father Baird in the other compartment, separated by a wooden lattice, and having to confess to her impure thoughts and misdemeanours.

'Why dinnae ye jist make stuff up, or dinnae tell him everythin'?' I had asked.

'Ah'm sure everywan does. When ah wis younger ah wis too scared tae no' tell him everythin'. Now ah jist tell him things tae keep him an' ma parents happy.'

I gently crouched down behind the table that was pressed up against the bannister at the front of the platform. It gave me some cover should anyone look up at the platform.

Father Baird sat upright and turned to look towards the back of the church where the side door had closed behind the newcomers. He was concentrating on whoever had just arrived below the platform and didn't look up in my direction. I must have managed to escape being seen by these new arrivals.

'Ah, Laura and Flora, do please come.' Father Baird gestured the new visitors towards him. I saw the top of Laura's head come into view; her dark hair was tied up and she was wearing a blouse and skirt. It was the first time I had seen her in anything other than trousers or shorts and a T-shirt. Flora followed her daughter and guided her towards the priest with a firm hand on Laura's arm.

'Thank you for taking the time to see us, Father,' said Flora.

Father Baird looked from mother to the daughter and broke into a smile. 'Not at all, Flora. One always has time for the Lord's children.' He put his hands on Laura's shoulders. She stood in front of him, her eyes cast down and shoulders slumped.

Father Baird bent forward and turned his face upwards to try and meet Laura's shadowed eyes. 'Your mother thought it best that we have a small talk, Laura.'

Laura didn't reply.

'Sit here with me.' The priest beckoned to the front pew. He sat next to her and Flora slipped into a pew two rows behind them.

19

'You committed a sin last week, Laura, and you haven't been to confession yet to seek absolution.'

I had to strain to hear the soft Irish accent that crept through the vaulted church. Laura didn't say anything or shout back or show any resistance but sat with her head bowed. She looked subdued for the first time since I had met her and the power that the priest held over her was clear. She could not question his wisdom or his authority.

'Do you know what that sin was?' he asked.

'Laura, answer the Father,' Flora hissed.

'Now, Flora, please.' Father Baird raised a placating hand towards Laura's mother. Laura's shoulders shook and I realised she was crying. Her small sobs drifted across the space between us. The bravado she showed towards the priest when she spoke to me disappeared when she was confronted by him inside the church. I wished she would stand up for herself, or that I was brave enough to stand up and say something in her defence.

Father Baird put an arm around her shaking shoulders. 'It is not polite to eavesdrop on adults having a private conversation. You know that, don't you?'

'We wernae eavesdropping,' Laura finally blurted out. 'We jist overheard by accident.'

'Laura! Don't talk to Father Baird like that.'

'All right, child, all right. Don't upset yourself. I can see that you know you have done something wrong. When you next take confession you will be absolved of your sin, and I'm sure you will not make the same mistake again.' He removed his arm and took Laura's hands in his. She didn't pull away from him. 'It's important that we talk about what you think you heard that night. Your mother and I are worried you may have overheard something you shouldn't have and have drawn the wrong conclusions.'

'Ah dinnae know wit ye mean.'

'Don't be shy, child,' he coaxed her, patting the back of her hands. 'I want you to understand that what you heard was nothing bad.'

Finally, the priest's lie sparked defiance from Laura. Her head tilted up and turned and she looked at him. 'Ah saw ye holdin' Mhairi Matheson an' tellin' her tae leave the island.'

'Now, Laura, I don't want you to lie to me. That would be another sin you would have to confess.' Father Baird tried to placate her and his hands reached for her shoulders again, but he paused. Perhaps he realised how it would look if he held Laura the same way he had held Mhairi Matheson. He withdrew his hands and folded them on his lap and looked at Laura.

'That's wit ah saw,' she said.

'That's what you think you saw.' His soothing tone added to the tension in the empty church. 'The adult world is a very complicated and complex one, Laura. You will learn that soon enough, but at the moment it may be difficult for you to understand. What you saw was a troubled young woman seeking guidance from God, through me. Mhairi Matheson has led a difficult and ungodly life. Some of it she has brought on herself and some of it she cannot be held responsible for. Poor Mhairi is not strong enough to rid herself of the ungodly side of herself, so I must help her. Do you see?'

Laura lowered her head again and returned to staring at the floor in front of her. I just caught her faint reply. 'Yes, Father.'

'When a child of God is lost in such a way it is my role – my duty, even – as a disciple of His son, Jesus Christ, to help that child. Now, you might not think it, but sometimes that might involve a priest acting forcefully. Do you understand? In order to help Mhairi, I must tell her things that she may not like to hear. That is what you saw at the hotel.'

Father Baird looked over towards Flora, who now had a tissue in her hands and was dabbing her cheeks. He gave her a reassuring smile. From my vantage point on the platform I thought it looked sinister. Then he turned back to Laura. 'Now, what's this I hear about you losing one of old Cameron's boats?'

'We didnae mean tae lose it, we jist used it tae git over tae Vatersay.'

'You were with Billy Matheson.'

'He followed us.'

'Us?'

'Me an' Ewan Fraser.'

'Ah, the boy from the mainland. Your mother has told me about your new friend. Well, fortunately, I believe he is only visiting us here and shall soon be returning to Glasgow, and the sooner we see the back of him, the better for all of us.'

I felt rising anger and bit my lip before I shouted out in my own defence.

'As for young Billy, you must stay away from him, Laura. He is a troubled child, much in the mould of his mother. I cannot allow him to worship among the congregation here, so devilish is his spirit. I confess I feel guilt about his fate and I have prayed to the Lord for guidance, but as yet there has been no answer. I tell you, Laura, only bad things will come from any friendship you form with that boy. Do you understand?'

'His father died, that wis hardly his fault. Shouldnae ye comfort those who have suffered?'

Father Baird cast an uneasy glance at Flora. 'His father, like that whole family, brought his fate upon himself, with his late-night drinking and revelry. Had he been closer to God, perhaps he would not have met such a tragic end.'

The priest stood up. 'I want to talk to your mother alone, Laura. Would you wait outside the church for her? It will only take a moment. I expect to see you for confession next week. Do you understand?'

Laura stood and looked at her mother. Her face was tear-stained and her eyes red.

'Go outside, Laura, and thank the Father for being so understanding with you.'

'Thank you, Father,' Laura muttered, and skirted round him while he made the sign of the cross over her. I wanted to get down the stairs and meet her, but I was trapped. Father Baird stood facing towards the back of the church and if I moved an inch he would see me. I had no choice but to wait until I was alone and could escape unnoticed. Father Baird already had a low opinion of me; I didn't want to make it any worse by being caught listening to his private conversations again. There was no denying I was intentionally eavesdropping this time. The main door opened and closed as Laura left the church. Flora left the pew she had been sitting on and walked to the front, where she sat next to the standing priest.

He waited until the door had completely closed before sitting down. Before he could say anything, Flora spoke first.

'She knows, Father. She isn't daft, she's figured it out.' She sounded anguished.

The priest raised a finger to his lips. 'Hush now, Flora. You must remain calm.'

'How can I, Father? I have prayed so hard for God to protect her.'

'And He will. He will not forsake you, Flora, but you must control yourself. Laura does not know the truth and she never has to learn it. We made a promise to protect her and we will continue to do so.'

'Everyone knows. It's all over the island. I see them looking and staring and I hear the rumours and gossip.' Flora broke down in tears.

'Enough!' The abrupt command made me jump. Father Baird placed a firm hand on Flora's arm and waited until she looked up into his face. 'Nobody knows anything. You must not let idle gossip upset you. Those that participate in such practices will face God's judgement in the end. You must get a grip of yourself or it will be you that reveals this horrid affair to them all.' His face relaxed and his tone softened again and he was calm. 'We decided at the beginning it was best that no one should know the truth and so we must now see it through. You have managed to forgive Hamish for his indiscretion. You will leave Mhairi Matheson to me. She cannot continue to live on the edge of society, shunned by all as she deserves to be. She will leave, I will make sure that she does, and with her the stain that she has brought to this island, and your family, will be gone. All you have to worry about is keeping your daughter away from Mhairi and that bastard child.'

I could feel my heart hammering in my chest and my eyes growing wide and my mouth hanging open. What were they talking about? A stain on the island? What had Billy done to be called such a thing by a priest?

Flora recovered herself. 'Lachlan knows,' she whispered up to the Father before repeating it and looking away again. 'Lachlan MacLeod knows.'

Father Baird sighed and took her hands and held them on her lap in the same way he had held Laura's.

'What happened to that poor boy was an accident, Flora. There is not a day goes by when I do not pray for him. I regret that moment all the time. I see it happening in front of me like it was yesterday. I have asked the Lord, why could He not have spared him? Why I could not have been quick enough to stop him falling? We must accept that it is the Lord's way. He will have a reason. I have spoken to Alec MacLeod and to the child himself, even though they have left our flock.'

'Is it true that the church helps to cover the cost of his care?'

'We are a charitable and broad church and we must help those in our community who need it, whether they seek God's grace or not.'

'Or is it a bribe to stop them talking?'

The priest stood in a fury. 'Flora Robertson, how dare you suggest such a thing under the Lord's roof!'

'Forgive me, Father, it's just I thought…' Her voice trailed off.

'That savage child, whom God has forsaken and the devil now owns, pushed Lachlan from that rock.'

'Because Lachlan told him the truth. That was all. Doesn't the Lord teach us that we should be truthful?'

'Of course He does and each day we must grapple with our conscience in order to serve Him as we see fit. Sometimes the truth will cause more damage than good. If we have learned anything from this whole mess, surely we have learned that.'

He made the sign of the cross and placed his hand on the top of Flora's head and the conversation ended. He closed his eyes and quietly intoned some words of prayer that I couldn't hear. My mind raced over what I had just heard. Could it be true? Could Billy have pushed Lachlan over the rocks? All because of some secret that Lachlan knew about that they wanted to keep from everyone else, something to do with Laura and her dad and Mhairi Matheson.

'I must go now; I need time to rest and reflect before the afternoon Mass.' The priest removed his hand from Flora's head and turned to leave. Flora reached out and caught the sleeve of his robe, forcing him to turn back.

'We have done the right thing, haven't we, Father?'

'Only God can be the judge of that. We have done what we saw fit.'

'She was of age, wasn't she? When it happened.'

'God does not judge things in such a way. That is a matter between your husband and the law of the land.'

'I keep thinking about the dates and when she gave birth...' Again her voice trailed off.

'I must go.' Father Baird withdrew his arm from Flora's grasp.

I had heard enough. Details fell into place. I was learning about the adult world of marriages and complicated relationships between people and about men who cheated on their wives and wives who cheated on their husbands. I had heard about plenty of affairs back home. There was Stevie Bell's dad, who worked in the Merchant Navy and boasted to us of the women he had been with when he had been away from home staying in some foreign port. There were a few kids at my school whose parents had separated, but it was still rare and frowned upon. Having an affair wasn't illegal, though, at least not in Britain. So what did Father Baird mean about the law of the land?

I keep thinking about the date and when she gave birth. Flora's words ran through my head. I thought about Billy and Mhairi. I thought about how old Billy was. He was a year younger than me, so that made him twelve. Mhairi was in her late twenties. I did the maths in my head. It was close. What if Mhairi wasn't in her late twenties after all; what if she was more in her mid-twenties, like twenty-seven or twenty-six? That had to be it. And it was Laura's dad, Hamish, whom she had been with. I remembered the night at the hotel watching the World Cup final. Everyone had stared at Mhairi Matheson and Billy when they came into the room. Except Hamish. He had stared out the window. It explained why Flora was so angry with us after she found out we had overheard Father Baird and Mhairi arguing. She was afraid her daughter would find out about her father. It explained that violent slap across her face. If I was right, if Hamish was Billy's real father, then that made Billy and Laura brother and sister. The enormity of it hit me. I remembered

Billy's dad, Angus Anderson, the man who Billy thought was his dad. His dead body found on the beach in Vatersay and no one could explain how he had got there. He had accidentally drowned, that's what people said. But what if it hadn't been an accident? What if Angus Anderson knew about Mhairi and Hamish Robertson? Had there been a fight? Had things got out of hand? I put my hand up to my mouth to stifle the gasp that escaped. My legs, aching from being crouched behind the table for so long, gave way and I toppled over. As I fell my leg kicked the table. It moved an inch across the platform floor, scraping the polished wood and banging against the bannister along the edge of the platform. Father Baird was halfway down the aisle. He stopped and looked up. Flora spun round in the front pew.

'Who's there?' called Father Baird urgently, standing listening for another sound. I stopped breathing. There was no way out without being discovered. I watched Flora. She scanned the length of the church and saw no one. She would surely look up to the platform next. I had to get out before she saw me. I jumped up and ran and threw the door open and flew down the staircase. I reached the bottom and raced through the inner door and then through the heavy outer door and I was outside. The bright sunlight blinded my eyes after being inside the dim church. I tripped and fell and banged my head against the low wall and pulled myself up and charged down the ramp, afraid to look back and see if anyone was chasing me. There was no way I would make it around the church without Father Baird cutting me off from the road. The cliff edge of the crag on which the church stood was in front of me. I ran to the edge and looked down. There was a ledge about six feet below the top. I hesitated until I heard the door of the church opening behind me. I had no choice. I jumped. One foot landed on the narrow ledge, but the other caught the edge and slipped over. My hands grasped the grey rocks, scrambling to find a grip. My fingers clutched at the rock and then caught in a tiny crack. I pulled my dangling foot up and was able to stand on the ledge with my back to the rock face. The wind gusted around and tried to pull me off the ledge and send me tumbling to the ground below. Beneath the ledge was another drop of about twenty feet and at the bottom lay jagged and uneven boulders. I pressed closer into the rock at my back. I heard voices above my head. It was Father Baird and Flora. Their footsteps on the gravel came close to the edge and stopped.

'He's gone,' the priest said.

'Did he hear everything?'

'I don't know.'

'Did you see who it was?'

'We can only pray that the Lord guides us.'

The footsteps receded as they walked away from the edge and I breathed out. Had I managed to get away with it? Looking down from the top they must have been unable to see past the cliff edge to the ledge. Had they not seen who it was? Flora must have suspected it was me, but perhaps she wasn't certain. If they knew it was me then Cathy and Tom would know before the end of the day and then I would know for sure.

I kept listening for any more footsteps. The wind chilled me through my T-shirt. I had to move. I had no way of knowing if someone was waiting for me outside the church, but I would have to take my chances; I couldn't stay on the ledge forever. Carefully, I turned round to face the grey rock face. The top of the crag face was too high above me to reach and there was nothing to use as a hand or foothold to climb up. To the side I saw a possible escape route. About three feet away was another ledge and beyond that a larger outcrop provided a path along the rock face that sloped upwards and met up with the foot of a grey slate wall that divided the church land from the farmer's field where the crag met the hillside. The most difficult part would be getting from my current ledge to the next one, but if I could do that I would be able to walk the rest of the way. I looked at the gap to the other ledge. If

I had a run-up, I knew I could get over the gap, but I would have to jump from a standing start. I looked down between the ledges and wished I hadn't. If I failed to make the other side the jagged boulders were waiting for me. I thought of Lachlan MacLeod and his wheelchair. I didn't want to end up like him. I looked for any hand grips that might help and the smooth rock face stared back at me. I was thinking about it too much now. There was a play park next to my house in Partick. It had an obstacle course made up of long wooden balance beams with gaps between them. I had always been too small to make the step from one beam to the next. I had learned to jump across the gap. This was just the same as doing that, I told myself. The only difference was that when I had missed my jump in the play park, I had landed on a soft carpet of muddy grass.

I stared at the ledge I was aiming for and raised my left foot. Then I pushed myself up with my right leg as hard as I could. For a moment I was airborne and over the gap between the ledges and my left foot came down on the very edge of the ledge. And then I was falling. I flung out my arms as the ledge disappeared above my head. My hands caught the rock edge and my body slammed into the rock face, knocking the wind from my lungs. I hung there with my legs dangling over the abyss. My fingers clung to the ledge. One hand was on firm rock while the other was clinging to a clump of long grass that grew out of a seam in the rock. I began to pull myself up and managed to get one elbow over the edge, then the other, and then I crawled forward on my belly until I was able to pull my legs up. The ledge was wide enough for me to lie on and gather my breath.

From there it was an easy walk along the wider ledge to reach the point where the outcrop of rock met the slope of the hillside and the wall that ran along it. The wall was made up of uneven pieces of grey rock and slate and provided plenty of handholds, and it was easy to pull myself up and over the top of it. The wall followed the churchyard round the back of the church and I walked in a crouch behind it to remain hidden. There was no one in the churchyard. Father Baird and Flora had gone. I clambered over a fence that separated one field from the next and stooped lower as the wall turned and ran alongside the manse. It was at the end of this wall that my bike should have been propped up where I had left it, but there was no sign of it. In my confusion I wondered if I was on the right side of the church. I was; the road ran along the side of the field as it should have done. Had someone taken it? If Father Baird or Flora had discovered it then they knew it was me that had been spying on them in the church. There was nothing I could do and there was no way I could make it back to Bruernish before Cathy now. It was a disaster, but I couldn't hang around outside the church all day. I jumped the fence out of the field and onto the road and ran away from the church. In the field, the two sheep stared after me.

20

I kept running until the road turned and continued down Heaval and levelled out as it reached the harbour. There was little consolation in the fact that I had evaded Father Baird and Flora. At least by not being caught I could deny I had been inside the church. Without the bike it was a two-hour walk back to Bruernish. Cathy might have already returned from her morning service and found the house empty and the outhouse unlocked and the bicycle missing. Perhaps I could get the bus back and still make it in time? But it was a Sunday and the service was less frequent and the bus would be full of islanders on their way back from attending church, so I would no doubt be seen by someone who knew Cathy and Tom. What story could I tell Cathy if I got back after her? What if I said I took Lennox for a walk and when I got back the door to the outhouse was open and the bike missing? That still wouldn't explain where I had been. Cathy would never believe that anyway. People left their front doors unlocked all the time on Barra because there were hardly any burglaries.

Sheltered by the buildings along the harbour, it was warm in the midday sunshine. I kicked loose stones over the edge of the slipway and heard them fall into the sea. They created small ripples on the calm surface. Sadness crept up on me as I looked out over the bay and the vast body of water beyond the castle. Over there somewhere was the mainland and my dad and mum and my home. Dad still hadn't been in touch for days. Mum was still in the hospital battling the cancer that was eating away at her. I was alone and would never see her again. I wanted to feel her holding me just now. Not the way it had been the last time she had hugged me, the day before she left for the hospital, when I had recoiled from the weak, clammy embrace and her thin, withered arms. I needed the warm embrace that I had grown up with that sheltered me from the world and all the silly, insignificant dramas that a child went through. The unconditional love that was always waiting when I got home from school. The feeling of safety and security when she comforted me after I had fallen down and hurt myself. There was nothing a kiss from my mum couldn't make better. I pictured the three of us sitting around the television on a Saturday evening, eating a takeaway off our knees, laughing and joking. I saw Dad and me play-fighting and Mum shouting at us to stop and all three of us in fits of giggles. I saw Mum coming into my room during the night after I had woken up from a bad dream and felt her cool lips kissing me gently on the forehead and her hand running through my hair and her soothing voice telling me everything would be okay. I needed to know everything was going to be okay. Who would be there to hold me if my mum wasn't? Who could I turn to? Now, when I needed it most, caught in the middle of something I didn't understand, there was no one. Whenever I returned home it would be Dad and me. The empty gap would be a constant reminder to us of what was missing. It would be everywhere around the house. We would sit having silent meals at the dining table and spend sullen evenings in front of the television. We would carry on doing the things we had done before without enthusiasm and without joy. We would go through the motions of living.

I sat on the wall of the harbour and dangled my feet over the side. Could I forgive Dad for sending me away? He thought he was protecting me by sending me to this place, without the chance to say goodbye. A sudden thought gripped me. What if Dad decided I should stay on Barra forever? What if he decided he couldn't cope having me back home? I could be stuck in this place with its dark secrets. That made me think about Laura and her dad, and Billy and Mhairi again and what I had heard. It seemed unreal now, outside the oppressive church, sitting in the pleasant sun with a view over the bay in front of me. It was absurd to think of anything sinister or bad happening in a place like this, but I had heard what Father Baird and Flora had said. I hadn't imagined it. What would I say to Laura if I saw her? I had to tell her something, and I had to see her again.

Around the other side of the bay a car engine broke the silence of the Sunday afternoon. A seagull circled overhead. I watched it swoop over my head and turned to follow it and ended up facing the buildings behind me. It was the back of the row of houses that led down to the ferry, the newsagent, the post office and the bank.

The bank. *Lachlan MacLeod knows.*

What could Lachlan, stuck in his wheelchair in the attic room above the bank, possibly know? There was only one way I would ever find out. I got to my feet and wiped the tears from my face and resolved to do what I knew I had to. I walked round to the front of the street until I drew level with the bank and looked up to the window of the attic room. There he was, sitting and watching. Lachlan looked straight at me and I looked back. I had to talk to him.

I knocked on the door. It was Sunday; the bank was closed. I knocked twice more. The handle turned and one side of the double wooden doors opened. Mary Margaret MacLeod looked at me. 'Yes?'

Had Alec MacLeod opened the door I would have turned and ran, but Mary Margaret was so small and frail-looking that I was able to control the urge to flee and stood my ground. She looked smaller than I remembered from the night at the hotel in Northbay. We were almost the same height.

'Ah wondered if ah could see Lachlan.'

She looked puzzled, 'Forgive me, he doesnae have many friends that call round tae see him. Dis he know yer comin'?'

'Aye,' I lied.

'Okay. Well, come oan in then.' If she was wondering how I had been able to meet Lachlan and make friends with him, she didn't say. Perhaps she remembered that I had been sitting near to him at the hotel watching the football match and assumed we had spoken to each other then. She opened the door wider and gestured for me to step through, then I waited while she bolted and locked the door and led the way through the empty bank. I realised now that I should have knocked at the door at the back of the building which led straight up to the living space above. We had to walk across the small foyer and through a hatch in the serving counter desk. At the rear of this area was another door which opened out onto a narrow hallway and stairs that led upwards. At the top of the stairs there was another door and beyond that a carpeted landing. A narrow stairway off the landing led up to the attic room.

'He's up there, jist knock before ye go in.' Mary Margaret pointed the way. On one side of the stairway was a bulky plastic bannister and attached to it at the top was a folding chair. There were red and green buttons on the end of the bannister. This was how Lachlan got up and down the stairs to his room.

'Dis he stay up there aw the time?' I peered up the dark stairway.

'Some days he doesnae want tae come doon an' join us. He likes tae be alone.' There was a blank look on her face. 'He used tae have lots a' friends before the accident.'

I could feel her sadness before a loud shout broke the moment of silence. 'Mary, are ye there?' It came from a room further along the landing and I remembered Alec MacLeod's hearing difficulties. Mary Margaret smiled at me meekly, trapped between caring for her disabled son and her deaf husband. No wonder she looked beaten down.

'Comin', dear,' she called back.

'Wit?'

'Coming,' she tried again, louder.

'Thank you.' I left her and started walking up the stairs.

'Ah'll leave ye tae it. Jist shout if ye boys want some juice. An' remember tae knock first. He doesnae like it if ye dinnae knock first.' She crossed the landing and entered the other room, where her husband must have been waiting.

It was dark at the top of the stairs when I reached the door. The light from the hallway below failed to reach up into the gloom. I knocked on the plain wooden door. There was no reply. I waited. I had come this far; I wasn't going to leave without speaking to him. Instead of knocking again, I turned the door handle and pushed. As the door opened I gave the wood another small tap with my knuckles and stuck my head through the gap.

Lachlan's head and shoulders showed above the grey back of the wheelchair. He sat facing out of the window. He hadn't moved since I had looked up at him from outside. There was no reaction to the door opening or my presence in the room.

'Hi.'

'The boy fae the mainland.' His head didn't turn to look at me. The voice was weak and hoarse, as it had been when he had spoken at the hotel.

'Aye.'

Lachlan's hands reached out and gripped the wheels on either side of his chair. With a swift pull on one side, he spun round a quarter turn and turned his head to the side and looked at me. A mop of dark hair fell over the side of his face. 'Come tae stare, have ye?'

'Naw, ah've come tae ask ye somethin'.' I stopped. That sounded selfish, even if it was true. I wanted to know about Billy and Mhairi and how it affected Flora and Laura. But faced with the crippled boy I realised how unfair it would be to just use him like that, as a source of information and nothing more. I couldn't just ask him straight out about what had happened. Laura had told me that no one visited Lachlan in his home and he rarely went outside. 'Ah thought ye might like tae talk,' I added, hoping I sounded convincing.

Lachlan peered at me from under his dark fringe. His eyes were sad, just like the atmosphere that filled the house and I had seen in his mum's expression. He pushed one wheel on his chair again, completing the turn to face into the room, and then wheeled across the wooden floor to his bed against the opposite wall. The roof of the attic room sloped upwards on both sides to an apex in the centre. He turned his chair round again and used his arms to lever himself from the chair onto the bed. I had sense enough not to try and help him. I knew he wouldn't like that. He sat across the bed and leaned his back against the wall with his legs hanging over the side.

'Wit makes ye think ah wud want tae talk tae you?'

'Ah kin go if ye like?'

He gave a vague shrug. Lachlan was a year older than me, but I felt like I was talking to an adult. I guessed the experiences he had been through had forced him to grow up. He had already faced a lifetime of struggle, wrapped up in the broken body of a teenager. I looked round the room. On the windowsill there were two model aeroplanes, a Spitfire and a Concorde.

'Ye like aeroplanes?'

The same vague shrug. 'Ah guess.'

'Ever bin in wan?'

'No' recently, naw.'

'Ye did before?' The words were out my mouth before I could catch them.

'Before ah ended up like this?' Lachlan gripped the thighs of his trousers and picked up his idle legs and let them flop back onto the bed. 'The last time ah wis oan a plane it wis the medical plane that flew me back tae the island fae the mainland when ah wis well enough tae come hame. Ah've bin oan a helicopter too, the wan that came tae take me tae the hospital.' His chest rasped as he rushed his speech.

'Ah didnae mean...' There was no point in trying to apologise so I gave up. 'Laura telt me about the accident. Ah'm sorry fir wit happened tae ye.'

'Ye've bin hangin' around wi' her.'

'Aye. She said ye used tae be friends.'

'Used tae be.' There was bitterness in his voice.

I walked over to the window and looked out at the view Lachlan had of the world. I could see the street below and a cove beyond and the rocks curving away along the coastline until all that lay beyond them was the vast expanse of the sea. I could see the top of the street and beyond that Heaval rising in the distance and Our Lady Star of the Sea Church sitting on her rocky outcrop. It wasn't a bad view, but it wasn't much if it was the only window you had onto the world.

'Why have you come here?'

'Ah saw ye lookin' at me out the window.'

'Ah wasnae lookin' at you in particular. Ah see lots a' people out the window goin' in and out a' the shop an' post office.'

'An' the bank.'

'So wit?'

'Laura an' ah've bin in a bit of trouble.'

'Wit dae ah care? Ah've never spoken tae ye before.'

'Ah'm tryin' tae help Laura. Ah went tae the church.' I pointed out the window towards the church up the hill. 'Father Baird gied her a talkin'-to.'

Lachlan glowered at me. Was it the mention of the priest? 'Wit did Laura dae?'

'We overheard Father Baird shoutin' at Mhairi Matheson an' tellin' her tae leave the island. Then we took a boat that belonged tae some guy called Cameron an' went tae Vatersay in it wi' Billy Matheson an' he showed us where his father's body wis found oan the beach an' the tide washed the boat away.'

The low laughter from Lachlan grew louder and I stopped talking and looked at him. His eyes were closed and his head arched backwards, his mouth twisted into a grin. He coughed and stopped laughing and opened his eyes. I had made a mistake coming and I had to fight my instinct to leave. Lachlan's face twisted again and the smile disappeared and a look of hate replaced it and I was glad that he couldn't cross the floor to reach me. I stepped back and bumped into the sill of the window and sat on it.

'Ye stupid wee boy. Yer as blind as the rest a' them oan this bloody island. Ah thought Laura might've been smart enough tae figure it out by now. Ah guess no.'

'Figure wit out?' The look of hatred disappeared and the broad shoulders slumped and Lachlan shook his head. He was close to telling me what he knew. 'Father Baird and Flora mentioned yer name. Ah know Father Baird wis there oan the day of yer accident.'

'Why d'ye keep callin' it an accident?' His voice was cold.

'Ye fell aff the rocks.'

'It wasnae an accident. He pushed me. Father Baird knows that; he saw it happen, but he willnae tell anywan.'

So it was true. Father Baird had said the same to Flora in the church. Billy had pushed Lachlan and made him fall on the rocks and into the sea. It was hard to believe; he would have been only eight or nine years old when it had happened. 'Why wouldnae he tell anywan?'

'Because if he telt everywan Billy pushed me aff the rocks, he wud have tae tell them why Billy did it.'

'Why did Billy push you?'

Instead of answering, Lachlan pushed himself off the bed and back into his chair. He wheeled himself back across the room and stopped next to me, looking past me and out into the street. Alasdair Campbell, the harbourmaster, was walking his dog.

'Ye git tae see a lot when ye have only wan windae out ontae the world.' He paused then faced me. 'Yer used tae the big city wi' lots goin' oan an' lots a' people an' cars, buses an' everywan rushin' around. We dinnae have that here. But when yer forced tae focus oan only wan small part a' the world, tiny details become important. It's like that oan Barra. No' much happens, so small events become big news. Little things out a' the ordinary are noticed.'

I had no idea where this was leading, but now that Lachlan had decided to talk, I let him carry on.

'Everywan knows everywan else's business. Even if they want tae keep somethin' secret, it's impossible because eventually somwan'll find out. There are two men in particular who find out everythin' because they work in the oldest institutions oan the island. Wan up there,' he pointed out the window to the church on the hillside, 'and wan doon there.' He pointed to the floor. He meant the bank.

'Ye mean Father Baird an' yer dad?'

'Ye've seen how this place works. Father Baird hears confessions, all the little secrets his congregation share wi' him. Ma da knows how much money everywan is worth. Who's rich an' who's no', who's in trouble an' who's payin' who. And, like Father Baird an' his confessions, he keeps it aw tae himself. Except, when the bank is also the hoose where the bank manager lives wi' his family, it's no' so easy tae keep everythin' private. Ah see an' hear enough tae know a little about some a' the customers, especially when Dad is moanin' tae ma maw about certain people. An' things kin be left lyin' around like bank books left oan the counter or letters tae customers.'

He paused, then continued his story. 'Most of the time it wis nothin' important an' ah didnae take much interest. Ah wis too young tae know or care much about money. Wan mornin' ah left fir school an' realised ah had forgotten ma lunch. Ah came back intae the bank tae git it. The back door to our hoose wis locked so ah came through the main door an' Dad let me in through the counter. As ah hurried past a cheque blew aff the counter. Ah bent down tae pick it up an' read the name. It wis made out tae Mhairi Matheson an' it wis signed by Hamish Robertson. Ah thought nothin' of it an' Dad snatched it out ma hand and ah went oan ma way. But no' long after that ma da left a ledger open oan the dining table. Ah dinnae know why ah looked at it, probably because ah knew ah shouldnae. Ah saw columns a' numbers an' dates an' amounts a' money an' running totals. Oan the first a' every month, the same amount a' money wis deposited intae Mhairi Matheson's account by cheque. An' aw the cheques came fae Hamish Robertson. At the top a' the page there wis the name a' the account that Mhairi Matheson put aw this money intae. It wis called Child Support.' Lachlan stopped and looked out the window at the view. A last whisper of his thin voice said, 'Ah wish ah had never seen it. After that ah made friends wi' Billy. Ah guess ah felt sorry fir him, thinking he didnae have a da, that his da wis dead, when his real da wis livin' oan the island. Ah never telt him what ah knew, until that day a' the church outing.'

So it was just as the priest had said in the church. Hamish Robertson was Billy's real father. That was the secret that Flora and Father Baird were determined not to let people know. But they did. Alec MacLeod knew because he saw the cheques each month, and Lachlan knew.

The wind gusted suddenly, echoing round the quiet room. The calmness of the day was over. The more I thought about it, the more pieces fell into place. Was Billy shunned by everyone because they suspected him of pushing Lachlan? I pictured Laura and Billy together, that same look of determination when they set their minds on something. Was I just imagining the similarity in their faces?

'How have they kept it secret? Disnae wan else know?'

'Everywan knows, or knows somethin', but nae wan says anythin', especially no' tae Laura an' Billy. Angus came along an' took care a' Mhairi an' telt everywan that he wis the father, even though he had bin away oan the fishing boat when she got pregnant.'

Everybody knows? I thought about what I'd heard in the church. Flora Robertson had pleaded to the Father to keep their secret safe. If everyone knew then who were they keeping it safe from? Did Tom and Cathy know the truth too? Was that why they warned me to stay away from Billy? Or was it just a rumour that no one wanted to acknowledge? If everyone knew about the affair, was that why Mhairi was treated the way she was? That made some sense. But did they know who Billy's real father was? Was everyone just pretending to look the other way? Ignoring the age that Mhairi must have been when Hamish had got her pregnant? And what did Laura know? She would have been only a baby at the time of the affair. Flora told Father Baird that she thought Laura knew. She told him she thought everyone on the island knew their secret.

'That day a' the outing oan the rocks. Ye telt Billy wit ye had found out about Hamish bein' his real dad?'

'He didnae believe me, so ah telt him again, louder this time, an' he shoved me. Father Baird wis standin' nearby an' heard what ah said an' came runnin' over. He knew the truth an' he didnae want Billy tae find out. He wis too late tae stop me fallin'.'

'Billy pushed ye?'

'Ah dinnae think he meant fir me tae end up like this,' he motioned to the wheelchair, 'but he wis angry. Deep down ah wonder if he already knew or had worked it out himself. He wisnae that big or strong, but ah wisnae expectin' it and ah stumbled oan the rocks an' lost ma footin' an' fell backwards.'

'Why'd'ye tell him?'

'Ah thought ah wis doin' the right thing. Ah thought he should know who his real da wis. Ah liked him.'

'And Father Baird telt everywan it wis an accident.'

'It wis, in a way, an' he wanted tae protect his precious wee community fae learning the truth about everythin'. Fae admittin' wit wan a' his flock could dae tae a young girl.' Lachlan's eyes were drawn to the window again. 'Yer girlfriend is lookin' fir ye.' Laura was walking down the street, pushing my rusted old bicycle alongside her.

'So Billy knows Laura is his sister?'

'Half-sister.' Lachlan shrugged. 'Ah dinnae know if he ever believed me, or wit his maw might've telt him.'

'Dis Laura know about Billy?'

'How should ah know? Mibbe she suspects somethin', or mibbe they've telt her now that she's auld enough. Or mibbe she doesnae have a clue. Ah never telt her. Ah never really had the chance after ah came back like this. She never came tae see me.'

'Ah need tae go an' talk tae her.'

'Are ye goin' tae tell her?'

I hadn't thought about what I would do. I backed out of the room. There was no goodbye between us. We looked at each other and I reached the door. I wanted to say I was sorry about what had happened to him, but something stopped me from saying anything. He was bitter and alone and who could blame him for being the way he was? Before I left, I saw him framed in the window, his blank stare watching me go. He was stuck there in his own small world, looking out that same window, seeing the life of the island pass by, holding on to all the dark little secrets of the community, trapped for the rest of his life.

21

The television was still blaring from the living room, turned up for the benefit of Alec MacLeod. The noise covered the sound of my footsteps and I escaped without meeting Mary Margaret again. Instead of retracing my steps through the bank, I slipped out the back door of the house which brought me into a small garden at the rear of the bank. I circled round to get back to the street to look for Laura, but there was no sign of her. The street was empty. I didn't look up at the attic window; I didn't want to see him staring down at me.

It was after lunchtime and there was little chance I would make it back home before Cathy returned from her church, even if I did get my bike back from Laura. I would have to explain where I had been. I walked towards the harbour and saw her sitting on the wall, dangling her feet over the water, where I had sat before going to see Lachlan. She was still wearing the blouse and skirt she had worn to church. The bike was lying on the ground next to her. She turned as she heard my footsteps approaching over the loose stones.

'Ah knew ye couldnae have gone far wi'out yer bike.' I stared at her smiling face, the red marks around her eyes that I had seen in the church had cleared away. What should I tell her? What did she already know? I wished I could go back to the friendship we had shared before today. She pointed at the bike. 'Ah found it outside the church. Where wer ye?'

'Ah wanted tae make sure ye wer okay.'

'It wis fine. Father Baird rambled oan about sins an' manners an' his usual nonsense. Ma ma wanted tae speak tae him oan her own. She's bin an emotional wreck since she found out about us goin' over tae Vatersay.'

'Ah wis hidin' outside,' I lied. It meant I didn't have to tell her what I had heard her mum and Father Baird talking about. 'Ah didnae see ye leave, an' then ma bike wis gone.'

'Sorry. Ah wasnie sure if ah should have left it, but ah thought somewan else might see it an' then ye might've got intae mare trouble, so ah cycled it away an' then waited fir ye doon by the school.'

Could she sense the awkward atmosphere, or did it just exist in my mind? Could she sense that something had changed between us? If she did, she didn't mention it.

'Ah best be getting back. Ma aunt is probably already back fae church an' wonderin' where ah am. Ah wasnie supposed tae leave the hoose.'

'Ah should head hame tae,' Laura replied, 'although ah bet they havenae even noticed ah'm no' there. They've bin arguin' a lot recently. A lot a' the time they jist sit in separate rooms an' dinnae talk tae each other.' She stood up and picked up my bike. 'Think ye kin gie me a backie?'

'No' up the hill. Ah cannae even manage that oan ma own.' The change of subject was a relief.

She smiled at my joke. 'We kin walk up it an' ye kin gie me a ride doon the other side.'

We headed round the harbour and along the main road, heading away from the bay and up the slope of Heaval. The church stood on its perch, grey and dull. The reassuring click-click of the wheels turning on my bike were the only sound that broke the quiet until we had left it behind us.

'Did Father Baird tell ye any mare about wit he wis sayin' tae Mhairi Matheson?' I already knew the answer, but I was trying to gauge how much Laura really knew.

'Nothin' at aw. Ah jist got the usual lecture about bein' a child an' no' understandin' adult things.'

'Wit's it really about? Have yer ma or da said anythin'?' I was prying now. Would she share anything more with me? Did she know anything more?

'No' really.' She shrugged. The slope beneath our feet got steeper. 'Ah jist know people dinnae like Mhairi an' Billy an' they arenae welcome in the church. Ah think it's somethin' tae dae wi' her gettin' pregnant so young an' no' bein' married. It's still pretty unusual around here. Ah expect it happens a lot in the city.'

I believed her. She didn't know about her dad. She didn't know that Billy was her half-brother. After a pause, I asked her the question that had been troubling me since I had found out about Hamish's affair. 'How old's Mhairi Matheson?'

'She's no' thirty yet.'

'How old wis she when she had Billy?'

'She could only have been sixteen or seventeen, ah think.'

I watched her out of the corner of my eye as we walked along side by side with the bike between us. There was no hint of suspicion about my questions. She definitely didn't know. Should I be the one to tell her? I was only a visitor, and an outsider from the mainland, and I'd only known her for a few weeks. Was it my place to tell her something as big as this? Would she even believe me? One day in the future, when she was older, her parents might sit her down and tell her the truth about her dad and her half-brother. Or would they? Flora wanted Mhairi and Billy gone, out of sight and out of mind. I felt sorry for Flora in some ways. I could see why she would want them to leave. Every time she saw Mhairi she would be reminded of Hamish's affair. Every time she saw Billy she would feel that sickening knot in her stomach.

We reached the top of the hill and below us the road snaked downwards until it reached sea level and headed off along the coast. Laura had been humming a song alongside me, without a care in the world.

'Come oan then. Backie.' She put her leg over the back wheel of the bike. I stood forward of the saddle so she could sit on it. At least cycling this way meant there was no pressure to carry on making conversation.

'Ye set?' I said over my shoulder. Laura wriggled around to get herself steady, her feet balanced on either side of the back wheel and her arms around my waist, clasping her hands together in front of my stomach. Her chest pressed against my back and her chin rested on my shoulder. Her warm breath brushed the side of my face.

'Let's go.'

I released the brake and stood on the peddles. The wheels began to roll slowly at first with the added weight of the extra passenger. We picked up pace as the slope descended and the wind began to blow into our faces. Laura's grip tightened around me and she pressed harder against my back. She let out a cry of joy as we belted down the road. I gripped the handlebars, terrified that I would lose control and injure her, and braked now and then while following the curves of the road. The speed and the closeness of Laura were intoxicating. In that moment we were light and free again.

Our momentum meant I could freewheel up the following hill, then pedal along the flat coastal road all the way to her house in Brevig. I stopped at the end of her driveway and the bike almost toppled over thanks to the imbalance of the extra passenger. She let go of me and hopped off. Through the window of the house I saw Flora in the kitchen, moving from one side of the room to the other, preparing their Sunday dinner. In the living room next to it there was a flickering light from the television where Hamish must have been sitting. Hamish Robertson, who had been kind and funny and had welcomed me into his home, had become some sort of monster in my mind. I couldn't help but dislike what he had done to Mhairi Matheson. Laura was not much younger than Mhairi had been when her father had had an affair with her.

'Ah'll see ye tomorrow, mibbe?'

'Mibbe,' I answered. I felt an impulse and let go of the handlebars of the bike so it rested on my side, and I put my arms around Laura and pulled her towards me in an awkward embrace. She stood with her arms by her sides, unsure how to react. I couldn't tell her the truth; I didn't know how to deal with what I knew. I let go of her and leaned back. We were still close and her arms came up and I felt her hands on my back as she looked at me with a puzzled expression. I was drawn to her lips and her cheeks that had reddened. I leaned forward and upwards and my lips brushed against hers. She let our mouths meet and we lingered for a moment together before she pulled away and stepped back and her arms fell away. As I stepped backwards, the bike fell over and clattered to the ground.

'Sorry.'

'Dinnae be. Ah'll come an' see ye tomorrow.'

'Okay.'

I wanted to tell her how I felt. I wanted to tell her what I knew. I had never kissed a girl on the lips before. Maybe it was the summer we had shared together, or maybe it was because I felt sorry for her and the secret that was being kept from her. There was something about her I couldn't describe. Was this what being in love felt like? When I was with her everything felt right. I could forget about my mum lying in the hospital and the cancer. Lachlan MacLeod had ruined it. So had Father Baird and Flora. I should never have gone to the church. Everything would have been okay. We could have gone on being friends for the rest of the summer and neither of us would have known anything and we could have forgotten about Mhairi and Billy and Father Baird.

She turned to go and took two steps before I called out her name. She stopped and looked back. It was now or never, but how could I tell her something so huge?

'Wit?'

'Ah have tae tell ye somethin.'

'Tell me wit?'

'It's about yer dad.'

'Wit about ma dad?' She stepped back towards me.

I searched for the right way to say it and opened my mouth. 'Yer dad had—'

Flora Robertson interrupted me. She was at the doorway of the house and started marching towards us.

'Laura, get yourself in here for dinner. Where on earth have you been?'

'Ah better go, we kin talk tomorrow,' said Laura, and left me standing there. Flora stared straight at me. She let Laura walk past her and then she turned and closed the door behind them without a wave or a goodbye. I couldn't tell whether she knew it had been me in the church or if she was still angry with me for what had happened the previous weekend.

I picked up the bike and threw my foot over the frame. I looked back at the house. There was no sign of Laura, but in the window of the living room Hamish stood looking at me. He waved and gave me a broad smile. He was saying he understood. He was apologising for the way Flora was treating me. He was saying if it was up to him he would have forgiven me and he would have let me see Laura as much as I wanted and I would be welcome back in his house. But I didn't trust that smile now. I didn't wave or smile back. I pushed down on the pedals and set off along the road.

* * *

Half an hour later, I rode down the hill that sloped back to Tom and Cathy's house. Tom's van was parked at the front of the house. My heart sank. Cathy would have been home long before me, but I had hoped to avoid Tom's anger. I thought he would have been away all day. I slowed down and let the bike crawl over the final few metres.

I put the bike back into the outhouse in the exact spot where it had been when I had taken it that morning. Lennox was still sitting in his basket and still looked depressed with his head on the floor and his eyes downcast. I patted his head and apologised for having left him alone in the house all day. Taking my shoes off in the hallway, I thought about sneaking up the stairs to my room rather than going into the living room. Anything to put off the row that was to come, but before I could, Cathy's voice called out from behind the door.

'Kin ye come in here, Ewan?'

I braced myself for what was to come. Cathy and Tom sat next to each other on the sofa. From the look on their faces, I could tell something had happened, but they didn't look angry with me. They didn't look like they were going to give me a talking-to. Instead, they looked at me with pity. I stood in front of them. Cathy's eyes were red around the edges. Tom looked at the floor and didn't make eye contact with me. I knew before either of them said anything.

'Yer father called, Ewan. It's about yer mum.'

Cathy carried on talking but it was only background noise beneath the screaming inside my head.

22

The water was choppy. Small crests of white foam rolled into the harbour walls and sent spray across the pavement around it. I watched the sea underneath me as I walked across the gangplank that took me off Barra and onto the ferry. Cathy and Tom stood outside the small terminal office. Tom's hands were buried in his pockets and Cathy's arms were wrapped round her chest to shield her from the morning breeze. Fine rain fell in a hazy drizzle, making everything damp and grey. I made my way up the stairs to the second deck of the ferry and then walked to the back, where there was a viewing platform. A few other passengers milled around, popping out to catch a final glimpse of Castlebay and then retreating inside to keep warm. It was not busy. Those who went to the mainland for work left on Sunday to be at work for Monday morning. The green-painted metal deck was chipped and rusty and the white barriers were tired and brown-stained. The wind buffeted against me, blowing my hair across my eyes, and I realised how much my hair had grown while I had been on the island. Dad would need to take me for a haircut before the funeral. The last of the cars clanked over the ramp underneath me and into the hold, and the crew busied themselves unfastening the thick, heavy ropes that secured the ferry to its berth while the ramp folded up and closed. It left the concrete floor of the harbour behind and the ferry detached itself from the island and I left Barra behind.

The ferry manoeuvred out of the harbour and Cathy and Tom waved one last time from the shore and then turned away. Tom put his arm round Cathy and they walked back towards their van. It felt like an age since we had got off the boat and Tom had driven me along that unfamiliar road. It had been less than three months ago, a handful of weeks, but I felt like a different person. I had learned about another place and other people separate from the life I had known, the life I was returning to now, and everything that had happened had changed who I was. A whole community of people that I would never see again but who had changed me from the boy I was when I had arrived. I didn't know if I would miss them, but I would never forget them.

There was Lachlan MacLeod, alone in his attic room, wheeling backwards and forwards to his lookout and dreaming of being able to fly away from the only world he would ever know. Had he been at his window this morning? Had he seen Tom and Cathy drive past on the way to the ferry port and guessed what had happened to me? Would anyone ever tell him that the boy from the mainland had gone and I had taken his secret away with me without telling Laura?

There was Mhairi and Billy. Would they carry on living among people that wished them gone? Would Mhairi give in and take her son away from all the rumour and whispers? I had thought a lot about Laura and forgotten about Billy. Should I have found Billy and told him who his real father was? Did Billy know about his mother and Hamish? He still called Angus his dad whenever he had spoken about him. Did he know that Angus was only the man who had stepped in to try and fill that gap in his life? Mhairi didn't seem like the sort of woman who would lie to her son. That was what made her different from the others on the island.

The ferry passed the castle in the bay and the village fell away behind us and the buildings became small grey blocks among the green hillside. One stood out distinctly overlooking the rest, the church halfway up the hill.

The previous night I had lain on my bed with the photograph of my mum on my pillow and thought about what life would be like when I got back to Glasgow. It would be just Dad and me. That was the biggest change that had happened to me. When I had arrived on Barra I had had a mum. Now I was leaving and for the rest of my life I would be without her. It was too painful to think about. Instead, I thought of Laura. Would I ever see her again? Probably not. One day she would find out the truth about her father and her half-brother. How would she react? She would hate her mum and dad for a while. Not because of the affair, or for their decision not to tell her about it, but because of the way they had treated Mhairi and Billy for years afterwards. Laura would love Billy as a brother. They would grow up together on the island and carry on being friends and cycle around together having adventures. Part of me wished I could be there with them. And I hoped Laura would forgive her mum. I didn't want her to feel what it was like to lose her mother. I didn't want her to feel like I did.

There had been no way to tell her I was leaving. I had woken up and Cathy helped me pack and we had a last breakfast together before driving straight to catch the early ferry. I pictured Laura pedalling along the road towards Bruernish, coming to find me and take me to another beach with her kite, or to the airport to see the plane coming in.

A flash of reflected light from the harbour caught my eye as the sun glinted off something metal. I made out her red bike coming to a halt at the end of the harbour wall, and her red jumper. The wind whipped her long, dark hair around her face. I waved, hoping she could see me. She didn't respond. It looked like she was looking straight at me. Was she wondering why I had left without saying goodbye? She would know the reason I had left the island suddenly. She stood there until I could no longer make out the harbour and the vast blue sea swallowed the island and I turned my back on it, and on her, and went inside to find the canteen and get a sandwich with money Tom had given me.

* * *

Five hours later the ferry docked in Oban. Dad was standing at the bottom of the walkway as I disembarked. He looked thin and tired and wore a black suit that hung loosely from his frame. His arm curled round my shoulders and stayed there and guided me to the station and we caught the early afternoon train back to Glasgow. He didn't say much and I knew if I tried to talk to him I would burst into tears. As the train pulled out of the station and into the countryside beyond Oban, I looked out the window across the sea to where that other world still existed. The Isle of Barra and Tom and Cathy and Mhairi Matheson and Flora and Hamish Robertson, and Lachlan MacLeod and Billy and Laura all faded away.

* * *

It rained on the day of the funeral. Another damp and grey day that was nothing unusual for the west coast of Scotland. They buried Mum in the Western Necropolis after a ceremony in the crematorium. There was no church service because we didn't go to the church. A few people were there, some of her friends and some of Dad's friends. Grandma and Grandpa came, and Tom and Cathy. They flew over a couple of days after I got home. Mum had no brothers or sisters, just like me. I sat on the front bench. A celebrant, who was like a minister for people that weren't religious, gave a short reading. I thought celebrant was a strange name for him; there was nothing to celebrate. Dad and Tom helped carry the coffin and lower it into the ground, and I threw some dirt on top of it and heard the hollow thud as it hit the wood. We got into the black car that drove us back to our flat in Partick and Dad told me it was better now that it was over, that she had been in a lot of pain at the end and now her suffering was over. I felt selfish for wanting her back and wanting her to be there to take away my own pain.

Tom and Cathy stayed for two nights to help Dad. The school holidays had another couple of weeks to go and as he wasn't working, he would be able to spend the time with me. When I went back to school and he found work again, he said the woman who lived above us had agreed to keep an eye on me after school each day to start with. After that Dad said he would figure something else out. We would just have to make do as best we could.

Tom and Cathy took the plane back to Barra. We took the bus with them out to the airport and said goodbye to them in the departure terminal. They disappeared through the doors and it was just Dad and me, and we took the bus back into Glasgow and walked home. On the way he asked me to tell him about Barra and what I had been doing all summer.

'Did ye make any friends?' he asked. I told him about Laura and Lennox and watching the football on television with Tom. I didn't mention Billy or Mhairi. It felt like I should keep them to myself. I carried their secrets around with me because no one on the mainland would understand life on the island. We got a chippy tea for dinner that night and sat in our small living room and watched television, and I curled up next to him on the sofa and felt his arm around me. That was how it was from then on. The two of us.

The photograph arrived two weeks later with 'Thank you' written on the back. I was back at school by then. There was my stupid smile as I looked at the camera. Laura wasn't smiling; she seemed to be looking intently at Mhairi Matheson taking the picture, and Billy was at the side of her, looking away as he spotted the car pulling into the car park.

'So that's Laura? Fine-lookin' girl. Ye should write tae her, keep in touch.'

I wondered why Laura had sent the photograph to me. I guessed Mhairi must have given it to her when she had got the film developed. It was the only picture we had of the two of us. Perhaps Laura had got a copy and wanted me to remember her and the summer we had spent together. I thought back to that day at the beach and her thin body and her laughter as we splashed each other in the sea.

Dad asked me who the boy was next to Laura and me.

'Billy.'

'Wis he a friend too?'

'No' really,' I answered. 'He wis jist a boy fae Barra.'

PART THREE

LAURA ROBERTSON

23

'Aye?'

The girl looked at me with suspicion. This wasn't London, or Glasgow, or any other city where strangers knocking on your door was a common occurrence. It probably didn't help that I was staring open-mouthed at the teenage girl in front of me. She was identical to the image of Laura I had been carrying around in my head for forty years. She had the same long black hair, deep brown eyes and pale skin. The only thing missing was the small birthmark on her cheek.

I recovered enough to speak. 'I'm looking for Laura Robertson.'

'Robertson? Ye mean ma maw? She's no' bin a Robertson fir a long time.'

Her accent was thick; I struggled to pick up her words. I could feel my heart drumming inside my chest. I had found her. She lived here. Could it really be that simple after all this time?

'Is your mum in?'

'Maw!' the girl shouted back into the house. 'There's a man here tae see ye!'

I tried to give her a polite smile as she turned back to me. She kept her hand on the door, barring my entry until she was sure I was someone her mum would want to see. There was an awkward moment as we stood looking at one another, waiting for her mum to appear. I studied the details of her face that reminded me of Laura. The photograph was in my jacket pocket and if I had pulled it out and held it next to her I would see the same thin nose and jawline. And those eyes. She was looking at me with the same expression Laura had in the photograph. Strands of her hair flicked around her face in the breeze and I was transported back to the harbour in Castlebay and that last glimpse of Laura as she stood watching the ferry disappear. But she was taller, almost the same height as me despite her youth, and her shoulders were broader, her figure fuller.

'Who is it?' Footsteps approached from inside.

'Some guy. I dunno.'

'Did ye ask his name?'

The girl let go of the door and retreated into the house, and an older woman took her place. I knew instantly it was her. She wasn't much taller than she had been then, which meant I looked down on her now. Her hair was shorter, coming down to her shoulders, and the dark black was now streaked with silver. It reminded me of Flora all those years ago. Her skin was still pale but no longer smooth. Lifelines crept around the corners of her eyes and mouth and across her forehead, and her cheeks were a ruddy red, the effect of a lifetime of exposure to the Barra climate. She was still slim and had not lost her boyish quality.

'Hello?'

I hoped to see a flicker of recognition in her eyes as she looked at me, but her look remained neutral. 'Laura?'

Now her eyes widened and she concentrated, her head tilting to one side as she tried to grasp a memory long buried in the back of her mind. 'Yes?'

She didn't recognise me. She hadn't spent months, or years, or her lifetime, wondering what had become of me. She hadn't been searching the internet or contemplating a mid-life expedition to try to find me. She hadn't thought about me since the summer of 1982.

'Sorry to bother you,' I stammered, unsure of how to continue. 'My name is Ewan Fraser and we knew each other once. A long time ago.' Slowly, realisation crept over her features. 'I'm not sure if you remember me.'

'Ewan Fraser,' she repeated. 'Ah remember a wee boy wi' a rusty auld bike.' She broke into a smile.

'The very same.' I returned her smile with relief. There was no embrace or cry, nothing that resembled the different ways I had imagined this moment would play out. There was just a pause as she raced through the memories of that summer. She was waiting for me to say something more, but nothing seemed like the right thing to say.

She broke the silence with the obvious question: 'Wit are ye doin' here?'

I had no sensible answer to that question. I decided to tell her the truth. 'I was on the underground in London, heading into work on Thursday and just as the train left Baker Street Station, out of the window I saw the face of a young boy. Just a glimpse, but it was Billy Matheson staring at me.' I stopped. She was staring at me in bewilderment, like I was a lunatic. 'I'm not explaining myself very well.'

'Naw, yer no'. Wait here.'

The door swung half-closed and Laura disappeared inside the house. I kicked myself. What an idiot! I heard her calling to her daughter, telling her that she was popping out, and then the door opened again and she was wearing an overcoat and was slipping on walking boots. I stepped back from the doorway as she straightened up and stepped outside.

'Come oan.' She set off down the path and I followed.

She waited while I closed the gate and then we walked along

the single-lane road. We fell into step together, both hunched up against the breeze with our hands inside our coat pockets.

'Ah kin tell ye it wasnae Billy ye saw in London, if that's wit ye came aw this way tae find out.'

'No, I knew it couldn't really be him.' I let out a nervous laugh. 'But seeing that face reminded me of that summer when I had been here and everything that happened and I wondered what had become of you, and everyone else.' I hoped it sounded like a casual enquiry.

'An' ye came aw the way up here fae London jist tae find out?'

'I know it seems a bit strange.'

'Ye could've jist phoned.'

'I suppose, although I didn't know if you still lived here or had moved away.'

I didn't say that I couldn't have called her over the telephone, that I needed to see her and confront the past and find out once and for all what had happened between her parents and Billy and Mhairi.

She seemed to accept my reason at face value. 'True. Yer uncle moved away, didn't he?'

'After my Aunt Cathy passed away, yes, he moved back to Glasgow. He passed too, a couple of years ago.' In the intervening years I had seen little of Cathy and Tom. They stayed on Barra and I had never returned. They visited the mainland on a handful of occasions when I was a teenager, but I had never asked them about Laura or Mhairi and Billy. There was no point in bringing up a sore subject with them and I had moved on to all the teenage concerns that adolescence brings. When they did come and stay with Dad and me, Cathy busied herself in the kitchen making teas and coffees and sandwiches and Tom sat on the sofa and spent evenings watching the television. Dad and he were never happier than when watching a football match together. Cathy died soon after I left Glasgow for London. Cancer, of course, same as Mum. Tom moved back to Glasgow and I saw him whenever I came home to see Dad. They had each other and there was me; that was all that was left of our family. Only the men; all the women had gone. Tom had kept going, living on his own and keeping himself busy with an odd job here or there. He even did a few jobs for the company he had once owned, driving a van with his name on the side of it again. My dad had found him in his one-bedroom flat. A heart attack during his sleep. He had lain in the bed undiscovered for three days before Dad had gone to find him.

'Sorry tae hear that. Ah liked them.'

I changed the subject. 'You have a daughter?'

'Two, an' two boys. That wis Eilidh, the youngest. She'll be sixteen next month. The rest have aw moved away. Nae doubt she'll follow them soon enough.'

I had never pictured her as the matriarch of a large family. She had been a loner like me when we spent that summer together, without particularly close friends and happy with her own company. Why had I expected to find her the same? Was it because I had been alone for my whole life?

'She looks a lot like you.'

'Thank you.'

'You're married?'

'Aye. Ye remember Callum Colquhoun? Ah dinnae think ah wis really friends wi' him when ye were here.'

I remembered the boy in the school playground, the one Laura had shouldered to the ground the first time I had seen her.

'He works at the fishery as wan a' the lorry drivers. He's away a lot. He's over oan the mainland at the minute. It didnae seem tae matter when the hoose wis full wi' the kids, but now it feels an empty place. Thirty years married this year.'

We reached the paved road at the end of the gravel path and carried on walking towards the coastline.

'D'ye have a family? Children?' Laura asked.

'No, never married.'

'Never foun' the right woman?'

'Something like that. A couple of close things, but I managed to keep my freedom.'

She laughed politely. 'Aw they women in that big city tae choose fae?' She could have meant Glasgow or London. 'It's different if ye live in a place like this. Ye have a limited stock tae choose fae. Ah got wan a' the gud wans.'

'You never moved away?'

'Naw. Ah thought about it, of course. Ah considered university an' work, but ah decided ah wud miss this place too much. Ah have too much a' it in me. Ah dinnae think ah'm cut out fir busy cities an' narrow streets an' aw that noise. Then ah fell pregnant wi' Angus, our eldest, an' Callum did the decent thing an' we were married an' here we stayed. Nae regrets about it either, ah wouldnae want it any other way. Ah dae visit the mainland, mainly tae see the kids. Angus is doin' a post-grad at Glasgow. Medical sciences. Mhairi shares a flat wi' him an' works at a law firm.'

We walked on. It didn't escape me, the names she had chosen for her children. Angus and Mhairi. I couldn't bring myself to ask the obvious question. It was safer to stick to small talk, filling in the everyday details of our lives. I told her about moving to London and being a solicitor and Lisa, and my dad still living in Glasgow in the care home not far from where we had once lived in Partick. We sheltered in the past, gradually regressing towards the one summer we had shared. It was Laura who eventually took us back there.

'Ye left wan day aw a' a sudden. Yer mother had died.'

'I had to go back for the funeral. I didn't get a chance to say goodbye to anyone.' By anyone, I meant her.

'Ah only found out fae yer aunt after the ferry had gone. Ah saw them drivin' away that mornin' an' guessed wit must've happened.'

'I saw you on the harbour. You had a red jumper on. I waved to you but you didn't wave back. I wasn't sure if you could see me or not.'

'Ah saw ye.' It made me feel better to know she had seen me that day.

'What about your parents? How are they?'

'Both gone,' Laura replied. 'Dad drank his sel' tae death years ago now. Ah wis only sixteen. Mum only last year, made it tae her ninetieth birthday.'

We had followed the road round the curve and faced into the wind. The stiff breeze stifled conversation and we walked along in silence until the road again turned and we were overlooking the narrow stone beach and the viaduct crossing the channel of water and Barra beyond. The modern-built cottage sat among its neatly trimmed garden.

'Isn't that where the old house was?'

'Aye, yer right, the wan we hid in.' Laura smiled. 'We were idiots that day. Every time ah saw auld Cameron after that, he reminded me about the rowboat ah owed him.'

'I wouldn't try rowing across that water now.' The channel looked wider than it had done then and more daunting. Perhaps experience and the fear of risk-taking that comes with age made it seem that way.

'Fortunately ye dinnae have tae.'

'You remember Billy Matheson showed us where his dad had been found on the beach?'

Laura must have sensed I wanted to talk about Billy and what had happened to him. I had told her he was the reason I had come to find her.

'Billy moved tae Canada when he wis auld enough tae git away fae here. Ah dinnae think he ever got over wit he did tae Lachlan. Still out there. Works as a lumberjack or somethin' fir the forestry department or somethin' like that. He's never visited London as far as ah know.' She smiled as she said it. 'An' he disnae have a son who might have been standin' oan an underground platform. He makes the odd visit back here an' stops in tae see me. No' bin here fir a good four or five years now, though. Used tae visit his mum.'

'Mhairi's still here?'

'Still lives in the same hoose in Bruernish, next tae yer aunt an' uncle's auld place. That's a B&B now, a' course, like a lot a' the places oan Barra.'

'She never let them drive her away.'

Laura pushed her hair away from her face and tried to tuck it behind her ear. 'Naw, she never left.'

Pebbles crunched beneath our feet as we stepped onto the beach. The tide was on its way out, exposing wet rocks as it went. Laura stopped by a group of large boulders near the grass bank and sat down. I sat on a boulder next to her, looking out over the channel and Barra beyond it. It took me a moment to realise where we were sitting. The dead tree that had been here before was gone, but the boulders were the same.

'This is where they found the body.'

Laura nodded. 'That's wit ye want tae talk about, isn't it?'

I turned to look at her. 'Billy's father,' I said. The corners of her mouth curved slightly upwards and all at once it was obvious. 'You know?'

'Aye, ah know. Ah figured it out no' long after ye left. Ah knew somethin' wis goin' oan.' She said it with a shrug, as though it was just one of those things. It wasn't the dark, monumental secret I had held in my mind all those years. It wasn't the earth-shattering scandal that would have destroyed her life. Perhaps it had been then, in that moment of childhood, without forty years of hindsight in which to come to terms with the revelation.

'What happened?'

'Billy an' I spent the rest a' that summer hangin' about together. We became friends. Ah didnae tell ma parents, a' course, although his maw knew an' we spent time aroun' her hoose. Mhairi never telt me we were brother an' sister. She wis jist happy when she saw us getting oan. Then Ma and Da found out that ah'd bin spendin' a lot a' time wi' Billy. Ah dinnae know how. Mibbe they followed me wan day, or mibbe somewan else telt them. We had an argument a' course. Ah couldnae understand why they wer so against Billy. Ma mum broke doon an' telt me the truth. "Because he's your brother." At first ah couldnae quite work it out. Ah wis still a fairly innocent thirteen-year-old girl.'

'I knew the last time we saw each other.' I made my confession to her. I knew it was safe to tell her now. No harm had come from not telling her when I had found out all those years ago. She had found out for herself soon after that anyway. It made my reason for coming all this way seem even more pointless. I had no big revelation about her life to tell her. 'I was hiding in the church the day Father Baird spoke to you, after we had seen him argue with Mhairi. Do you remember? After you left he spoke to your mum and I heard everything they said. They almost caught me. They talked about Mhairi and your dad and Billy. Your mum kept saying Lachlan MacLeod, the boy at the bank, knew the truth so I went to his house and spoke to him.'

'Poor Lachlan,' Laura sighed.

'It was an accident. Billy pushed him but he never meant to hurt him. He just lost his balance.'

'He never forgave himself.'

'Did your dad ever talk to you about it?'

'Da wis a terrible drunk. When ah wis born he got worse an' wud leave Mum tae look after me an' go aff oan his own. It's nothin' special. Jist that age-auld combination a' alcohol an' depression an' lack a' attention at home, an' round here there's no' much chance tae escape. Wit bothered me mare wis that it wis Mhairi that he had the affair wi'. She wis so young.'

'Was she too young?'

'Ah never found out. Ah asked her wance an' she jist telt me it wis in the past an' she had known wit she wis doing.'

'Did you believe her?'

'No' really. He took advantage a' her. It wis so wrang, whether it wis legal or no'. But wit choice do ah have? Ah refused tae let his actions turn me intae a bitter woman. Like Mhairi, ah refused tae become his victim.'

'But no one knew about it, did they? That's why your mum was desperate for it to be kept secret.'

Laura squinted at me with a confused expression. 'Everybody knew. Aw the people at church, aw the gossips. Ye cannae keep a secret like that in a place like this. They kept it fae Billy an' me an' the other children, but everywan knew wit had happened an' who Billy's real father wis.'

'I don't understand.' My brain picked over half-remembered conversations. 'If people on the island knew, why did no one do anything?'

'They did. They chose tae believe that Mhairi an' Billy were the problem. No' my da.'

'But what was your mum so afraid of if everybody already knew the truth? What was it that Father Baird was trying to stop people finding out about?'

I looked at the beach on which we sat on the rocks. The place where Angus Anderson's body had been found. The body of the man who became Billy's father despite everyone knowing he wasn't. Did he do it for Billy's sake alone? The clouds closed in and the sunlight faded and a long shadow crept across the beach. A feeling stirred in the back of my mind, a sense that the real truth was finally emerging. I grasped at it, trying to clear the fog and reach the clarity that had been hidden from me, in my ignorance and denial, all this time. The real secret, the real dark tragedy that hung over the island. The truth that I had come back to find.

Laura was watching my face. 'Ye didnae know?'

'It was an accident,' I stammered, 'Billy's father. Billy told us so the day we came here.'

'Because that wis the secret they had managed tae keep. That wis wit Father Baird wis talkin' about. He wis talkin' about wit happened tae Angus.'

'Your father killed him?'

'Ma father?'

Not her father, not Hamish. I grasped again and the truth finally hit me. Her mother. Small, thin Flora Robertson.

'Ma father wis a drunk. He had bin brought hame fae the pub by Alec MacLeod, too drunk tae even stand oan his own feet. Maw an' him had a huge row. Angus Anderson had bin in the pub, jist back aff a fishin' boat an' lettin' aff steam, shooting his mouth aff about Billy an' goadin' ma da. Talkin' about how he wis takin' care a' his bastard son fir him, how he wis providin' a hame an' money fir Hamish's son. How Hamish liked tae take advantage a' young girls. Everywan in the pub heard him. They quietly drank an' ignored Angus. Everywan knew about Billy an' Mhairi an' ma dad. They looked the other way until it almost came tae blows an' Alec stopped Dad doin' anything he might regret an' brought him hame.

'Ah wis in bed sleepin'. Ah wis only a toddler. Dad got home an' argued wi' Mum. When they calmed doon she made him coffee an' put him tae bed tae sleep it aff. Then she left the hoose an' went lookin' fir Angus an' found him coming out a' the pub after closing time. Nae wan else wis about. Nae wan saw them. She wanted tae talk tae him, tell him tae leave her family alone. Tell him tae think a' Mhairi an' Billy, tae concentrate oan lookin' after them. Angus wis still drunk. He threatened tae go tae the polis an' tell them that Hamish had raped a fifteen-year-old schoolgirl called Mhairi Matheson an' got her pregnant. Said he wanted money or he wud dae it.

'Ma mum wis frightened. She panicked. She went after Angus up the steps behind the pub that led up tae the church, tae the side a' Our Lady Star of the Sea. She wis never clear about how it happened, but she maintained it wis self-defence. She pushed

Angus an' he lost his footing oan the cliff edge. He fell, only twenty feet or so, but he landed headfirst oan the boulders below an' died instantly.'

I remembered the boulders at the bottom of the cliff on the rocky crag that the church sat upon, and how close I had come to landing on them while escaping from Father Baird and Flora. I remembered the flash of temper when Flora had lashed out at her own daughter, striking her across the face. 'Do you think it was an accident?'

'Mibbe it wis, mibbe it wisnae. Ah have nae idea. Ah wis eighteen by the time Ma telt me the truth. Dad wis already dead.

'She ran tae the manse an' banged oan the door an' Father Baird answered an' saw how distraught she wis. She pleaded wi' him fir help. He calmed her doon an' took a flashlight out. They saw the crumpled body wi' blood aw around it at the bottom a' the drop. He helped her.'

'They moved the body?'

'Dumped it in the bay. The next mornin' it had gone. They thought it wud be found there an' people wud assume Angus had fallen intae the sea oan the way hame fae the pub. But the current had taken the body and it wis foun' here.' Laura pointed to the spot on the beach in front of us. 'People still thought he must've fallen intae the sea. They wondered how he could've ended up here, but nae wan ever thought too hard about it. The polis found nae evidence a' wrang-doin'. They put his injuries doon tae hitting rocks when he fell intae the sea.'

My mind reeled as I tried to take it all in. I pictured Flora's kind face and her hospitality, her smile and her warmth. And Hamish, with his quiet, downbeat presence, his silence and sullenness. And it all fitted. His adultery, the question over Mhairi's age, Billy and Angus and his murder and the silence and guilt and the secret that followed. No wonder Flora had been desperate for Father Baird to persuade Mhairi and Billy to leave the island. They were a constant reminder of the sins she and Hamish had committed.

'You never told anyone?'

Laura shook her head. The light in her brown eyes dimmed 'Wit gud wud it have done? Father Baird had moved oan by then, Dad wis dead, an' nae wan else knew wit really happened. Mhairi suspected.'

'What about Billy?'

'Ah thought he had suffered enough. He had lost a father already. Two, if ye count my da. Wit gud wud it dae tae tell him Angus wis killed by his real father's wife? Besides, he soon moved away.'

'He has a right to know.' I sounded indignant and regretted it. Who was I to come stumbling back into her life and tell her what she should and shouldn't have done?

'Perhaps. But ye dinnae come fae here. Ye dinnae even speak like ye come fae Scotland anymare.'

'You're right,' I agreed, and realised I was glad I didn't belong to the island.

Laura stood up. I reached out and took hold of her wrist to stop her walking away from me and looked up into her tired face.

'I wrote to you when I got back to Glasgow. After you sent me the photograph. You never replied.'

She looked confused. 'Ah never got a letter fae ye. Ah never sent ye a photograph either.'

It was my turn to be perplexed. 'The photograph of you, me and Billy on the beach. I have it with me.'

I took the old photograph from my pocket and held it out to her. She took it from me and looked at it and smiled.

'We wer so young.'

'You remember that day on the beach with Billy and Mhairi. We swam in the sea.'

'Aye, ah remember. A lifetime ago.'

'If you didn't send it, then who did?'

Laura turned the photograph over and saw the writing on the back. 'Whoever wanted tae thank you, ah guess.' She handed it back to me, and I knew. It wasn't her or Billy. It was the woman who had taken the photograph on her camera.

What had Mhairi to thank me for? Was it just to say thank you for giving her and Billy one afternoon of joy on the beach where she could forget about everything else and watch her son play with his half-sister and another boy without the stares and whispers of the islanders that followed them everywhere else?

'Ah better be gettin' back. Sunday dinner needs cookin'.' Laura began walking back across the beach to the road.

'You never got my letter?' I called after her.

She turned and walked backwards, the wind blowing her hair around her face. 'Naw.' She shrugged. 'Probably ma parents kept it fae me an' threw it away. Or mibbe it wis jist lost in the post.'

'Would it have meant anything to you if you had got it? Would you have replied?'

'Who knows? That's life.' She spread her arms wide.

I watched her retreating steps, unsure if I should follow her or turn and head back to Barra. I noticed a slight hunch now; she no longer stood as tall and defiant as she once had. I was trying to process what I had learned, what she had known and kept to herself and how it impacted on everything I thought I had known when I was a boy.

She turned back when she realised I had not followed her. 'Yer welcome tae stay fir dinner if ye want. It's jist Eilidh an' me. Plenty tae go roun'.'

She stopped at the edge of the beach where the grass verge met the road. I stood up and looked at her and knew this would be the last time I ever saw her. Our eyes met. There was an understanding. I had found what I had come to look for, more than I had expected, in fact, and she had finally unburdened herself. We could both let go of that summer now, and of the memories we held of each other. She had found someone she could talk to and admit the dark secret of her past and she knew I wouldn't tell anyone else or do anything more. She was right; they were all gone now. Her mother and father, Angus Anderson, and Billy, the boy from Barra who had escaped to the other side of the ocean. Perhaps I should have come back sooner and let her unburden herself before now. Was it the tragic past of her family that had made her stay on the island? Had she felt unable to leave it all behind? If she could have shared her secret sooner, would it have made any difference to her? Perhaps, as she had said, her life was exactly as she wanted it to be.

Would it have made any difference to my life? I didn't think so now, but how can one ever tell? She had been my first love, although I had been too young and inexperienced to realise it at the time. I had been left an image of her, an ideal, a false perfection whose flaws I overlooked and who existed in the sentimentality and vitality of youth. And now I knew that nothing can ever live up to those perfect memories we create. Not even her. We are all flawed people trying to make our way through life as best we can.

We didn't say anything more. There was no warm embrace, or 'take care'. There was no 'pleased to have seen you' or 'thank you for coming to find me'. We just looked at each other across that barren, grey beach with only the sound of the wind and the waves between us and we each understood that all that needed to be said had been said.

She broke the gaze first, with a nod and a slight smile and a small wave. Then she turned and stepped onto the road and walked away from me.

I watched for five minutes as she receded along the tarmac until she was just a dot that disappeared around the curved hillside. I walked along the beach and threw some stones into the water and the ripples swirled like the thoughts running through my mind. That summer ended with my mother's funeral. The two inextricably linked moments that took me from childhood into adolescence. I had lost my mother and my innocence at the same time.

I stepped up onto the causeway and crossed the channel of water without looking back and began the steep climb back up the hill that took me to Castlebay.

24

The sun had not broken through the yellow curtains of the bedroom window when I woke up. I lay in bed and watched the weak autumnal rays gradually reach across the floor and up the opposite wall. It would be a fine morning on the Heaval. There was an absence of sound; the breeze that had been constant since I had arrived had gone and a calm quiet fell over the island. I had a ticket booked on the flight back to Glasgow that afternoon. I didn't have to take it, but there was nothing to stay here for. I had found Laura and the answers to my questions. What would be the point in hanging on?

The previous day I had walked back to Castlebay and around the bay and remembered more of the sights and sounds. Some things had changed. There were new buildings here and there, and new pavements and roads and new paintwork and signs of modern life, like the mobile phone mast near the pier. The individuals had changed and yet the people looked the same. There was nothing more to do on the island, nothing more to see. I could visit the old house that Tom and Cathy lived in, but what would I do there?

The photograph was on the bedside table where I had left it. I picked it up now and looked at it. Laura and Billy and my younger self stared back at me. I turned it over and traced the scrawled message on the back. 'Thank you.' Not from Laura, but from Mhairi. Was it just a thank you for spending some time with her son? Or did she know that I had found out the truth about her and Hamish? Was she thanking me for not telling Billy who his real father was? I wondered if she had another reason for wanting to take the photograph of the three of us together, or more specifically Laura with Billy. Did she send a copy of the photograph to Hamish and Flora to taunt them with it? Would she do something that calculated? The way she was treated by the people of the island, could you blame her for wanting to fight back in some way? There was one way to find out for sure. I could visit her. I could go to her house at the end of the road in Bruernish, the house before the fence and the rough path down to the cove, and I could ask her. She would be in her mid-sixties now. Would she even remember me? Or had I seen and learned enough? Everyone had moved on and, like Laura had said to me the day before, what was the point in dredging up the past? I couldn't change anything that had happened. I couldn't have changed it then. I was, after all, only a visitor here. My life was not here, my present, or my future. The past that was here was linked to the death of my mother. That was why I couldn't let it go. All I needed was to say goodbye to my past, to bury it. I looked at the young Laura and Billy and my past self again. There was nothing left for me to discover on Barra.

But what was I returning to? A bachelor flat in London with a few friends and a job I was coasting along in, waiting for retirement. Then what? A slow decline until the care home? Laura Robertson had never left Barra, but she was happily married and had a large family. Billy had escaped over the Atlantic Ocean, escaped Barra and set up a new life for himself. Was I the only one who had wasted my life? Should I have done something different? Had I been expecting Laura to provide some sort of closure or future or meaning? There was so much I hadn't done. I had been content and nothing more. Was that enough?

I knew what I had to do. I packed my bag and locked the house. Mary MacNeil's house was quiet. I popped the keys through her letterbox and began walking along the road with Castlebay behind me and the sun hitting the castle in the bay and the church still standing guard. I took one last look behind me when I reached the crest of the hill before the road wound down the other side. I followed the road north and remembered the bicycle journey. After half an hour, I passed Brevig and the house that Laura used to live in. There was a new extension on one side and the windows and doors looked new and it no longer stood in isolation. Houses had been built on either side of it. From the end of the driveway, I could see through the window into the kitchen where a woman was making breakfast and next to her a boy was trying to put on a school tie. The door opened and a man appeared, dressed in overalls. He got into a van and started the engine. I walked on as he passed me at the end of the driveway and turned towards Castlebay.

In another hour I reached the turning from the main road that would take me to Bruernish. One last temptation brushed over me, but I had no need to go back. If Cathy and Tom and Lennox had been waiting for me over the crest of the hill I would have delighted in their company for a few hours, but they were long gone, from Barra and from the world. Only one person remained down that path that I had known forty years ago, and there was nothing I could say to her that would make any difference, to her or to me. An apology for the wrongs done to her decades ago from a stranger, a middle-aged man she may not even have remembered, would mean nothing.

* * *

As the airport came into view, my phone beeped and a deluge of notifications and messages were delivered. Between leaving Castlebay and my arrival here I had been out of mobile-phone reception. I looked at the messages. They were from Lisa. She had tried to call me too. I was about to call her back when the phone started ringing. I reached the terminal building and stood outside the entrance and answered the call.

'Lisa, is everything okay?'

'Finally. I've been trying to reach you all morning.'

'I haven't had a signal. What's wrong?'

'Are you still on Barra?'

'Yes, I'm at the airport.'

'I'm in Glasgow.'

I felt guilt wash over me. I didn't deserve her. 'Why are you in Glasgow?'

'I was worried about you. The way you rushed off on this trip, the way you were acting before you left. I just wanted to make sure you were okay. It was silly of me to come all this way.'

'Of course not, Lisa.' I wanted to tell her how happy I was that she had followed me. I wanted to tell her how much I wanted her in my future. I wanted to tell her how much I would make up for the idiot I had been for the last year. I didn't know how to start telling her all these things, especially not over the phone. She was the answer to the questions I had been asking myself since arriving on Barra.

'Ewan?'

'Sorry. I was just wondering. When I get back to Glasgow, I was going to visit my dad in the care home. I was wondering if you would like to come and meet him too.' It wasn't much, but it was a start.

'I would love to, if you think it's a good idea. Would he like to meet me?'

'I think he would like you, probably more than he would enjoy seeing me.'

'Don't be silly.'

'And after that I could show you round where I grew up.'

'That would be great.'

'And another thing.' I couldn't stop myself now. Now that I had decided how I wanted to spend the rest of my life.

'What?'

'When we get back to London, should we move in together?'

There was a worrying pause.

'What happened to you on that island?'

'Nothing, really. Nothing much at all.' Which was true.

'Let's talk about it some more when you get here.'

Not a total rejection then; there was hope, which was more than I deserved. We signed off in our usual way. I had spent the last few days in the past. Now it was time to look forward.

* * *

The propellers turned and the aircraft thrummed and taxied across the sand to the far side of the bay and turned to face south and begin its take-off run. Without ceremony we moved forward and gathered speed before lifting into the air. We flew over the island as we gained altitude. From my window I looked down on blue sea and golden beaches and the rocky green-brown landscape. The road snaked along the coast and through Northbay and passed the fish factory. Just beyond that was Bruernish. The plane banked to the east to follow the flight path back to Glasgow. I picked out the roof of the house that I had once lived in. It still stood on its own and the single road still led over the slope towards the sea and forked at the junction and further along was the row of houses where the road ended. There were more houses here than I remembered. Perhaps I had remembered it wrong, or perhaps more houses had been built. The house at the end of the row was the same, though. The fence ran along the side of it out to the small cove. In the garden of the house on the end of the row was a woman wearing a long dress that billowed in the wind. She looked up at the sky as the plane flew overhead. Her hair was white. She was hanging out washing on a line in her garden. A white sheet billowed out from her hands. The plane bounced as it hit air turbulence. The white sheet escaped her grasp and took off across the garden and over the low wall, blown along by the Barra breeze, heading for the small cove. A ghost trying to escape.

My last glimpse of Mhairi Matheson was of her striding from her garden to chase after that ghost. Did she ever think of me? Would she have welcomed a visitor from her past? She had sent me the photograph that was still inside my coat pocket and thanked me for being a friend to her son. Had I really been a friend to the boy on Barra? Could I have done anything more for him that summer?

I wondered how many times she had looked up at the sky and seen the small plane passing by and wondered if she should have escaped too, as Billy had done. But she chose to remain, defiant until the end, as she had sworn she would do. They would never chase her from the island.

We passed over the coast and Barra was left behind us, and soon I was looking down at the blue water and the stray crops of rock that interrupted the surface. I leaned back in my seat and closed my eyes and let the steady hum of the engine lull me into a fitful doze. I dreamed of Lisa and London and Glasgow and my father and faded memories of my mother and the happy family we had once been, and my life beyond that summer long ago.

A JUSTIFIED STATE

Book One of *The State* Trilogy

The future. The socially reformist Central Alliance Party rules unopposed.

Poverty and homelessness have been eradicated, but overpopulation, an energy crisis and an ongoing war jeopardise the stability of the country.

When a local politician is assassinated, Detective Danny Samson finds himself at the centre of an investigation that threatens not only his life but the entire future of The State.

Praise for *A Justified State*:

– 'the action is pacey and exciting, the characters fleshed out, nuanced and believable, the mystery… is genuinely intriguing and alarming.'

– 'the writing brought to mind Phillip Marlow, *Do Androids Dream of Electric Sheep?*, the world of George Smiley, and Robert Harris' Fatherland'

– 'This is a superbly well written fast paced, suspenseful mystery. A page turner as the action… makes you gasp'

ALSO AVAILABLE

STATE OF DENIAL

Book Two of *The State* Trilogy

Election time in The State, the citizens prepare to vote.

A journalist from the Capital City heads north to report on growing resistance to the powerful ruling Party.

An ex-police detective returns to the City he once fled.

Together they become entangled in a burgeoning opposition movement.

Soon they learn the Party will do whatever it takes to remain in power, and one life is all it takes to spark a revolution.

Praise for *State of Denial*:

– 'Well paced and full of drama. A great sequel.'

– 'Well written, the plot flows effortlessly… A gripping sci-fi that is a little bit horrifying and a lot entertaining.'

– 'Get lost in the pages… through passages that may have you holding your breath.'

ALSO AVAILABLE

STATE OF WAR

Book Three of *The State* Trilogy

The State is at war at home and abroad. While the global First Strike War continues, a civil war threatens to bring down the ruling Central Alliance Party.

Daniel Samson – Citizen, Traitor, Survivor.
Gabriella Marino – Soldier, Assassin, Fighter.

Caught between the State Forces and the rebels, hunted by both sides, they must choose between their own survival and protecting the city and the citizens trapped within the war zone. Are they willing to sacrifice their own chance of happiness to save a city from destruction?

The thrilling conclusion to *The State* Trilogy sees Danny and Gabriella join forces against their enemies in a fight that will determine the fate of the State, and the lives of all those who live there.

– 'A lot of writers could learn how to create a believable future by studying Kelly's novels.'

– 'More action, more emotional stakes and this time the wrong move will not only end their lives but take a city with them.'

For writing and publishing news, or
recommendations of new titles to read,
sign up to the Book Guild newsletter: